GABE BAKER
MAN OF THE WEST

HUGH PIXLER

Print ISBN: 979-8-35091-815-1

eBook ISBN: 979-8-35091-816-8

1

GABE HAS A VISITOR

Gabe Baker got up slowly to put another log on the fire. Just two hours before, a torrential downpour had started in Boulder, Colorado, the likes of which Gabe had not seen since his slave days back at Heavenly Hills, Maryland. That was a long time ago. A lifetime. Now the storm settled into a steady, driving rain that would from time to time surge with a whooshing sound that seemed to come from all directions at once. Sheets of water assaulted his small, but sturdy house. Then the storm would retreat only to return with renewed strength. October 1873 had been a wet month, but this was the worst of it so far.

As Gabe sat in his favorite rocker, his two fat cats, Tex and John Henry, yawned and stretched in front of the fireplace. They had long ago given up on the excitement of the changing sounds of the weather outside.

It was times like this that Gabe allowed himself the twin pleasures of sipping rye whiskey and reading a good book. These two diversions now conspired to weigh down on his eyelids as he passed into a pensive, contented state. He started to drift. Tex and John Henry were partly to blame. They gave no end of comfort and solace to his agitated mind. And to the loneliness, too, that Gabe had recently realized was becoming his lot - in spite of the good friends he had in town.

Was it because he was the only black man in town? Should that matter? I mean, considering, he pondered, the strength of his friendships, the respect he had earned and was shown by his employers and by local law? He had always done his part and maybe more, when it came to his responsibilities as a worker, a friend and a citizen. Had more been required of him because of the color of his skin? No, no, surely he was just being petty. Having grown up under horrendous conditions, with the daily mental and physical abuse visited upon himself as well as those whom he loved, he wondered, though, if he thought and felt the same way as his current friends did. Maybe he was being too sensitive. But he couldn't help but think that all of the hurt and humiliation, great and small, that accumulated somewhere inside of him, must have made him different somehow.

The laundryman Lin-Chi had told him along with his friends Billy and Harley that they suffered from "soldier heart". This was a kind of damage to the mind - or to the soul, maybe - as he understood it. It was caused by the horrors of war. How did his friends suffer? Hadn't they suffered the same depredations he had lived through?

Well, no, he admitted to himself. He had grown up hiding and watching as his mother was beaten and ravaged by an old white man. A man who owned her. A man he called "master". His friends had not grown up wearing a grain sack for clothes and working in the fields from the time they could walk. They had not worked for a man who could legally do anything he wanted to his human property, including inviting friends over to beat and force themselves on their mothers. And Gabe's friends had never been whipped and beaten, a couple of times near to death, even as children, as he had. They had not been raised under the shadow of purposeful humiliation and constant fear. And they had not lived under the watchful eyes of one who thrived on the sadistic power he had over those under his control. Yes, the slavedriver, Sikes. That was his name. And he, Gabe, had killed that man. He had killed Sikes and his master and his master's sons that moonlit night so many years ago when they had all come together to do their filth on his Mama in the stable. The night when he came out of hiding and could no longer just watch and sob at what he was witnessing.

He had told Billy and Harley that that was the night he stopped being just a slave and became a man. But what price that manhood? He had to escape that night and leave behind his mother and brother and sisters, not knowing what would happen to them. Maybe carrying around all these thoughts, and this pain, was the source of his loneliness. He knew he could talk to Billy and Harley, and, of course, Lin-Chi about any and all of these troubles without holding back. But, how could he possibly make them understand?

Gabe's eyes became heavier as he slipped past the agitation of thought and entered into a state of calm, on the verge of sleep. He could feel himself going down, down and inward and down. He was enjoying the forgetting and the momentary weightlessness of the descent.

Bam! Bam bam! The moment was lost in an instant. Someone was outside, in the storm, banging on his front door. The calm was over. The sound was sharp and loud enough that whoever was there was not using his hand. Maybe a gun. None of his friends would knock like that. Should he answer? Or, close his eyes and hope the disturbance would go away? No, he was up now. He grabbed his Navy Colt .36 and glanced at the cats. He took the two steps towards the door and slowly crossed his left hand under his right to unlatch it so he could point the gun with his better hand. He held it so the barrel of the Colt would be the first thing the person outside saw as he opened the door a crack.

The tall, rangy man on the porch immediately put his hands up. They were both empty, but Gabe saw through the man's open slicker. He wore a shoulder holster, the butt of his pistol now peeking out from behind the coat. It was dark and the man had his collar up around his ears. He had on a gray cowboy hat with a single brown strap running around the base of its crown. Gabe couldn't see much else.

"Evenin', stranger," Gabe said in a calm monotone. He pushed the Colt a bit further out the door. "Why don't you just state your business so's you don't 'ave t' stand out on my porch all night?"

"I'm hopin' you're the man called Gabe Baker," the stranger said as he started to lower his hands. Gabe cocked the Colt. The man put his hands back up high.

"I am. Now, like I said, state your business or you're like t' drown out there."

"You don't know me, but I know you. Or, about you, that is. My name's Heck McCabe and I come from St. Louis. And I always heard western hospitality was of the best sort. Mind if I come in? It won't take more'n a minute or two to tell my business."

"Mister, if you hand me that pistol you got up high real slow and butt first an' then shed the slicker and hat, drop 'em right there on the porch, you can take one step inside my house. Then I'll hear ya until I judge you're not bein' straight with me." The man called Heck quickly handed Gabe his gun and dropped his gear as he was told.

"All right, Mr. McCabe, come on in," Gabe said, indicating with his Colt. Heck took a step inside, while Gabe reached around him and shut the door. Gabe could see the man better now. He was a white man, tall and straight. Gabe figured he was in his fifties. He had plenty of gray mixed in with the thick tousle of brown hair that now showed with his hat off. He also had a noticeable scar just above the ridge of his left jaw. He may have been from St. Louis, but he looked like a man who had spent a good deal of a hard life in the sun. He was bronzed, with wrinkles around his eyes and mouth. He didn't talk like a Missourian either. Gabe was quite familiar with that deep south twang in Heck's speech, and it sounded more like South Carolina. The man didn't appear to be missing much as he did a quick survey of the room.

Gabe backed up a bit, leaned against his kitchen table and lowered his gun. As he looked Heck in the eye he lifted his Colt, pointed it off to his left, and made a point of showing Heck that he was easing the hammer back down. Click-click. He reached behind him and placed it on the table. He nodded, "All right, Mr. McCabe – "

"Please, just Heck is good enough. Can I call you Gabe?"

"That's fine so long 's you know how t' be quick an' to the point," Gabe said, still wary and now watching the man's hands. Gabe crossed his arms.

"Of course. I know this is comin' outta nowhere far as you're concerned. I understand you bein' careful and all." He took a deep breath and looked at Gabe. "Like I said, I heard of you. I know somethin' about you. I know somethin' about Fort Wagner, too. I know - "

Gabe flinched and his heart started pounding. He stood ramrod straight and grabbed for his Colt. "You better say why you're here right now, Mister," he growled as he pointed the gun at him again. Gabe had succeeded to some extent in keeping the war, the 54th Massachusetts and especially the battle of Fort Wagner in the back of his mind for some time now. In the back, but always lurking, always there. Under the leadership of Colonel Shaw his regiment had shown the South, the North, and yes, the whole doubting world, that the black man could fight with or against any other and not be caught short. It was the prejudice of the South as well as the North that the black man could not, or would not, fight. Shaw knew better. The heroism and dogged determination of the 54th in the face of terrible odds were noted by Americans of every stripe. There could be no question. And they suffered mightily for their efforts, too. Near half of their number was lost between sunset and 10:30 that fateful July night in 1863.

"Hold on. Hold on now, Gabe," Heck said, holding the palms of his hands out and wagging them back and forth. Now he spoke more quickly. "I come a long ways to see you. I'm just askin', hear me out. I got a proposition for you. A job offer, with top wages, maybe more, maybe a bonus."

Gabe took in a breath and let out a big sigh. He crossed his arms again and looked down at the floor for a second, then back up into Heck's eyes. He cocked his head slightly to the left. "Mister – Heck – I *got* a job. Couple of 'em, ya might say. Now, who could be so all-fired interested in me t' come lookin' me up way out here in Boulder, Colorado, you comin' from St. Louie an' all?" Gabe couldn't help but being curious now.

"I'm sure you remember a certain Captain Calley, Gabe. You and a couple of your friends worked for him on his wagon train from Westport to La Junta, 'bout six years back. He recommended you to my boss. I work for a man named General Burke. Well, Avery Burke now. He was a general in the war and a friend of your Colonel Shaw. You should know, Gabe, I was there at Fort Wagner too. You'd figure it out anyway, so I'll tell you. I was shootin' from *inside* the fort. That didn't matter to General Burke and I hope it don't matter to you neither."

Gabe's shoulders slumped a little. "Go ahead, Heck. Let's hear it," he said, giving in.

Encouraged now, Heck dove in. "Us Johnny Rebs didn't know it at the time, but Jeff Davis was keepin' gold down under the fort. Way down under. We don't know if your bluebellies – er, I mean, your federals, ever knew it. After the war, some in South Carolina heard about it and went after it. Well, it seems maybe it ain't there no more."

"Well, what you want with me? My work with Cap'n Calley was ridin' guard, shootin' meat and fightin' when it came to that."

"Your General - er, President Grant is interested in findin' this gold. And seein' that the thieves get what's comin' to 'em, too. The way the gov'mint looks at it, whether North or South got it, it was stolen."

"That don't answer my question. Why me?"

"Well, fact is Captain Calley says you're a good man and reliable. And, you were with the 54th. You know the fightin' men, the ones who got out. If someone on your side got the gold, or knows somethin' about it, you'd have a chance to find out. You could ask questions. You could get close to them who took it. As you can tell by lookin' at me, I couldn't."

"*If* it was on our side. And that's right, all I know is the fightin' men. We went in with about 600, come out with three. Then, we left. The North didn't take your fort until September, I'm recallin'."

"That's right. If. We're workin' the other side, too. And I was still there in September. We abandoned after Union guns plumb tore us apart. And the gold was prob'ly not on anyone's mind right then. We barely got out at night under heavy fire. Only thing came out then was all the cannon we could still move and the garrison itself. That's it."

"Seem like you'd be lookin' at mebbe some southerners, gold hunters, officers who knew about it. Or locals. Mebbe Jeff'son Davis hisself." Heck stiffened up at that suggestion. Gabe noticed. "Or even 24th Massachusetts, the ones who drove your bunch out in September. Fifty-fourth was gone near two months afore that."

"Um, yeah, you know we been workin' some of those angles, for sure. But, now we got a tip. It appears one of your ironclads that was shootin' up the place, tryin' to soften us up before the 54th charge up the hill, made some mighty big holes down under the works and in the moat. Those 32-pounders packed a wallop." Then he smiled and loosened up a bit. "They couldn't move the Rebs out though. Anyways, word is they hit around where that gold had been stored months earlier. There was some gold coin found out there among your boys when we came out to bury 'em. 'Course, I didn't know about it at the time."

"Yeah, I heard 'bout how you buried 'em," Gabe said with a scowl. Heck didn't have anything to say about that.

The rain continued to pound the roof and walls of Gabe's house. The two men were silent as they regarded each other. Tex and then John Henry jumped up on the table behind Gabe, and stared at Heck, ears at attention.

"Mebbe you bein' straight with me. I don' know for sure. How can a man know? He only use 'is best judgment. So, here's me bein' straight with you. Onliest reason I'd even consider such a thing is I still have my Mama and mebbe a sister and brother back in Maryland. If I was goin' back east

I'd have to use that trip to see 'em, see how they doin'. And if th' pay's good, I could set 'em up for a better life than what they got. 'Cause see, Heck, I'm doin' fine here for m'self without no rebel gold."

"General Burke thinks you're important. I'm sure that kin part can be worked in there."

"How important? I'd say most of th' 54th still back aroun' east. You do better t' get someone there. It don't seem quite straight, Heck."

"Here's what is straight, Gabe. I think – I mean, we think we know some of them who found some gold coin, maybe they know what happened to the rest. We know that you know 'em and they'd trust you."

"Jus' what makes you think if I get a line on that gold, I won't join up with my brothers from the reg'ment and take up with 'em?" Gabe asked, lifting his chin, but still looking directly at Heck, but now looking down on him. "I ate and slept and marched and fought and sweated and cried and bled with *them*. Not you."

"I know it, Gabe. But General Burke says that Calley spoke up good for ya. Says you're a good man. We'd have you sign a paper, says you owe the gov'mint your good faith and such-like. You do that and we figure you'll join up 'cause you ain't goin' back on your word. And you'd do it for General Grant. Plus, like you said, you might be able to help out your Mama and sister."

"I don't like you talkin' 'bout my Mama, Heck, you don't know nothin' 'bout 'er," Gabe scowled, as cold shiver went up his back.

Heck crossed his arms and flashed an unfriendly smile at Gabe. "Fact is, I do know somethin' 'bout *your Mama*," he said, sneering out the last two words. "I talked to that nice Mrs. Belcher back in St. Louis. Your former boss back at the boardin' house? Seems your kin found out you were workin' there. She sent letters addressed to you out here, and you sent news back to her 'bout how they were doin'. Mrs. Belcher thinks highly of ya, Gabe. When I explained I wanted to help the whole family, she opened up plenty. Even told me where I could send any bonus money you might get, you know, just to help out the family."

Gabe reached back and grabbed his Colt again. He cradled it in his lap, holding the barrel with one hand and the grip with the other. He squeezed it until his knuckles were near as white as Heck's as he considered how the conversation was going. Heck saw something in Gabe's eye that made him uneasy.

"Well, now, no need for any worry on your part, Gabe. I mean, word could be out already you'd be helpin' us, but I got a couple of real good boys out there prob'ly keepin' an eye on your Mama's place in case any of your old friends drop by. No need to worry! 'Course, unless you can't help us. Then I'd have to use those boys to help with the gold-huntin' part down in the Carolinas."

Gabe pointed his Navy Colt at the center of Heck's belly and cocked it. His hand shook slightly. There was an interesting target right there below where he was aiming. He hadn't noticed it before. Heck's belt buckle was larger than most, and rectangular in shape. In the middle was a gold-colored triangle.

"Don't do nothin' rash there, now, boy – er, I mean *Gabe*," Heck said, his speech now rushed. He gestured with his hands straight out. His tone had changed. He quickly added, "Those boys don't hear from me you hired on with us, they're gonna pack up an' meet me down to Fort Wagner. Won't be there for protectin' duty any more. Sorry, just have to use 'em best I can."

Gabe's finger was tightening on the trigger.

"All right, Heck," Gabe said through clenched teeth. "You who you say you are, let's see your papers. What they call credentials."

"I've got identification papers and a letter from General Burke in his own hand," Heck said, reaching into his breast pocket. Then he looked at Gabe, "With your permission of course, I'll reach right in here and show 'em to ya."

"Bring 'em out, Heck," Gabe said. Heck slowly pulled the papers out and handed them to Gabe.

"All right, says the man carryin' these papers is Heck McCabe, you got orders from Avery Burke t' make an offer t' me. All I heard so far was some threatenin' words from you, Heck. No offer."

"Oh, no, Gabe, I didn't mean it threatenin', no sir," Heck said. "All I meant was - "

Bam! Bam bam bam! Another stranger?! Someone else was now banging on the door. The sound startled Gabe out of his concentrated anger. It may have saved Heck's life. Gabe motioned with his Colt for him to move to his right so he could keep an eye on him. He gave Heck a quick glance and a scowl and opened the door a crack. "Who's there bangin' on my door?"

"I followed a man here," came the muffled response from outside in the blustery wind. He might be dangerous. Best let me in. I'll explain."

"Who are you?"

"Name's Heck McCabe."

2

GABE HAS
ANOTHER VISITOR

Gabe immediately looked back at the first Heck and told him to stand still. Then he yelled out to the second, "Drop your slicker and hat outside next t' the other ones." The second Heck complied, revealing an Army Colt in a side holster. "Now, hand that Colt on over butt first and you can come on in an' join th' party." Second Heck complied again, and followed Gabe inside.

Gabe backed up against the table again and motioned the first Heck to stand by the second in front of the door. The first Heck complained, "Man, this son-of-a-bitch is a faker. A low-down fortune hunter of some sort. I don't care who he says he is, I'm Heck McCabe."

"You know this man? Why's he saying that?" Second Heck asked, looking flustered and waving his hands around. Second Heck was six inches shorter than First Heck, had a round head and red, bulbous nose. He was also round in the middle. His gunbelt rode on top of his rotund belly. His medium-length hair was combed straight back, wavy and jet black. Gabe also saw that he had stubby, well-manicured fingers. He wore city clothes, now rumpled and wet.

"Well, Heck, this here's Heck McCabe." Gabe gestured back and forth. Heck McCabe, meet Heck McCabe," he said with a wry smile.

"Now listen, you," the First said to Second, towering over him. "I don't know who the hell you are, but you ain't Heck McCabe, and anyone messin' in my business is gonna *get* messed up." He started to grab Second's collar.

"Oh, no – uh-uh, Heck," Gabe said, nodding his head back and forth. "You let go 'o Heck right now and move over a step while we all have a little talk. That all right with you, Heck?" he asked in the Second's direction. Second Heck nodded.

"Both of you quiet now 'til I ask a question. This here is an interestin' uh - *conundrum*, as they say, you'd have t' agree," he said, looking from First to Second. Gabe was gaining back his composure. "I'd advise both o' you Hecks be on your best behavior. If'n I have to shoot one o' you, that would kinda fix th' problem, wouldn't it?"

First Heck couldn't hold himself back. "This man is a damned imposter! Can't you see that, Gabe?" He took another step toward Second, who stood his ground.

"I told you t' hold it, Heck!" Gabe pointed his Colt at First's face until he stepped back. "I'm getting' tired o' pointin' this thing at you and not pullin' the trigger. You understand?" He scooted back so he was sitting on the table now, next to Tex and John Henry. "Now, let's start like this, boys. Heck," Gabe said looking at Second Heck, "state your business here. You must o' been right smack on this man's trail. What d' you want?"

"Like I said, I followed this man here. He's obviously using my name because he knows I got good information on missing Confederate gold. He's here to trick you. You help him out, you'll never see one gold piece of your own," Second Heck said. "All he'll ever give you is the deep end of a dark hole."

"Thing is, Heck here just showed me his papers. Looks like he's got one up on ya, Heck," Gabe said.

"This jasper here didn't show you *his* papers," Second Heck blustered, "he showed you *mine*. He snuck up on my camp two nights ago, beat me half to death, and took my official documents."

"Well, now, you can see he's a damn liar, can't ya, Gabe? He doesn't look like no kinda gov'mint man you ever saw," First said.

"Look here, Gabe," Second said, indicating the right side of his face. That's got to be the man who snuck into my camp, coldcocked me with the butt of his Winchester right here, and took all my personals with him. Probably left me for dead." Second's face was heavily bruised on that side.

"Looks like you did get some kinda beatin', there, Heck," Gabe said, looking. "How we know who done it?"

"I'll tell you how. Same scoundrel who snuck up on me and took my papers took my gold watch and chain, too. Says 'from A.B. for courage under fire' on the back of it. I came from St. Louis, straight from the offices of one General Avery Burke. That's the A.B. General Burke sent me to recruit you for an important job. And that includes a good offer, including possible bonus. He's commissioned by President Grant himself to find Confederate gold that was stolen from Fort Wagner. The man here calling himself by my name is the imposter. He - "

Gabe held up his hand to stop him. "All right, Heck, that's enough. Looks like you two not only have the same name, you're in the same business. Must get confusin' 'round the office back there in St. Louie."

"No, we ain't, Gabe. This man here's in the business of lyin' an' cheatin'. I'm here on gov'mint business," First said.

"Heck, you don't pipe down, I gonna stuff a rag down your throat an' tie you up. Understand?" First nodded and frowned in the direction of Second, who stood calmly with his hands together in front of him.

"All right, Heck," he said to Second, "I don't see this man has a gold watch on him. Heck, raise up your arms, I'm gonna search ya and you're gonna be good. Not so much of a twitch or my trigger finger's gonna twitch."

First Heck did as he was told. Gabe didn't find anything. Then, he said to Second Heck, "You say those papers are yours? Why don't you describe 'em for me?"

"There are three pages. One's a letter from General Burke. The other two provide my identification and describe our mission. Also, says I have authority to make an offer to you."

"That don't mean nothin', Gabe. He can see the papers on the table there and he already knows why I'm here. This man is a fake, I tell you, you too thick to see that, Gabe?"

"Flattery ain't gettin' you nowheres, Heck. I know somethin' could though. Heck and I gonna go out on the porch while you get your horse and walk 'im over here. I saw him. Right across the street tied up there by the print shop. Under the tree."

"What the hell's the purpose of that?" First Heck grumbled.

"Well, now what you think, Heck? Let's see if you got that nice watch and chain out there?"

"I'm not gonna - "

"You're gonna and right now, Heck," Gabe said. Then, indicating to Second, "You and I will go out on th' porch and watch 'im. Onliest way t' keep an eye on the both o' you. And Heck," he said, indicating First, "Anything you do I think is jus' a little bit slick or a little bit funny, I be shootin' you down right there in the mud. Your mama wouldn't want t' see ya go out like 'at. Let's go, Hecks."

As soon as he emerged out onto the porch, First leaned down to pick up his slicker. Gabe refused him but allowed him to put on his hat. The rain had lightened a bit, but was still steady. Second Heck and Gabe stood watching. First Heck slopped across the street to his horse, lifting his feet high as the thickening mud started to suck at his boots as if to pull them off. He made it to his horse and looked around him. He tugged at his hat to bring it down farther onto his forehead. He started to lift the flap on the left side of the saddlebag and gave a quick look back at Gabe before he stuck his hand in. Gabe didn't like that look.

"Heck!" he yelled across the street. "Just untie that critter and lead 'im over here. Keep your hands where I can see 'em. I'll do the lookin'."

Heck dawdled and fumbled untying his horse. It was too slow and deliberate. Gabe was now on high alert.

Heck grabbed the reins with his left hand and jerked the horse around just far enough to give him some cover. He reached into the saddlebag, flashed a pistol out and went to his knees, aiming it back towards the house. Gabe cocked and fired before Heck could get off his shot. It hit him in his right shoulder and turned him half way around as he was pulling his trigger. Heck's shot went high and wide.

"Damn you, Heck!" Gabe yelled as Heck struggled to raise his gun again. "Don't do it!" But he did. Gabe fired again, this time his bullet hitting his target in the chest. Heck jolted backwards under his horse, his grip on his gun now loosening. The street around him was quickly darkening as Heck's life-blood pumped hot into the mud.

Gabe's breath came hard and fast. He looked at Second Heck and let his gun hand go limp. His eyes started to glaze over. He put his hands on his knees, still holding the gun. He'd had to do a lot of it in his life, but he never liked killing. He stood up, gathered himself and looked at Second Heck again. With a nod of his head he motioned for Second to follow him out in the rain to check on First.

"Tie that horse back up, will ya, Heck?" Gabe asked, while he leaned over First Heck. Gabe turned the man onto his back. Second came over and said, "Damn, Gabe, that second shot went right through the man's heart. But I think he deserved it."

"Well, I don' know. Mebbe deserve got nothin' t' do with it. An' deserve or not, mebbe I'll never know the man's name that I just done for, neither. Gabe stood up straight.

"Actually, Gabe, I believe I know his name," Heck said with a boldness Gabe hadn't seen in the man yet. He let out a deep breath. "Fact is, this man is – or, I should say, *was* one Oliver Sweeney," Heck said. "Leastwise, that's what I believe. He's one of those who had spied for both sides during the war. "You probably just did a great favor to the Secret Service, President Grant and the whole country today, Gabe," Heck said. "If this was Sweeney, he was a bad one – devious, cunning and a killer without a conscience."

3

WHO WAS THAT MAN?

The rain started to taper off as the two men stood on Gabe's front porch. Heck looked Gabe in the eye, and said, "I'm not a fortune hunter like the man said. And I'm not a fake. And the job I'm proposing is real." Just then, though, he stopped and pointed down the street towards Gabe's friend Harley's house. "Gabe! Do you know that man? Standing there with the gun in his hand?" he asked, nervously.

"That there is m' friend Harley. He heard the shots and come out t' see I'm all right." Gabe waved his hand at Harley, now coming out of the mist and the dark of late afternoon.

Gabe gestured Harley to come over while he again looked at McCabe's credentials. Harley holstered his Colt as he approached and looked at the two men standing there. "United States Secret Service," he said as he read the document and looked up at his friend. "Harley, this here is Heck McCabe of the U.S. Secret Service – anyways I reckon 'e is. I mean, that's what the paper says. So . . . anyway, Heck, which I'll call ya for the time bein', this is Harley Cobb outta Fairfield County, Ohio and points west."

"How do, Heck," Harley said, nodding and shaking McCabe's hand. "And, uh, that unfortunate gentleman over there lyin' in the mud?"

"That is one Oliver Sweeney, formerly known as Heck McCabe - I think," Gabe said, giving Heck a little smirk.

"You just shot the man. You don't know? I mean, you usually get past the howdy-dos before the shootin' starts. Wait a minute. But this other gentleman, the one still standin', he used t' be Heck McCabe too?"

"Used to be and still am," Heck said.

"It may be 'bout time t' get Sheriff Taylor involved and mebbe make sure we got this all straight now and get this mess cleaned up out here," Gabe said, "then also mebbe get some more answers from Mr. Heck McCabe here."

"You bring me to your sheriff, I can clear anything up," Heck said, sniffling and wiping rainwater out of his eyes with the back of his hand.

"Won't have t', Heck," Harley said. "That's our sheriff comin' down the street right now, totin' 'is Winchester."

"What sort of a sheriff do you have here in Boulder? I mean, do you gentlemen trust him?" McCabe asked, looking back and forth between them.

Gabe nodded at Harley. Harley knew what that meant. "First thing, Heck, we don't like bein' insulted like that. Second, yessir. Our sheriff is of the finest kind."

"What? I didn't insult anybody!"

"What 'e means is, we *ain't* no gentlemen," Gabe said, looking down at Heck. "And afore the sheriff gets here, I'd feel a might better if you could reach int' them saddlebags an' pull out a nice gold watch – careful like."

"I'll remember," Heck said, as he started rifling through Sweeney's bags. Sheriff Taylor came up slowly, boots sucking mud.

"I see one man lookin' bled out and lyin' there in the mud. I heard three shots. I see three of you standin' here. Oh, and then there's two horses, neither of which do I recognize. Who wants to tell it?"

"I did the shootin', Sheriff. Mebbe I best do it," Gabe said. "Before that, though, this here's mebbe one Heck McCabe outta St. Louie, Missouri."

"Evenin', McCabe," the sheriff said, sizing the man up. "May be? You see the shootin'?"

"I did, sir," McCabe replied.

"Was it a good shootin'?" Sheriff Taylor asked.

"It was."

"All right then, I'm askin' you to go sit inside the house there, while I talk to Gabe, then I'll talk to you. That all right, Gabe?"

"Surely, Sheriff," Gabe said, then yelling out to McCabe, who was starting for the door, "Heck, just have a care with them critters in there. You make any sudden moves, they'll cut ya." Heck placed the gold watch in Gabe's hand as he passed by on his way to the door.

"Harley?" Sheriff Taylor asked.

"No, Sheriff, I came out just a bit late," Harley said.

"All right, then, would you mind gettin' Mr. Dankworth over here to collect this body up? It won't do to have him lyin' out in the street now with people comin' out after the rain."

"Sure, Sheriff," Harley said as he slowly started up the street, looking for a good, walkable path.

Gabe told the sheriff the story. With their history together, Taylor knew to just listen, not interrupt, and he would get the whole truth of it. He stood, arms crossed, nodding, until Gabe was done. He said, "That's the whole of it, Sheriff," when he was done. They headed into the house.

Heck McCabe sat on the hearth in front of the fireplace. Tex and John Henry were sitting together on Gabe's reading table beside his rocker. They were singularly focused on McCabe, who was looking back at them. Tex was letting out a low, guttural growl.

"Looks like they got you surrounded, Heck," Gabe said with a chuckle.

"Yeah, I took your advice," Heck said, with a faint smile. "No sudden moves."

"All right, Mr. McCabe, let's hear it from you. From the time you knocked on Mr. Baker's door until this moment right now," Taylor said, looking down on Heck.

"Of course. Three things first, Sheriff. First, my papers are right there on the table. You're welcome to look at them. Second, I'm going to tell you everything you want to know, but with the understanding that when I tell you something is confidential, as a fellow law enforcement officer, you'll keep it confidential. Third, I'm not going to sit here and look up at you the whole time I'm talking. I'd appreciate if you'd sit, I don't think Mr. Baker will mind."

Sheriff Taylor looked at Gabe, who was nodding. He sat on a straight-backed wooden chair close to the door. "Agreed, so long as you convince me what side of the law you're on."

"That's good enough, seeing as how I've already figured you for a reasonable man," McCabe started.

He then related how the Grant administration had chosen Avery Burke to track down the missing Confederate gold. General Burke knew of Heck's undercover work during the war and wanted him to be his lead man to take on the task of searching for the gold as well as the thieves who took it. His work for the Union had resulted in a lot of Confederate pain and loss.

Heck told Sheriff Taylor that if he had any outstanding questions or doubts, he should wire his boss in St. Louis. Taylor decided it would be in Gabe's best interests to do that and they all went down to the telegraph office. Heck sent the wire, drafted in collaboration with Taylor. Burke's description of Heck and what Heck had said about his mission were confirmed.

Now, Gabe had a decision to make. He wanted to do what was best for his family. He wanted to reconnect with his mother and sisters, and try to find his brother. The last time he had seen his mother was when he and another slave lay her down in some hay after she had been beaten by his master at Heavenly Hills. The night he first had killed. The night he threw off the shackles of bondage and became a man.

4

THE DECISION

Gabe knew that the family members he knew about were living better lives than when he had last seen them. But he didn't know how much better. He thought about where his loyalties lie - to a family he barely knew, or maybe to Harold Douty, who depended on him down at the Red Rock Flour Mill. His other work was not as important, and he knew the stage line could find another guard. He decided he would just talk it through with Douty. And what would become of Tex and John Henry? They were, after all, his family in Boulder.

Gabe had also started to confide in Lin-Chi, the one Harley called a "'splicable". His friends Billy and Harley put a lot of stock in whatever he said to them and he had learned to appreciate his wisdom, too. Lin-Chi had helped them all deal with "soldier's heart", the affliction that so many warfighters had come back home with after years of fighting and killing.

Gabe asked Billy and Harley to meet him at O'Neill's Saloon after work the next day. Billy was the smartest man he knew and was quickly becoming the most sought-after attorney in town. Harley was the toughest. And the two of them were his best friends.

"I'm buyin', 'cause I'm payin' for your advice and expertise," Gabe told them.

"Sounds right," Harley said. "We do 'ave plenty o' that. 'specially after a couple o' those ryes, right Billy?"

"Especially. If you want the real good, top quality advice, you had better buy the real good, top quality rye, Gabe," Billy added.

"Yep. That's all right, then, boys," Gabe said. The first round came and then the second. Billy and Harley knew it was best just to wait until Gabe was ready.

When he was, he spoke up. "Boys, seems like the United States Secret Service can't get along so good without ol' Gabe Baker. I have a job offer. Money's good. Work looks to be honorable, though there may be some question 'bout that. Harley, you met Heck McCabe, you know somethin' 'bout who I'd be workin' with. I hate to leave Mr. Douty after all he's done for us, Harley."

"We done plenty for him, too, Gabe," Harley noted.

"Yeah, you two have become indispensable to his whole operation. But he's a smart man and can figure something out, too," Billy said.

"Well, I talked to 'im today some, told him nothin' was decided yet," Gabe said. "But, man, he was takin' it hard. I felt bad."

"Yeah, I heard somethin' 'bout it, Gabe. He thought you were, uh, you – what's 'at, Billy?"

"Negotiating."

"Yeah. Yeah! Negotiatin' for more money. You'd get it too, Gabe," Harley said.

Gabe gave his two friends the basics of what the job would be and why the Secret Service had sought him out. Billy thought it looked like really interesting, if risky work. Harley thought it sounded like a great adventure.

"If you take that job, Gabe, you think Heck would need an extra hand?" Harley asked.

"Well, if you came along, we'd just 'bout ruin poor ol' Mr. Douty, eh, Harley? I mean, it's been tough on 'im just you goin' part time ever since you put money down on that new horse ranch o' yours," Gabe said, sinking lower in his uncomfortable chair.

"Gabe, I'd just have so many questions. What kind of guarantees are you getting from this McCabe fellow? Does he have a contract I can look at for you? Are you paid by the day, week or month? How much? Anything up front? What expenses are paid for and what equipment is provided? What happens if you want out early? What about if you are hurt? What about a bonus? If you find gold you should get a good piece of it. Is there any paper out on these thieves so you'd have a chance at bounty?" Billy ruminated out loud.

"Whoa, Billy, them are some good kinda questions. I tell y' what," Gabe said, jerking his head over towards the front door. "There's the man to ask, right there." Heck McCabe walked into the barroom, sniffling and holding his hanky in his left hand. He pushed his hat back on his head and strode over to where Isaac was polishing glasses. "Good afternoon, my friend, might you have a good sherry in this establishment?"

"Do have a sherry, sir. Can't say anything about 'good'. I mean, is there such a thing?" Isaac asked, with a smile.

"The answer is 'yes', and I'd be most happy to give yours a try," Heck said, with a slight nod.

"Ah, yes," Heck said, "I can see you are a man of refinement and education, sir. You have found the proper glass for it," Heck said, with a smile.

"Educated, some. Refined? No. I mean, I might get run out of town!" Isaac answered, chuckling.

Heck laughed. He turned his back to the bar and raised his glass to the table of friends sitting in a dark corner. His pudgy fingers made the glass appear even smaller than it was.

Harley was the first to motion for Heck to come over and join them. "Here's our chance to give you advice and expertise, Gabe," he said.

Heck came over, still lifting his glass and smiling. As he sat down, he said, indicating Gabe and Harley, "Well, now I have met this gentlemen here," he said, indicating Harley, "and I am willing to guess that you, sir, are the able attorney, Billy Forest."

"I do like to think of myself as one of several, but, yes, please just call me Billy."

"My attorney has questions for ya, Heck, if'n ya don't mind talkin' bus'ness at this late hour," Gabe said.

"Of course. Seems like in my line, business hours are never over," Heck said, downing his drink. He frowned.

Isaac called over to the table, "Well, sir, what did you think of our sherry?"

"I believe I'll have what these gentlemen are having, friend," Heck yelled back, over his shoulder.

"That's plain enough," Isaac said to no one in particular, then brought over a glass of rye.

"And how 'xactly d' you describe your line o' business, Heck?" Billy asked.

"Well, it started during the war. You could call me a scout. Some called us spies. I was a part of a group that reported on arms and ammunition shipments, gold transport and caches and when the opportunity arose, troop movement. After the war when the Service was established, I became a 'special agent'. Still looking for gold," Heck said, then nodded and took a gulp of his rye.

Billy started asking some of the questions he had put to Gabe before. Heck answered all the questions he could. Gabe would not work directly for the Secret Service, but his work would be like that of an agent. He would make more than actual employees, close to $100.00 a month. All expenses would be paid. He would get a bonus, as yet undetermined, if the gold was found, and more if the thieves were apprehended.

"I'd 'ave t' 'ave time t' see m' kinfolk while I'm out east," Gabe said, looking off at the far wall.

"General Burke thinks you're important, Gabe, and so do I," Heck said. "Whatever reasonable time you'd need would be arranged."

Heck left the group after a while so they could talk among themselves. "Well, what d' you fellers think?" Gabe asked. "It'd be a big change for me."

"This is definitely not the expertise you asked for. Lin-Chi would say, 'follow your heart'. Maybe that means your instinct, whatever your inclination is right now. Because, after talking to your man Heck, he does seem like a straight-shooter," Billy said.

"Sounds right, Gabe, although it wouldn't be just Mr. Douty misses ya," Harley said. "And by the way, since that old redbone hound has been bunkin' with me lately anyway, I wouldn't mind takin' in Tex and John Henry neither. We might just make up a tight little bunch." Harley looked off into the distance for a moment before he caught himself. The horrible loss of his sweet Isabelle three years earlier was obviously on his mind. "We'd make up a good little family, I'd say," he added.

"Thanks, Harley, figgered I could count on ya. Both of ya," Gabe said, looking down into his glass. "I guess I'm just a little wary 'bout goin' east. It's not like here for a black man. I hate thinkin' o' fightin' all those battles all over again. Walkin' into a bar, or a store. Folks lookin' away or crossin' the street t' the other side. Disapprovin' and hatin' faces ever'where. Can't look here, can't stay there, can't go in somewheres else."

"Hmmm. Yeah. We saw some of that on the way out here, didn't we Harley? I guess that is a struggle, though, one Harley and I can't wholely appreciate. And a sign of our times. Just think, though, Gabe. You're a pioneer. Things are so tough for you, but maybe in 100 years, they won't be so bad," Billy said.

"Yeah, that'd be worth it. But I don' know. No one does. That kind o' hate goes on from one generation t' the next. And I reckon ya can't jus' go shootin' your way out of it ever' time it happens, though that is kinda *my* way," Harley said with a twinkle in his eye. "You could cut down on them lowlife mongrels doin' all th' killin' and lynchin' down south right now."

"Thanks for the expertise and advice, boys. Reckon I gotta do it. Gotta do what I can for m' Ma and sisters is what it comes down to," Gabe said. "Mebbe even get t' know 'em some."

"Gabe, you find trouble - just send us a telegram!" Harley said, chuckling.

5

THE TRAIN ROBBERS

Gabe put his affairs in order. When he ducked his head into Harley's front door to say his final good-bye, he saw that Tex and John Henry were cuddled into Red's belly and all were fast asleep. He knew they would be fine.

He and Heck rode to Denver. They planned on taking the Kansas Pacific to Kansas City and the Pacific Railway on to St. Louis. The Denver station was now built up with a large, two-story depot, a wide, flat promenade between it and the three lines of track that curved off into the distance, towards the mountains, or deeper into the expanse of the Great Plains.

Gabe looked forward to talking to Avery Burke. He wanted to get more comfortable about the mission he and Heck were on and hoped for more detail about travel and logistics. He especially wanted to visit with his old boss Mrs. Belcher. And he had an inclination to go out to Bloody Island. Knowing of the horrors visited upon black folks in that remote place, he had declined to go out before when he worked so close by. But now, thinking of visiting family in the east, he wanted to visit and connect with some ex-slaves who probably still lived out there.

He was thinking of this when he and Heck McCabe stepped up into the "first-class" car Heck had booked for them. Heck told him it appeared much more like "second-class", but was the best they could get on this particular day. Gabe felt relieved that there were no incidents outside where he felt exposed amidst a sea of white faces. But then, the conductor eyed Gabe suspiciously and when they entered the car, several passengers immediately started to whisper among themselves, one of the ladies pointing at Gabe. He watched as she summoned the conductor and spoke softly in his ear with a contorted look of disgust and hate on her face. He saw the conductor nod in agreement and put out his hands palms up, demonstrating that he could not do anything about this most regrettable situation. Gabe's hand had instinctively gone to the butt of his Navy Colt before he caught himself. Somehow this lady would have to withstand his presence, and for hours to come. McCabe wore his badge on his jacket for all to see. This seemed to work to prevent any escalation of trouble.

Heck McCabe was observant and curious by nature, but also as a habit of his profession. "I see maybe I've got some to learn, Gabe," Heck said, having watched and understood the whole situation. "I hope you can be patient with me."

The whistle blew two short blasts, the car jerked and clanked into motion and the journey began. Gabe relaxed a bit now. "Jus' you sayin' that makes *me* patient. An' mebbe that's the big word for now, eh, Heck? I mean, we're talkin' 'bout 36 hours to Kansas City?"

"Yep, this is a pretty fast train, but Kansas is a lo-ong state."

The men started to get comfortable with their surroundings as the train left Denver behind. Their car had 12 rows of seats and a narrow aisle, big enough for one person to get through at a time. Heck would have to squeeze and struggle. The seats were situated so that each row faced the one behind it, except for the first and last rows. Passengers could trade places and look ahead or behind. Each row had two connected seats on each side so that full, the car could accommodate 48 passengers. Their car was less than half full. There was a water dispenser on a wooden pedestal to the right up front and a privy at the rear of the car. The bench seats had a thin cushion covered with leather to sit on but the backs were of bare wood and too short to lean one's head on. Sleeping would be difficult.

Gabe had also noticed that theirs was the first of three passenger cars. In front of them was the express car, the coal car and then, the engine.

Gabe and Heck sat on the right side of their car, just behind its mid-point. The agitated lady and her party filled the third and fourth rows ahead of them on the left side. Gabe wondered if she was still thinking about him, hoping that the excitement of their departure had by now distracted her attention. But he knew the trouble wasn't likely over. Sooner or later, some of the passengers would start showing signs of "prairie fatigue". If a scapegoat was needed, attention could fall on him again.

After a couple of hours of travel, the conversations among the passengers started to die down and the monotony of the swaying of the train, the sounds of the track and the sameness of the prairie, mile after mile, started to set in. After watching the plains roll by for several hours, Gabe started to watch his fellow passengers again.

There were two men of indeterminate age sitting together in front of the ladies who had made their complaint known to the conductor. Their faces were brown and creased, but they held themselves like younger men. They spoke together in hushed tones. Gabe saw that they both wore their Colts down low on their legs, their holsters tied down tight. One of them kept a Winchester close to hand.

There was a young family, husband and wife, with a boy and girl, all dressed in clean, but somewhat worn clothing. They were gregarious together but kept to themselves. The husband was carrying a pocket pistol of some sort on his belt. They sat three rows in front of Gabe and Heck. Once in a while, Gabe would catch the young boy, who appeared to be about six, sneaking a peek at him. Gabe smiled and the boy smiled and giggled. Behind them there was a group of three who appeared to be cattlemen. They all carried sidearms. There were also several passengers traveling alone. One appeared to be a drummer, and he kept his samples case close by his side at all times. There were two others who could have been businessmen of some type. Gabe could not see any obvious weapons on them.

Gabe's attention turned back to those two in the front. Their demeanor had changed slightly. They were talking less and sitting up straighter. One of them was clenching his jaw. He repeatedly lowered his head and looked out the windows of both sides of the car. The other looked at a pocket watch he held in his left hand every couple of minutes. Gabe elbowed Heck and nodded in their direction.

"Yeah, Gabe, I've been watching. Maybe this is their first train trip and they're just a bit nervous. I mean we are steaming along at 20 miles an hour," Heck said, smiling, then wiping his face with his hanky. "Anyway, it's good to know my traveling companion has a lawman's eye."

"Onliest experience I have is shotgunnin' for th' stage t' Cheyenne an' a bit o' backup for the law in Boulder and Denver when they call on me."

Heck followed one of the men's eyes out along the prairie, wondering what he was looking for. Then, he said, "Experience helps but it is the mettle of a man that makes for a good lawman, I figure, from the sheriff on the street all the way up to the attorney general."

"Well, I never figgered on doin' too much of it, lotta folks, talkin' 'bout some white folks, don't take so kindly t' black man with gun or badge. They're gettin' stirred up even afore I can get t' the heart o' th' matter at hand, if y' know what I mean?"

"I think I do," Heck said. Then he motioned with his head towards the gunhands up front. "They're about to make a move and I don't think it's going to be a friendly one."

Gabe and Heck heard horse hooves coming up beside the train. The two men slowly started to stand up to face the rest of the passengers in the car. "Heck, earlier's better 'n later?" Heck gave a slight nod.

The badmen stood, each holding onto the seatback in front of him. Gabe and Heck stood up at the same time. The men drew their guns. Suddenly, it was too late for words. Gabe and Heck drew faster and fired at the same time. Gabe's man clutched his chest, dropped his gun and fell back against the front of the car. Heck's doubled over, grasping at the seatback. He lifted his gun to shoot, his eyes desperately searching for a target. Gabe and Heck's guns again blasted at the same time. This time the man crumpled to the aisle floor.

Two of the women in the party in front who were facing the men who were just shot half stood and started shrieking. The woman and her male friend facing Gabe and Heck ducked down below their seatback. "Get down up there! Get down!" Heck yelled. Gabe got down on a knee to find the riders now fast approaching the train. As he pointed out the right side of the car, the young family man in front grabbed the Winchester that was now laying on the floor. He rushed back to Gabe and Heck.

"I can shoot this thing. Just tell me where you want me," he said in a strangely calm way, looking back and forth between Gabe and Heck.

"Looks like the riders are all on this side," Heck said, looking back at Gabe for confirmation. Gabe nodded his head. "If you want to help, son, get down by this window here and wait for something to shoot at," Heck said pointing at the seats just behind them.

"Name's Rogers, Sir. Casey Rogers," the young man said as he settled into position on one knee.

"Glad you could join us, Casey. I'm Gabe, and this here's Heck McCabe," Gabe said, still watching out the window. Then he looked at Heck and pointed at the ceiling.

"Yeah, I heard that," Heck said. "One on the roof. Now we have a problem, with all these citizens in here. And they might not take too kindly with how we abused their partners. Gabe, can you check out the back? See what you can see? Might help if we knew what's happening in those two cars behind, too. I'll go up front on the baggage car, maybe we can squeeze our man between us."

"So long 's we don't shoot each other. On m' way, Heck."

"Don't get yourself shot. Your president needs you," Heck said, with a somber smile.

Casey gave Heck a questioning look. "Casey, can you protect this car? Bullets could come from any direction," Heck said.

"I can do that, Sir," he said, with a quick nod, lifting the Winchester to waist level." He walked over to reassure his wife and kids and make sure they were as protected as possible under the seats.

Gabe went to the back door and watched until Heck was ready at the front. He nodded and they both went outside. Gabe gave a quick look into the car behind. He could see several passengers ducked behind seats. He figured he'd better attend to whatever was happening up above before checking into the different cars. Maybe he would get a better idea of what was going on, too. But he didn't want anyone coming out and shooting him, thinking he was a train robber, either. He opened the door and yelled inside, "Ever'thing all right in here?" There was no answer. "Just so's y'all know, I'm with the law. Anyone hear any noises up top?" No Answer. "All right, damn it, just don't shoot me," he said, disgusted. He slammed the door, turned around and climbed the little half-ladder so he could poke his head up over the roofline of his car.

At the other end of the car a man knelt on his left knee and held a pistol in his right hand. He was looking straight ahead. Gabe pulled his Colt out, aimed it at the man, and shouted through the noise of the train, "Best give it up now, cowboy!" The man turned, flopped down to his belly and took a wild shot at Gabe. After ducking, Gabe reached back up over the roof with his Colt, and followed with as little of his face as he could to see the man again. The man shot again, clipping the edge of the roof right in front of Gabe. Well, damn, Gabe thought, I didn't play that one very well.

Then he heard, "Throw that gun away, or I'll blast you for sure, you damned scoundrel!" The cowboy jerked his head around and shot at Heck. Heck's shot hit him in the shoulder. Gabe fired at the same time and hit him in the back of his head. He went limp and rolled off the car, hitting the ground with a thump and a cloud of dust that Casey could see from in the car.

Heck looked over the top of the car as Gabe was doing the same on the other end. "I'm thinkin' two more, you?"

"Yessir! Two more. They have got to get one up to the engine. Any ideas of their whereabouts, Gabe?" Heck said with a big smile. Gabe thought, what's wrong with this crazy man, is he having fun?

"No sir! Mebbe I'll go back, you able to get forward?" Gabe asked.

"Hey, now! You think just 'cause I'm a little bit heavy around the middle I can't move around?"

"Nothin' o' th' kind. Just don't know how you'd do it," Gabe said.

"If I get to the engine and I've got the other two, we'll give two blasts of the whistle. If I get one, one blast. If don't see them, three blasts."

"What if you see them and don't get them?"

"Then they're all yours," he laughed, and disappeared below the lip of the roof.

When he got back down the ladder, Gabe poked his head inside the car. Casey Rogers was standing with one hand on the seat where his family had been so comfortable some 20 minutes earlier. He held the Winchester in the crook of his other arm. "Casey, ever'thing all right in here?" Gabe asked.

"I reckon, Gabe, just stayin' put 'til this is all over."

"Good. Two o' them jaspers left. Heck's lookin' up front, I'm goin' back. It ain't over yet." Gabe wasted no time. He closed the door, turned around and looked into the next car. He slowly opened the door, his Colt out in front of him. He saw no movement and no passengers until a man poked his head out from behind a seatback on the second to last row on Gabe's right. The man must have seen Gabe as he immediately ducked back behind again. "You. You in the back! Stand up," Gabe yelled over the sound of the wheels on the tracks. He waited. Nothing.

"Stand up, back there, or I'll blast you right through that seat. This Colt'll do it. Stand up, man!"

The elderly gentleman lifted his head up so his eyes were showing. "Rest of the way, Sir!" Gabe yelled. The man complied. He had black, slicked-down hair and a bushy gray beard, turning white under his chin. He had on a white shirt under his gray vest, and wore a black western bowtie around his ample neck. Gabe thought, this guy has to be a banker. His eyes darted down to his right and then to Gabe.

"Are you here to shoot me, is that it? I already told the other, uh, gentle-man, I don't carry a lot of money, you boys can have everything I've got," the man grumbled, nervously.

"I ain't here t' shoot nobody 'at's not shootin' at me, Sir. I'm lookin' for train robbers. You got 'ny in here?"

Gabe's demeanor and manner of speaking put the man at ease, but he still looked shaken. "N-no. I mean, there was one here – you, know, before. He – he left, maybe he went back. Yeah, could be behind us. And there was noise – up on the roof, you know? Then we heard some gunfire up ahead, where you came from," the man said.

"All right, I'm comin' through for a look-see. Then I'm checkin' the car behind. Ever'body stay down. I see th' flash o' gun metal on m' way through, I'll be shootin', not talkin' – so, stay down an' be careful." He started walking, grabbing a seatback on each row with his left hand, holding his Navy Colt with his right, looking from side to side. Three rows down a dusty-looking, middle-aged cowboy was hiding on the floor next to a pudgy older lady dressed in her best for travel. When he looked up, Gabe could see the man's pock-marked face and red hair. Gabe gave them both a nod and said, "How do, ma'am, ever'thing gon' be all right real soon, you'll see," to the lady. She stared up at him with a terrified look on her face. Her hands covered her mouth as if to stifle a scream. Her seatmate nodded but avoided Gabe's eyes.

He nodded and said "how do" a couple of times when he came across the other passengers laying low on the floor. When he got to the back of the car, he nodded at the elderly gentleman and gave him a pat on the shoulder. The man stooped back down. Gabe whirled around to give the car one last look before he went out the door. He looked to see where the man's eyes had darted when he first came in. A small lady's traveling bag lay in the corner. When he got outside, he looked back into the car again, through the window in the door. Something was not quite right.

Gabe started to look through the window into the last passenger car before going in. At that moment, the train lurched and screeched as it came to a sudden, violent stop. He slipped and lost his footing. He grabbed onto the hand bar to stay upright and not fall all the way off. He barely held on. He dropped his Colt on the floor in the process. Just as he was trying to get steady again, the whistle blew. Gabe waited a moment. Only once. All right, if that was Heck's signal, there was only one badman left.

As he slowly moved through that last car now, his mind went back to what was bothering him. That fine lady who was dressed up so much had no rings on. He had seen both of her hands. For that matter, she had no broach. That must have been her bag in the back with the banker. Why hadn't he done something to signal Gabe that the lady, probably his wife, was in trouble? He may have been too scared to think straight. Or, Gabe just hadn't noticed. That last car held only two sets of passengers. Neither seemed suspicious. He wheeled around and made his way back to the second car. It was empty. Except for the dusty cowboy. He was now standing at the front of the car facing Gabe as he opened the door. The man had a wide stance and his arms dangled at his sides. At the end of his right one was a Colt peacemaker.

"All right, cowboy, good to see you ain't hidin' behind the lady's skirts no more. I came back for ya, and I'm hopin' you'd know better'n t'give me grief," Gabe said in a conversational tone.

"You'd be Gabe Baker outta Boulder, Colorado and St. Louie before that," the man said. "I'm Briggs. Percy Briggs." He slowly raised his gun and held it on Gabe.

"I don't know why ya know me, but common courtesy would be t' holster that gun and talk to me man t' man. If'n ya can do it without the Colt."

Briggs shoved his gun into its holster and gestured with his arms out wide. "All right, Gabe?"

"All right, Percy. Now, what're you after here on this train?"

"I'd think that'd be clear by now, Gabe. *You.* We're – well, it may be just me now; anyway, I'm here to take you to my boss. Just so's he can have a brief conversation with you, though. No more than that."

"No more'n that. You and your boys just attacked and stopped a train with a couple dozen innocent passengers on board, just t' have a talk. An' now, mebbe your boys are dead, too. You couldn't just ask, that right, Briggs?"

Gabe tried to keep the conversation going. He saw Heck McCabe come up between the cars behind Briggs. Heck would need the surprise factor to get a hold of him. But Briggs heard the door squeak as McCabe slowly opened it. He quickly turned and kicked the door open, knocking Heck backwards and down. When he turned back, Gabe had his Colt pointed directly at his belly.

"Well, now, doesn't that common courtesy work both ways, Gabe?" Percy demanded, now breathing quickly.

"Not after you knock my friend down and tell me you're here to force me to go with you. I had enough o' that back at Heavenly Hills Farm. Now, unbuckle that gunbelt there and let it drop. That way you won't scratch that fancy new Colt o' yours."

Briggs frowned, but having no choice, complied. And when the gunbelt dropped, it uncovered the belt behind it. Its buckle was in the shape of a large rectangle with a golden triangle in the middle. Just like Sweeney's.

6

ABILENE

Heck McCabe had been knocked off the car and onto the ground when Briggs hit him with the door. Once Gabe had gotten Briggs into a seat he peered out to see what had happened. Heck looked up at him, shaking his head.

"You all right, Heck? That's a long fall!"

"Are you kidding me, Gabe? With all this padding I have on me, it didn't even hurt." Gabe could see that he was shaken, but he was getting up and dusting himself off when Gabe went back into the car.

Once the train got rolling again, Heck handcuffed Briggs to the arm of his chair. The banker and his wife sat quietly in the back, whispering to each other every now and then, all the way to Abilene. There, the Kansas Pacific allowed the passengers two hours for dinner. When they got off the train, they immediately encountered the sights, sounds and smells of a recently arrived herd of 2,000 longhorns that had just survived the long and difficult drive up the Chisolm Trail. Cowboys and cows had suffered three months of heat, dust and the occasional torrential downpour. There was also an attack on their herd by rustlers who had come over from Oklahoma for some easy money. The town was full but eerily quiet just now.

"The calm before the storm," the banker told them, as they stepped down from the train. "It won't be safe for man, woman or child in a few hours. We'd all best be back aboard on time."

Heck had thought the best thing to do with Percy Briggs was to see if the town marshal would take him. Maybe he would accept him into his lockup, at least while the train was in Abilene.

Gabe and Heck walked off to their left down the wide, dusty street where Heck thought the marshal's office was. Broadway Avenue wasn't much more than three blocks long. The largest building in town was the Drover's Cottage, built to house the cowboys coming up the Chisolm Trail with their longhorns from Texas. Huge holding pens alongside the tracks kept the beeves under control until they could be loaded into stock cars, on their way east. There was a small bank, and a new two-story brick hotel. There were a couple of saloons, but it looked like the real action in Abilene was down Texas Street.

And that's where one of the marshal's deputies sent them. "Oh, marshal's down at his real office about now. Things'll start to liven up a bit soon," he told Heck. "Just down the street, turn left on Texas Street down to Cedar, then on your left, second block. Alamo Saloon, you can't miss it, from the sight, the sound or the smell."

"Haha!" Heck laughed. "Sounds like my old friend has not changed much. While we're down asking him about leaving our prisoner here on a more permanent basis, I hope you can put him up for the time being?" Heck asked. He is the sole survivor of the attempted robbery of the train we just came in on. We also have some business for your undertaker, of course, too."

"I'll take the live one. Uncle Marvin – that's our undertaker - will collect the rest if you can find him," the deputy said.

Once Percy Briggs was behind bars, Heck and Gabe started down the street, Heck pulling out his watch to see how much time they had left. "Well, we'll give the marshal notice of what we've left for him to deal with before we go. He's an old friend of mine, you know. You may have heard of him. James

Butler Hickok. Lots of folks are calling him 'Wild Bill', you know he's been in the dime novels they're all so excited about out east."

"Yeah?" Gabe said, "Well I 'ave heard of him. They say he's just about the fastest there is with a gun. And you know 'im, eh, Heck?"

"You could say we worked together once, yeah, it'll be good to see old 'Wild Bill' again. And I don't know about that 'just about' business there, Gabe," Heck said with a sly smile.

"I haven't seen 'im in action, so hard t' tell, but I just can't see anyone could be faster 'n my friend Billy Forest. Or, lately now, Harley Cobb neither. I been learnin' from both o' those fellers m'self," Gabe added. Heck smiled and shook his head.

The Alamo had two entrances along Cedar Street. The two men pushed open the double-glass doors at the west end and stood for a few seconds to get their bearings and adjust to the dimly-lit room. The ornate bar was just to their left. It was made of dark mahogany and featured elaborate brass fixtures and rails. Behind it and looming over the backbar was a large polished mirror which aided in the illusion of how large the room was. It also highlighted the great variety of whiskey and other spirits available.

Wild Bill was not hard to find. There was a jumble of gaming tables set around the large room, but only one with a crowd of men around it. And Heck could hear his booming voice as well. Gabe and Heck ordered large whiskeys and took them over to see the main attraction, Bill Hickok playing cards with a group of young cowboys.

Bill looked up from his hand when the two men approached. He immediately laid it down, slapped the table with his right hand and bellowed, "Well, I'll be damned! If it ain't ol' Heck McCabe, lawman extraordinaire and a helluva saddle partner to boot!" He stood up and gave Heck's hand a vigorous shake. The cowboys seemed to take pleasure in the spectacle, Wild Bill, tall and muscular, with his long, flowing locks tucked behind his ears, and short and squat Heck McCabe, meeting as equals. Something like long lost brothers.

"And if it isn't Wild Bill Hickok, fastest gun in the west, famed far and wide in the annals of American fiction – well, er – literature?" Heck said as he broke himself up laughing. "Good to see you, Bill. And this gentleman with me is my current saddle partner, Mr. Gabe Baker," Heck added, nodding over to his left.

Bill Hickok extended his hand and Gabe shook it. "Very good t' meet ya, Marshal. I've heard some good – well, some *things* - about you, yeah. I reckon you are famous."

"Hahaha!" Bill Hickok roared. "I do like your friend, Heck." He turned back to Gabe, "Of course, it can't all be good now that I'm on the side of law and order, can it? I've got a feelin' that could be a temporary problem though." He laughed again. "Heck, it would be my great pleasure to buy you and Gabe here whiskey until we've had our fill or until trouble starts, whichever comes first."

"Wish we could, Bill. Gabe and I are on a short layover courtesy of the Kansas Pacific, and we'll have to be off soon. But we wanted to know if we could leave some of our cargo at your accommodations down the street before we go."

"Sounds interesting," Bill said, sitting back down and looking at his hand again. "Anyone I know?"

"He calls himself Percy Briggs, we just put a crimp in his and his gang's plans to rob the train. Rest of the bunch is over at, well, Uncle Marvin's?"

"Good. Less trouble for me to deal with," he said to Heck. He looked back at his cards. "I'll see that and raise $20.00." He threw two small gold pieces into the pile in the center of the table. "Hmmm. Briggs, huh? I think I know him. I'll take him if you two will write out a report of what happened. I'd guess you're on your way to St. Louis?"

"That's right, appreciate it, Bill."

"That's fine. I'll wire your office in a couple of days if I need anything else. Any crew or passengers hurt?"

"I'm happy to say no."

"Sounds like you and Gabe did a good job." He stood and shook their hands before they swallowed their drinks and headed for the door.

The men stepped outside into the late afternoon sun. "So, that was Wild Bill Hickok, huh, Heck? Seem like a right nice feller. An' he look just like I thought he would. You and him partners? Well, 'at's jus' somethin'," Gabe said, shaking his head back and forth. "Jus' somethin'. I notice he got Navy Colts - .36s, jus' like mine. Well, 'ceptin' for the ivory handles. Like t' see how fast he is with them shooters someday."

"I saw him once. He gets them both out in a hurry and shoots straight. The thing is, even if someone else was faster, no one I ever saw is cooler under fire. That includes during the war," Heck said. The two walked around the corner back to the jail, where Heck quickly wrote out his report. They also made sure the young Casey Rogers would be able to collect the bounty on each man in the gang who had a sheet out on him. Then they went to the Drover's Cottage for a quick dinner before boarding the train.

They were greeted by some of the passengers as heroes for the work they'd done in handling the outlaws. The passengers in the group at the front of their car, however, averted their eyes and maintained their distance. Everyone soon fell back into the rhythm of the rails and the travel across the prairie. Initially, the passengers at the front of their car had seemed captivated by the utter vastness of a landscape that went on forever until at some, unreachable distance, it met the sky. That magic was now long forgotten. They quickly settled into the tedium of mile after mile of prairie that to the untrained eye appeared unchanging.

This trip *was* monotonous for most. It seemed dull and dreary, even desolate. It was mostly treeless, and the colors rarely changed. It was yellow and gray and dusty brown. But the careful observer could appreciate a stark beauty in this land, like one finds in the desert. And at times sagebrush, sunflowers and even colorful patches of wildflowers would appear. Prairie dog "cities" were numerous. One buffalo herd they came across started running with the train. Thousands of the "big shaggies", as Gabe had learned to call them, spreading out and flowing across the broad expanse of the prairie like a murmuration of gigantic starlings, making and remaking forms below the horizon.

Gabe watched all of this in a state of wonder. He had seen this country at a much slower pace coming out west with Captain Calley's wagon train just five years earlier. Even then, he had immediately felt an attraction to the wide open spaces of Kansas and eastern Colorado Territory. He had an awareness that his affinity for this world had something to do with his captivity growing up as a slave at Heavenly Hills. There, his world had been crushingly small, his routine grinding, his torment relentless and his life without hope or joy. This place was an antidote for all that. This world was unfathomably huge, both the land and the sky. It was made for freedom. And the possibilities in a life here seemed endless. He remembered what his friend White Crow, the half-Cheyenne with whom he had worked and fought on these plains, had told him. He believed that they could not be free without their tie to this land. He pondered these things as the train chugged along. And he thought of what it would be like to see his mother and sister.

7

ST. LOUIS

Although St. Louis was becoming a big and thriving transportation and industrial hub by the 1870s, the railways that served the area still had their own individual depots. Gabe and Heck's train hissed and screeched to a stop at the Kansas Pacific station in Mill Creek Valley at around 6:00 a.m. The passengers slowly picked themselves up and staggered, glassy-eyed for the doorways of their cars. It was warm for October, and, humid. As the two men stepped down to the platform, the slight morning breeze brought with it an exotic blend of fetid water, industrial smoke and decaying refuse, some of it visible along the streets in the morning light. Gabe's memories of his time in St. Louis came flooding back with the familiar and singular smell of the city.

"General Burke is a man of habit," Heck said as they started walking away from the depot, bags in hand. "He should be at the office at 7:00. It's only a mile from here. We might as well walk and stretch our legs. There's a good place for breakfast on the way."

"I know it, Heck," Gabe said. "Weidmann's!" The two men ate and regained some energy. They arrived at the Secret Service offices a little after 7:00. The building housed a variety of banking and financial enterprises as well as the government agencies that filled the top floor. It was a modest four-story structure, with open views to the east and west. Heck McCabe announced their arrival to the General's assistant, who sat in an open reception area at the top of the stairs. The two stood as he disappeared into the General's office for a minute before emerging and inviting them in.

The General's office was dark, but with the Mississippi River visible through the morning smoke and haze. When his assistant led Gabe and Heck in, the General stood and stepped around the end of his heavy, imposing desk, and extended his right hand. "Good morning, gentlemen, good morning," he boomed, shaking their hands. "Good to see you hale and hearty, still, Heck. Very good to meet you, Gabe," he said, as he leaned on his desk to get back to his swivel chair.

General Burke was a stout man for his age, apparently in his mid-60s. He had a long face framed by a full head of brown hair, swept back, half-covering his ears, and falling down over his collar. He had an ample, full beard, which had grown down to the third level of buttons on his clean, light-brown shirt. The only gray he was showing was around the edges of his whiskers. His eyes were a piercing blue, and attentive to both of his visitors.

"I imagine you've had an exhausting trip all the way from Denver. I'll have Leonard bring some coffee. Leonard!" he yelled out the open door.

"On its way, Sir," came the quick answer. After the coffee came, Burke offered the men a cigar. When they declined, he said, "I know, it's just a nasty habit. But, if it's good enough for the president . . ." He interrupted himself, making a show of turning it against the match and puffing it lit before blowing out the first pall of smoke. "Anyway, I want to thank you Gabe, for agreeing to see me. I know you want to get right down to business, and maybe get some questions answered. Most likely first would be how we found you and what we're asking you to do."

Gabe sipped his coffee. He hadn't drunk out of such a small, pretty cup since his days at Mrs. Belcher's and he fumbled with it trying to use the handle which was too small to get his finger through. Gabe gave the General a weak smile and nodded. Then he said, "Yessir, and mebbe even a little of who you are. I was just a gun-toter, didn't know too many gen'rals." Heck sat back so Gabe and Burke could get to know each other.

"Yeah, yes, all right. The Secret Service is a new agency within the Department of Treasury and not many have heard of us. Our first task at the end of the war was to clamp down on all the counterfeiting of U.S. currency that was going on right after Appomattox. We're now being used to investigate other financial misdeeds, most importantly, the theft of gold and valuables belonging to the United States government. And gold, Gabe, is what we're after now. Confederate gold," he said, drawing the words out for emphasis. He blew out a plume of cigar smoke. "I should say 'formerly Confederate gold'." He chuckled at his little joke.

"Heck tol' me a stash of it was hidden under Fort Wagner. Not only Heck, but a gen'leman who went by the name o' Oliver Sweeney, too. That gen'leman happened t' be at my house in Boulder when Mr. McCabe here first came by."

"Yes. Sweeney? Heck sent me a telegram. Seems like Mr. Sweeney finally met his match. In you, Gabe, for which, I can tell you, the Grant administration is grateful."

"Good t' hear, Gen'ral, but I was just tryin' not t' get shot, or mebbe t' keep Heck here from gettin' shot." Gabe looked at Heck. "You know, Heck, I'm still not sure which one of us that varmint was aimin' at."

Heck smiled and nodded. "I'm thinking you saved my hide, Gabe. He wanted me out of the way and you in the gang he had come out west to put together."

"And the reason he wanted you is the same reason we want you, Gabe," Burke continued, now chomping on his stogie. "Some of that Confederate gold was in the form of coins, some dollars, some specially minted CSA double eagles. Could be some gold bars, too. Someone put at least one of those coins into circulation a few months back around Maryland, maybe Baltimore area. With some hard work and a lot of luck, we traced them to an area close to your old home, the Heavenly Hills Farm. Sounds like a nice place."

Gabe stood and looked over at Heck. He gently put his cup in its saucer, his hand shaking. And the look in his eyes was anything but gentle. He leaned against the fingertips he stretched out on both sides of the cup. He glared down at the General, who instinctively scooted his chair back before Gabe said anything. Then Gabe spoke. "Heavenly Hills. That was a *white* man's home. The man who owned me. It was also home to that man's white trash boys. Those sons-of-bitches beat and raped my Mama in front of me for years. I was jus' a tadpole, havin' to watch it. Too young and too small and too scared to do what needed doin'. Too many times t' count. With all due respect, Sir, you must know somethin' like that happenin' most any big farm you can name south o' the Mason-Dixon line. That ain't no home to a black man. No. That is surely just as much hell as you can conjure up and picture in your mind. Opposite of home, opposite of 'nice'."

Gabe looked back and forth between the General and Heck. He was shaking a bit, slightly, but noticeably. Heck crossed his arms, opened his eyes wide and cocked his head as he looked the General in his eyes. Gabe exhaled loudly and sat down, not knowing what to expect next. Then, he apologized. "Sorry, General," he said, taking a moment to inhale. "I guess you didn't mean nothin' by it."

Then it was Burke's turn. His face was red and his cigar shook slightly in his right hand. He leaned forward, glaring at Gabe. "If you were under my command in the army, I'd have you court-martialed before the dinner bell rang and in the clink before the sun came up. Nobody talks to me in that tone," he blustered. He flung the cigar into the ash tray to his right. He stood up, aiming his imperious gaze into Gabe's eyes.

Gabe returned the look, regaining his composure. "I said I was sorry, Sir, and I meant it. But my commanding officer was Colonel Robert Shaw. And Colonel Shaw *never* woulda said what you jus' did. And may he rest in peace, I never saw a better man or soldier."

General Burke's posture softened. He put his fists on his desk, let his head droop slightly and sat down. He looked straight across at Gabe again and said, "I knew your Colonel Shaw. You are right about him, of course. You'd be in a better position to know him as a man and as a leader of men than I would anyway."

The storm had passed. But General Burke had learned something important about the man who sat across the desk from him. Burke's tone and demeanor changed. He leaned forward and started again. "Anyway, we know that some of the 54th was made up with escaped slaves and freedmen who came from Maryland, many from the Baltimore area. We also know that some of them were members of your Company D. And we believe those gold coins that were put into circulation in that area may have originated with some of your compatriots." General Burke held up his hand as if to stop Gabe from speaking, and continued, "I'm not saying any of these men are thieves. We just don't know. But we have to go to where the gold showed up. We need somebody these men will trust. That's you, Gabe."

"General, that Sweeney fella, threatened if he didn't send word I was helpin' him out, could be some harm done t' my family. An' 'e seemed t' know right where my Mama and sister are livin'. I need t' know they gonna be all right."

"Hmmm," the General's chair squeaked as he leaned back and then forward again, now with his elbows on the desk and his hands steepled in front of his chin. He started to tap his hands against his mouth and chin. "Leonard!" he yelled out the partially closed door to his assistant. Leonard rushed in dutifully and stood beside Burke while Burke wrote out a note. Leonard read it and said, "Got it, sir."

"All right, send that as a telegram to the Chief. Right away. Wait for a response. When you get it, come back here and report."

"Yessir," Leonard said as he escaped with the note out the door.

"We will have a man looking after your family, Gabe. And what you've said may help us find more of Sweeney's gang. If, indeed, he had any yet. Is there anything else you can tell us about what this Sweeney said to you before, well, you know, before you sent him along to his just desserts?"

"He didn't say it, but I did notice somethin' peculiar. His belt buckle. I'd never seen one before. It was dark except for a gold triangle in it."

"Heck, I didn't see that in your report," General Burke said with a raised voice and a more serious look.

"I have to say, sir, I didn't notice it myself," Heck said with a weak smile. He drew out his handkerchief and mopped his brow as the morning, and the room, warmed.

"Well, if that means somethin', mebbe this means somethin' else. That man we left in Wild Bill's lockup, the man called Briggs? Well, he had on the same buckle. And he knew m' name and said 'e wanted t' take me t' his boss. Sorry Heck, in all th' excitement it slipped m' mind."

"Damn!" the General pounded his fist on the desk and looked Heck in the eye. "At least we know they're around and on the job. This isn't just some gang put together by that lowlife Sweeney, then."

"Yeah, General," Heck said. "Good to know." He sat up on the edge of his chair. He wiped his chin and neck. "Chevaliers du Triangle D'or. Gabe is right. Something about that train robbery didn't seem right. There was nothing in the express car worth committing four men to."

Burke caught Gabe looking puzzled. "The Knights of the Golden Triangle," Burke said. "A military and political society of the Confederacy. The worst of the worst. Shameless, bloodthirsty killers all. Their aim was to ally the CSA with several Caribbean and South American countries to create a new social order – a new empire. They would use white southern elites to control an empire built on the backs of every last black African they could find and put in chains. Sugar, tobacco and cotton would make them rich and powerful." He paused. "They don't accept that the South lost the war."

"Yeah, Gabe," Heck added, "They probably have an army of owlhoots and petty criminals around the country. Ex-soldiers who haven't learned how to make a living other than what they can pick up toting a rifle around the countryside. Their plan would require a lot of funding. It seems we now know where they're looking for at least some of it."

"That does seem clear, Heck," Burke said. "But this won't change what you and Gabe are doing except to make it that much more dangerous. For you, Heck, because you are a known man and a hated man in the South and these men want the South to rise again. For you, Gabe, because you may be the key that unlocks the whereabouts of that gold. And the ability of these treasonous bastards to realize their dreams." He hesitated and sat back. "Gentlemen, let's keep this Golden Triangle thing under our hats. Even within the Service. You don't know where their spies might be, as Heck well knows. But if you find anything more about them, send me a telegram. Refer to them as something else. Uh, maybe, let's call them - the Johnson Gang. Yes, that'll do."

"General Burke, that man Sweeney found out 'bout my family from talking to my former boss here in St. Louis. I worked at the Belcher House for a good year. I'm thinkin' mebbe we could see if Mrs. Belcher got t' know anythin' 'bout him."

"Fine. That's good. I think you'll make a good special agent with the Service, Gabe." He reached into his desk and retrieved a badge and an official-looking document with Gabe's name on it. He handed them to Gabe, who reviewed the paper and nodded his head. Burke continued. "Now. I've got you men scheduled on the mid-morning train out to Cincinnati tomorrow. You'll go from there straight to Washington. As you know, Heck, headquarters is still in New York just now, but the Deputy Chief is working in the capital and that's closer to where you'll want to start your work.

You have rooms tonight at the Barnum. I have a carriage to pick you up at 9:30. Leonard will accompany you and help you with baggage. Speaking of which, he will bring you each an extra bag with equipment you need. I think you'll be happy with it. And an expense report form for each of you. The Deputy Chief will expect to see you on your arrival in Washington to brief you on any new information we may have. Any questions?"

Gabe and Heck looked at each other and nodded. No questions, they were both exhausted. It was a good time to take their leave.

8

THE DEPUTY CHIEF

After a pleasant, but fruitless conversation with Mrs. Belcher, Gabe and Heck settled into the Barnum. They enjoyed a long night's sleep before Leonard picked them up with the carriage in the morning. They would catch the ferry across the river to East St. Louis and catch the train from there.

They were pleased upon boarding to learn that the General had booked them into a Pullman car. This provided the travelers with a compartment similar to a small cabin on a ship. There was a sofa at floor level and a second sleeping berth made up at night by the porter fixing a board above it, with ample bedding for each of them. At meal time the porter, or one of his assistants, carried in a small table. The railroad offered a variety of fare, such as mutton, ham, mackerel and chicken. Water and fuel stops usually included the option of eating at a diner and enjoying coffee or tea. This leg of the journey would be much more civilized than their trip through Kansas and Missouri. But it would be long - 14 hours to Cincinnati, and another 18 to Washington, D.C. They would have plenty of time to talk about plans.

They did more eating and sleeping than planning. But they did plan on hiring a ride to find Gabe's family in Baltimore after meeting with the Deputy Chief. Gabe started to get nervous about seeing his mother and sisters. His master and owner at Heavenly Hills had used his mother as a breeder. She was young and strong and attractive. And he made sure she was pregnant most of the time. He kept her away from her children as much as possible. Gabe's grandmother tended to the young ones. She was old enough that her field hand days were over. Gabe knew her better than he did his own mother.

The last time he had seen his mother was the night he killed his master and his master's sons. And the slavedriver Sikes, with the help of a friend, even while Sikes held his big Bowie knife to his Mama's throat. His lasting memory was of her lying limp on the ground with glassy eyes, staring into some unknown void. And he had left her in the hands of those who refused to escape with him. Now, maybe the woman he was to meet was someone else. Would she know him? Would she be able to smile or laugh? Was she physically healthy? She hadn't revealed much in her letters. Gabe just knew that she had survived. He was nervous, but hoped for the best.

Anyway, first they must have their meeting with the Deputy Chief. He was using an office across the street from the capitol building. They decided to walk as it was only a few blocks from the station. It was a fine November day, sunny and cool. The building was easy enough to find. It was an imposing Greek Revival-style government building, of white stone that appeared to be marble. The façade was impressive with elongated pediment and columns. The elevation seemed designed to impress as they walked up the wide steps towards the front entrance. Although covering most of a city block, it was only three stories high.

Upon entering, Heck was immediately struck with the atmosphere inside. "Gabe, a blind man would know he's in a federal building from the smell. I tell you, I don't know how they do it. They're all the same."

"I noticed, but it wasn't familiar to me. Seems like old papers, maybe mold. I was in a library once in St. Louis had that smell. Maybe old books or files?"

"Haha! Could be, my friend."

They checked the office register and saw that their man was on the first floor and around the corner in front of them. Heck looked at Gabe. "Well, Gabe, I don't know this man too well, just by reputation. He did some detective work during the war for a certain Lieutenant Colonel who was stationed in New Orleans for a while. But the kind of work he did, most of it was kept secret, so it's hard to judge the man on that, but he's known around the agency as a man of some competence. Um, Gabe, I should tell you, he was once thought to have some Southern sympathies, but I don't know the truth of that."

"Thanks, Heck. You know me by now. I'll mind m' manners," Gabe said. Heck shook his head while giving him a broad, disbelieving smile.

They found a closed door with a bronze plaque on it that said, "Hon. Hiram J. Flynn – Deputy Chief". Heck knocked and slowly opened it, poking his head around the edge. The man sitting behind the desk had his booted feet up and was leaning back hard against his chair. His arms were crossed and his chin down against his chest. It was dark in the room. The man cleared his throat, put his feet down with two hard clunks and leaned forward. He waived Heck to come in, saying, "Come on in. Heck McCabe, I presume?"

Gabe followed him in. The place smelled of stale whiskey and cigar smoke. The Deputy Chief was a middle-aged man with slicked-back long, dark brown hair which curled slightly around his ears and over his high collar. He had a high forehead with a prominent vein running along its side on the left. His dark, bloodshot eyes flashed and darted, even in the dark, from their deep sockets. These were in constant motion under the shadow of long, thick brows that had apparently never been clipped. The man wasn't just white, he was pallid. He wore a well-trimmed, medium-length goatee that seemed to cover a weak chin. He was thin to the point of bony. Still, Gabe couldn't help thinking something was familiar about the man.

Heck and Gabe stood side by side in front of Hiram Flynn's desk while Flynn looked them over. "All right, all right, come on ahead and sit down," he rasped. He cleared his throat again and held up a kerchief to cover his mouth for a moment.

"Yes, Deputy Chief, I am Heck McCabe, and let me introduce my new associate, Gabe Baker," Heck said, sitting down. Gabe offered Flynn his right hand. Flynn hesitated, then waved him off, putting the kerchief back to his mouth.

"Sorry, gentlemen, I had heard, but didn't really believe that we were now working with a dark-, uh, I mean, a black man," Flynn said in his weak, breathy voice. He looked at Gabe. "No offense, I'm sure, uh, Gabe, is it? But you don't usually think of a Nig–, uh, a Negro, having, shall we say, the *bona fides*, for such a position? You know, the *necessities*, is what I'm sayin'." Flynn's speech revealed an unmistakable Tidewater twang.

Gabe and Heck exchanged a knowing glance. Gabe was determined not to get Heck into trouble with his higher-ups. He held his annoyance in check.

It was Heck who frowned and squirmed. Then, seemingly unable to control himself, he spoke up. "Sir. Not only does Mr. Baker have the 'necessities', as you say, I have found him to be, thus far, the best man I have worked with in the agency." Heck sat up on the edge of his chair, his back as straight as he could make it. His ample neck glowed red and strained against and spilled over the clean, white collar of his shirt. He pointed his right index finger across the desk into Flynn's face. "What the hell did you think that damn war we just fought was all about, Flynn? I don't understand people like you. You've had the best of everything, Harvard education, all the books you want to read, the smartest people around to talk to. And here you are, still can't see what matters in a man. It's in here," and he pointed to his head, "and in here," he growled, as he pointed to his chest. "The color of his skin doesn't have any more to do with a man's character than the color of his eyes. Or," he sneered, "the cut of his chin."

Flynn started to shake. His hand trembled as he held his kerchief against his mouth. His eyes darted back and forth. He gathered himself and stood. He stretched his long, skinny arm out and pointed to the door. "Out!" he squawked, "Out of this office now! The both of you!" he gasped and shook. "You, sir, dare to speak to me that way," he wheezed, pointing at Heck, "And right in front of this – this - " he struggled for a word, then started coughing. Gabe slowly rose to his feet, as did Heck. As Gabe exited first, Heck looked back at Flynn, who was reaching for a breath. "You know, Flynn, you were instructed to give us the latest intelligence for our mission. What have you got?"

"Here!" Flynn swept a single piece of paper off his desk and flung it at Heck. "This is all you get. Now get out!"

The two men walked back towards the entryway in silence. They stepped out into the bright sun. It was as if they had been in a dark cave for a long time and had just found brightness and warmth. Heck crossed his arms and looked around at their surroundings, now alive with bustling activity. Horsecars clattered by, their steel-clad wheels causing echoes to bounce around among the walls, columns, towers and domes of the city's governmental architecture. There was a feeling of a new energy of American power in this place. Pedestrians, all in a hurry, walked and talked at an ambitious pace. And - there was a whiff of breakfast in the air.

"I didn't know the man would look that sickly," Heck said with the slightest smile. "You know, the rumor is he had some kind of accident, when he was young. Lost the use of a lung. Been unhealthy ever since. Anyway, I don't know, Gabe, but somehow, looking out at all this, even after dealing with the likes of Hiram J. Flynn – well, I still feel good about where this country is headed."

"Could be right, Heck. I mean, here we are, a short, fat, angry white man, and a mean ol' ignorant black man fresh off th' plantation, standin' out here together – in front o' God and ever'one else, pretty as you please. Nobody can do nothin' about it."

Heck suddenly realized he had a friend. When he flashed a broad smile, so did Gabe. "What do you mean, 'angry'?" Heck said with mock seriousness. They broke up laughing and started down the stairs.

9

MRS. JEFFERSON

Gabe knocked on the door to the modest, green clapboard shack on the outskirts of East Baltimore. The house was no more than 15 feet wide. It had three steps up to the front stoop. The door was on the left and there was a single window to the right. He knew this type of house from the trips he had taken into the city with his master years before. The white man had called it a "shotgun shack". Gabe wasn't sure why, but he could be sure it was derogatory. His master did say he could level a shack like that with one blast of his 12-gauge unless the front and back doors were open. In that case, he wouldn't hit a thing worth worrying about.

Heck waited in the carriage they had rented for the day. After knocking, Gabe stood on the stoop, with a jittery stomach and a light head. He hadn't known what to bring until Heck had suggested a loaf of bread. He squeezed it hard between his left arm and his side. Again, the questions came up. What if she doesn't know me? What if she's sick? What if he betrayed some kind of shock by the way she looked? He readied himself.

He heard the creak of floorboards. Then, the groan of the door as it started to move slowly, caught on something, and then opened the rest of the way. Gabe stood in front of small, black woman dressed in a bonnet and floor-length skirts with pleats. She was a full foot shorter than him. And rail thin. She looked up at him, puzzled, but unafraid. Her face was familiar, as he thought it should be. But he shouldn't have to have that thought. Her nose was wider and her lips thicker than he remembered. And she was darker standing in that door than she had been in his imagination. He seemed to be experiencing her features with a critical eye. When he caught himself, a wave of shame poured over him. He was half-white because he was his mother's rapist's son. Was he seeing her through white eyes? He couldn't bear the shame. His heart raced and his whole body shuddered. Gabe let out a wail loud enough for the whole block to hear. Heck looked on, knowing it was not his place to interfere – yet, anyway. Gabe's tears flowed, and he fell to his knees before this, his beloved mother, whom he barely knew.

"Son. It's all right, son. Bad people put bad things int' yo' head. It ain't no fault o' yours they're still in there. You can't do nothin' 'bout it," she said in a surprisingly calm, motherly manner. She put a work-worn hand on his shoulder. He looked up at her, eyes glistening. How does she know? Is she some kind of a saint? Gabe had a quick thought of the folks Harley always called "'splicables". "Yeah," he thought, "she was one of those. Come by it sufferin' so much and comin' out th' other side still able t' love."

She extended her tiny, crooked hand. He grabbed it lightly and stood up. It was a strong hand. Mother and son hugged. He was careful not to hurt her. He knew she must have the same kinds of scars he had, inside and out. He knew she had some that were worse.

"Mama - "

"Shh-shh," she admonished him with a finger to her mouth. "Gabr'l, is 'at yo' friend out there a-waitin'? You wants t' aks 'im in?"

The voice was unfamiliar. He'd never heard her use his name. His mind was racing. "Mama – uh, Mama, I'll go talk to 'im and be right back."

Heck jumped down from his seat on the little phaeton when he saw Gabe coming in his direction. He took off his bowler hat and wiped his brow with his handkerchief. He smiled at Gabe. "A right handsome woman, your Mama, Gabe," he said.

Gabe drew a deep breath. He looked down as he let out a sharp exhale, then looked his friend in the eyes. "Thanks, Heck. Do y' want t' come in and sit a spell? Or, jus' give me an hour, mebbe you can tour the highlights of the neighborhood."

Heck noticed that Gabe's eyes were wet. "I would like to meet your Mama, Gabe. But this time is for you and her. I believe I will take that tour. Might be nice to know if there're any unsavory characters hereabouts."

"Thanks, Heck." Gabe turned around and plodded back up the walk like he was in pain. His usual, upright posture now appeared as an old man's bent-over lean. Heck was concerned about him but didn't really know what was happening in his head or his heart. He would ask his questions later.

Gabe entered his Mama's dark house timidly. He stopped and looked around while his eyes adjusted. "Reading the room," as his friend Billy said, but this usually applied to stepping into a hostile room like a white man's saloon.

"Gabe, come on in. I ain't gonna bite ya, boy," his Mama said, with her hands at her sides. "I already has th' coffee goin', I'm gettin' us some right now. You jus' sit there, Gabe, an' I'll be right back." When she came back, she handed Gabe his cup and sat in a rocking chair next to the heating stove.

Mother and son sipped their coffee. They regarded each other. Gabe tried to hide the fact that he was still sorting out who this person who was his Mama was. He stole furtive glances in her direction. What was she like? His Mama looked him over unabashedly.

"Gabe," she said, "Your letters was a real treat fer me. An' when I seen how good you're a-doin' an' what kinda good friends you have, it's made me real proud and real happy, too. 'Course, most o' what I know come from the book. Yeah, your sister, she read th' whole thing t' me an' I was jus' so proud."

"Mama – what? What you mean, the *book*?"

"Well, the book. You know. All 'bout you, son, and you an' your friends out west."

"Mama, I don't know nothin' 'bout a book. Are you sure?"

"Shore, I'm shore!" She stood up and started walking into the back room. "I'll show it to ya."

She reappeared carrying a small salmon-colored paperback with a block print design on the front. She handed it over to Gabe. "Jus' look at it, Gabr'l. It's a real book an' it's all 'bout you. You didn' know?"

Gabe looked. The cover showed a black man holding a Colt pistol with smoke pouring from the outsized barrel. He was leaning back, his eyes concentrated and malevolent. And he had a stupid-looking smile. Sure enough, the title was "Gabe Baker: Black Man of the West". He leafed through the pages of the nearly 100-page volume. He stopped when something caught his eye and read a little. Some of the chapter headings showed that the author knew something about him. One was called, "Gabe Baker shoots it out with Evil Railroad Men". Another was, "Gabe Baker: Hero of Mayhem Gulch". Then there was "Baker saves the Day in Trial against Denver Pacific". Then, Gabe remembered. There was a reporter from Denver at that trial back in 1867. He had talked to him briefly. Others must have talked to him too. He remembered seeing him hanging around Earl at the livery. And that Earl could talk.

"Mama, most of this stuff is jus' made up. It ain't real," he pleaded. "This is what they call a 'dime novel', they have some 'bout Wild Bill Hickok. He'll tell ya, it's mostly jus' made up."

"I don' know 'bout that, Gabe. Sound like from them letters from you, it's mostly true."

"Anyway, Mama, I'd like t' jus' take it with me t' see all they're sayin'. An' 'bout those letters. I didn't know how t' address 'em, you know, proper-like," he said, looking down at his feet before he looked back at her. "What's your name, Mama?"

"My name at the farm was Jane. They called me Jane. 'Jane, do this', 'Jane, fetch that', 'Jane, Jane, plain Jane', 'don't you dare hide now, Jane'. But Gabe, I have a real name. Your grandma name me Adamma. Not 'plain Jane', but 'beautiful daughter'."

"Adamma. Adamma?"

"Yes."

"It's beautiful. Mama, did I have a real name?"

"Your name always been Gabriel, or Gabe. You were taken 'way from me, and we weren't allowed t' name our babies. You know your grandma took care o' you. Best she could. An' I think she liked the name on account o' it was a angel name. You are now Gabe Baker, I seen in your letter an' th' book. An' you was doin' law work. I was so proud."

"Thank-you, Mama," Gabe said. He waited and thought, looking out the window. Then, he finally said what was on his mind. "'Course, if I 'ad a real last name, I s'pose it'd just be Haney, master's name, an' I wouldn' want that."

Now it was her turn to look out the window. Then she looked at the floor for a full minute while Gabe waited patiently. She looked up at him with shining, wet eyes, and said softly, "No Gabe, no. It wouldn' be Haney."

"Mama?"

"No, not Haney. One o' his friends from up Alexandr'a way - Virginnie. Come down for Christmas."

"Mama!"

"Son, I swore t' th' preacher I would never tell it. Preacher said it was bad. Can't tell."

Gabe started to shake, ever so slightly. He tried to control himself. He didn't want to cause his Mama pain. But he wanted - needed - to know.

"Master's friend come visitin' few times. He and master get so drunk. An' I know what's gon' happen then. They always after me. I hid. I went int' the fields. They send th' dogs. He finally get me, 'e beat me, that time somethin' awful. I fight good. Get that hay fork up under 'is ribs, right here," she said, indicating her left side with her right hand. "'ppeared like, make three nice holes, deep. That man still 'ave is way with me an' I can't do nothin', but 'at's last time 'e come. Then, you come late next summer."

"But," Gabe started again. No, it was too painful, as much as he wanted to know. And he wouldn't make her break her promise to a preacher. That would make it worse.

"Do you have a last name, too?"

"They call me Mrs. Jeff'son aroun' this neighborhood. I don't mind a'tall. Some say it mean freedom-giver. Some say jus' 'nother slave owner. I jus' like t' think 'bout the freedom part, since I has some o' that now."

They sipped their coffee in silence for a minute. "Mama, I'm out here doin' more law work now. That man Heck, out in the carriage, 'e's a gummint man, but a good man. He wants me t' help the gummint get back gold stolen by them graybacks after they knew they was whupped, or, mebbe, after the war. Could be, some o' my ol' Comp'ny D knows somethin' 'bout it. Gonna be pokin' aroun' here lookin' for a while, so I hope t' come back an' see ya, Mama."

"Oh, I'd like that, Gabe," she said, "Oh, some much," now with a sparkle in her dim eyes.

"Mama, do I 'ave any sisters livin' 'round here? Even a brother, mebbe?"

"Your sister Bilah, now she's aroun', but I hardly know when, 'xactly. She work some in th' city. She stay with friends some. I worry 'bout that girl somethin' awful, Gabe. She come here sometimes, I just never know when. She's a good girl. I know she got her troubles, though. Your brother, Amos, he can't write so I don't hear. Last I know, he's traipsin' aroun' up north somewheres, mebbe got hisself a job with th' railroad. Wish I knew."

"They call themselves Jeff'son, too, Mama?"

"Mm-hmm. Yes, I might say."

Gabe heard the clatter of the carriage outside. "I'll be lookin' for 'em while I'm tryin' t' dig up that slaver gold, Mama. I got so many questions. I'll be comin' back. I'm so glad to 'ave a real Mama now. Even at my age. Yeah, it's a good feelin'."

"An' I'm so glad t' 'ave a real son. A man. You didn' know, but I saw you becomin' a man that night. An' I knew you would. I did see some o' what 'appened, not all. Then, it was real confusin' an' real dark after."

Gabe set his cup down and went over to kiss his mama on the cheek. "I promise. I'll be back, Mama." Mrs. Jefferson bowed her head and smiled broadly.

When Gabe opened the front door to leave, he was surprised to see Heck standing there on the stoop.

"Gabe, I think it's time I meet your Mama."

"I see you must o' found somethin' on your scoutin' trip," Gabe said.

"Just so. Something. Something is not right in your Mama's own neighborhood. I couldn't quite put my finger on it, but then I saw a man hurry for cover when I was approaching. And I saw another man quickly close his blind when he saw me. There are some folks around here who know who we are and maybe what we're up to. I'd say we've already made a good start. First thing though, we need to get that full-time guard over here for your Mama. I didn't see anyone on the job yet. But before we go back in, can you tell me – um – how is your Mama, how much should we tell her?"

"Ever'thing necessary to 'er well-bein', Heck. I reckon she's seen more'n most in the torment an' affliction department. She can handle anything we got."

"Haha! Gabe, you know you are always coming up with a most pleasing turn of a phrase."

The two went back in to talk to Mrs. Jefferson. Heck immediately decided Gabe was right. They talked to her about potential danger, even in her own neighborhood.

"Mr. Heck, it so good t' meet one o' Gabe's friends, I'm thankin' ya, I ain't afraid o' no bad men aroun' here, though. Even if'n they come a-callin', I got me a big ol' shotgun in th' kitchen an' Gabe's brother Amos taught me how to shoot it. An' I got some good neighbors, too."

"Just the same, ma'am, I'm sure we'd feel a lot better if you had some professional protection. You'll hardly ever see them, may not know they're around. If they make themselves known, though, you should know their names are Smith and Jones."

Gabe lifted his eyebrows and looked at Heck incredulously.

"Those're their names," Heck said, nodding and smiling. "I swear it," he added, with a little wink at Mrs. Jefferson.

"I ain't much afraid anyways, these days. I've 'ad a couple o' Gabe's old buddies from 'is soldierin' days come over, sayin' if I needed anythin' - " Gabe's Mama just remembered.

Heck sat up straight, but Gabe spoke first. "Mama! Who were they? Did they give their names?"

"No, no, they jus' said they know you, Gabe. Seem t' know somethin' 'bout that fort you was fightin' at down there with your Colonel Shaw. Seem like nice enough boys."

"Mama, did they ask questions?"

"Oh, yes, son, they was all int'rested in meetin' up with ya an' talkin' 'bout old times, I reckon."

"Anything you remember, how they looked?"

"No, no, well, one tall an' one short, both skinny as a reed. Look like they not eatin' reg'lar. They jus' give me piece o' paper with writin' on it, they ask where you livin', something weren't right, so I don't say. So they say send it t' you. I don' know, Gabe, I reckon over time I just plumb forgot. 'Course you know, Gabe I can't read nor write none."

"Mama. Do you still have that paper?"

"Yes, an' I plumb shore forgot t' give it to ya earlier too, glad you come back." She slowly got up and limped out through the kitchen to the back room. When she got back she handed it to Gabe. The note read:

> gab this nat and dundee we member you dun rite
> at fort wagner and you hep we can get gold but
> white men come for us we hole up two months in
> field behind old railroad stashun so cum fast dont
> tell nobody

After he read it out loud, his Mama said, "Oh, lord, Gabriel, them boys is up t' no good, ain't they? I didn' know. They seem like good boys, but still – somethin' not right. But, oh, my, them boys was int'rested in your book, too. Your sister read to 'em, too."

"Mama, how long ago did they leave this note?" Gabe asked.

"Now, 'at's why I forget, I reckon, been most a year."

"Thanks, Mama."

Gabe and his Mama said their goodbyes again. Gabe climbed up into the carriage beside Heck and waved to her. She seemed so small and so vulnerable. Heck slapped the reins gently on the old bay and the two friends rattled down the cobbled street for a couple of blocks in silence.

"Um, Gabe, I guess that book your Mama just mentioned – that's the 'Black Man of the West' book, huh?"

"Heck! You knew about that? Why didn' you say nothin'?"

"Well, Gabe, I thought you might know about it. Maybe I should have said something. It may have been the spark that caused our friend Sweeney to seek your services."

"Hmm. Didn' even know I was a famous feller. Wild Bill an' me, huh?" he chuckled. They rode in silence for a while.

Then Heck asked, "What is this station, Gabe? Old station they referred to? Where did they want you to meet?"

"I'm workin' on that right now, Heck. Got a couple ideas.

"What sort of men are these, this Nat and Dundee?"

"I only knew 'em from trainin' with th' comp'ny and th' reg'ment, then I knew somethin' of their fightin'. Didn't know 'nough t' trust 'em with m' money, but would o' trusted 'em with my life – if y' know what I mean?"

"I do. After I get Smith and Jones on the job, we can start checking on some of these ideas you're coming up with. Sound right?"

"Sound just right."

10

ROAD TO ROCKVILLE

Heck left Gabe at their hotel for three days while he made arrangements with Smith and Jones. Gabe walked around the city and thought. He read and reread Nat and Dundee's note and wondered whether even if they did find the "station" it would give up any clues. He toured around Washington and Baltimore, looking at every railroad station he could find. Nothing prompted a memory or even an idea why they would think Gabe would know where to go. What kind of clue could possibly still exist? But, they had to try. The paper the Deputy Chief had given them was as worthless as he had turned out to be.

When Heck returned, Gabe felt as if he had let him down. Heck told him, "Well, Smith and Jones are in place and happy to be employed." He smiled, and added, "Don't have any worries, Gabe, these guys are the best of the best. Mrs. Jefferson is well-protected. She won't even have to shoot that 12-gauge of hers."

"Thanks, Heck. If she did ever 'ave t' shoot that thing, I'd think it'd knock her plumb over."

"Haha! It would," Heck agreed. "Well, Gabe, what's our next move?"

"I don' know, Heck, I been thinkin' 'bout this thing over an' over. I jus' don' know what these boys are talkin' 'bout with th' railroad station. And why would they think I'd know. Onliest railroad station I ever went to was . . ." He stopped mid-sentence. He looked down at his feet. "Heck! Heck, I got me an idea. These boys escaped jus' like I did. They went through Rockville, same as me."

"I don't get it, Gabe. They caught the train north from there?"

"Well, yeah, in a manner o' speakin'," Gabe said. "Ever' slave in this part o' the country, I reckon, knew 'bout them Quakers there, helpin' black folks t' freedom. But the main goal was t' get t' the Episcopal Church. It was a station there, see?"

"I'm starting to," Heck said, in a low voice, grabbing his handkerchief and scratching the back of his head.

"Yeah, that was the last station on the underground railroad before some o' us folks got over towards the promised land. Everybody'd celebrate when they got 'cross the border t' Penns'vania. Then, most didn't stop, headed for Canada. Still had t' worry 'bout slave catchers, even where all those Quakers come from."

"Ah! Nat and Dundee had to be referring to that Rockville station!" Heck exclaimed, brightening. "Yessir!"

"Yessir!"

"If we start out on a couple of horses early tomorrow, we can be there in time for supper," Heck surmised. "Hmmm. Late supper?"

Even eight years after the war was over, now in late 1873, Heck and Gabe drew a lot of stares along the pike up to Rockville. It wasn't unusual to see a white man and a black man riding together, it was unusual to see them side-by-side, both dressed well and apparently treating each other as equals.

Reconstruction had started to falter and some believed that President Grant had lost his ability to continue to make progress. And that which had been made was being reversed by the federal government leaving decisions to the states. Mass lynchings and "disappearances" were happening all over the South on the slightest pretext. Frederick Douglass had found his voice again when it became clear that *de jure* freedom was not the same as *de facto* freedom. He was out on tour again.

As they rode along, Gabe told Heck how he had escaped from Heavenly Hills. He told how one night when he was almost 16 years old he saw his master draggin' his Mama into the barn by her hair. He stripped her and threw her down like he'd seen him do so many times before. His master said he was going to give his Mama a special treat that night. He was going to let his two sons have her.

Gabe told Heck how he had killed the father and one son with a pitchfork and shot the other one. He then told how he killed the slavedriver Sikes. And how he then took up his master's gun, filled up a sack with food and headed to Rockville. All the slaves of a certain age in Montgomery County had heard the stories and memorized where all the landmarks were said to be so if they got the chance they could find their way. Now, telling the story of his escape, Gabe remembered just how alone he had felt heading out into the deep, dark woods. By himself. But with no white man with gun, knife and whip behind him, at least for the time being. *He* had the gun. He was so young. He knew very little of the larger world outside, except what he had learned by finding newspapers that had been thrown away and from his several forays into Baltimore. He had experienced fear and exhilaration at the same time.

As they approached Rockville, Gabe offered to Heck, "If you want t' make it easier, I'll just ride behind and keep my head down."

"No sir. Let's just do what we can to help put those times behind us," Heck said, facing straight ahead.

"Thanks, Heck," Gabe said, drawing his Colt out and checking his loads. Heck saw that, smiled, and did the same.

"One thing, though, Heck, we don't want to cause too much of a disturbance. Mebbe we should make camp and ride into town tomorrow."

"Well, Gabe, I was looking forward to a nice, warm bed and some tavern cooking."

"I don't mind at all, Heck. Just the same, I'll be campin'."

"Why are you so all-fired anxious to sleep on the cold, hard ground tonight?" Heck asked, pulling off his hat and wiping his brow.

"Heck. You try to check a black man int' that inn you're thinkin' 'bout and there gonna be some kinda row. That won't help us tomorrow a'tall."

"All right, Gabe, all right. Sorry. Let's make camp over by those trees over there. There's good cover, a likely creek, looks like grass for the horses," Heck said pointing off to the right side of the road. "I'll ride into town and get us some good grub and we can make a night of it."

11

CHRIST EPISCOPAL CHURCH

Gabe woke up the next morning, listening to his horse cropping the grass by the creek. It was still dark. He looked over at the snoring Heck. What would this day bring? Were they making any progress? Heck had bought enough provisions for breakfast at camp. Gabe started a fire and got the coffee going.

The coffee was boiling when Heck turned over on his side, and said, "Now that's a fine way to wake up. Smells mighty good, Gabe." He sat up and looked around. A little pink and gray streaked the eastern sky. It wasn't freezing but felt close to it. Heck threw off his blankets and sat up, rubbing his eyes.

"This'll help," Gabe said, handing him his cup filled with the fresh brew.

"Certainly will. You know Gabe, I slept like a baby. Better than I can remember. Since the war, I haven't slept so well. Saw too many things that I can't make go away. Last night? I don't know, I just had a calm come over me. He slurped from his cup. "Oh, Gabe, yeah, this'll do."

"Yeah, you know I got a kind o' reputation for makin' the best camp coffee. All m' friends say so. I'll tell ya my secret. I use more coffee than they do."

"Gabe, your secret is safe with me."

"Well, sure. You make it as good as me, an' soon enough folks'll be askin' *you* t' make it. Wouldn' want that."

Gabe started to get breakfast cooking in the one big skillet they had brought. Heck stood up and stretched. "Gabe, I'll go out behind those bushes over there to do my business, check on the horses and come back with some more firewood." Gabe nodded.

As the two sat eating their fried pork and biscuits, they talked of many things. Heck told Gabe about some of his missions during the war. "The army, in its infinite wisdom, decided I was too fat to fight. Can you imagine? I can outshoot and outride most any man. Of course, I did need a stout horse. But I wanted to do my part, and with my education, was able to convince them to let me do spy work."

"What kind o' ed'cation, Heck? I always wanted a chance at that."

"Well, I had four years at Rutgers University and then Yale Law," Heck said. "I hope you get your chance, Gabe. I know it'd be hard t' get in and tough once you're there. As an alumnus, I could help out, but the way things are . . . well, you know better than me," Heck said.

"What sorts o' things they have you doin' in the war, Heck?" Gabe asked, chewing on a stringy piece of pork.

"I started at the bottom. I would check the corpses after a battle. I searched them for papers, maps, anything that would be evidence of future plans, or position and strength of Confederate units. You can imagine, it was dreadful duty. Sometimes I couldn't get out into the field until those poor boys had been lying out there for a few days. Even worse, a couple of times, the corpse wasn't a corpse yet if you know what I mean. Scared the daylights out of me. I worked my way up to providing estimates of enemy strength and drawing maps. From there, I learned interrogation techniques. And, finally, I went deep south and what I call deep undercover to infiltrate one of their own intelligence networks. I was able to report on the inner workings of the top tiers of the Confederacy."

The two friends ate in silence for a few minutes. Then, Heck continued, "After the war, I stayed on by working with the newly formed Secret Service. I like the work. It feels like I'm doing something positive for the country. Something it needs after the horrors of the war, the assassination, then the Johnson administration . . ." He trailed off, looking off at the horizon. The day was cold but with the new sun coming up, he felt invigorated. "Well, my friend, what say we go visit this train station of yours and solve the case. Then, maybe some rye tonight to celebrate."

"Hahaha! That's good. You sounded just like my friend Harley. 'ceptin' the way you pronounce the words all proper, o' course!"

Heck washed the dishes while Gabe broke camp and got the horses saddled. It did feel like a bright new day. The last time he was here was night time, he was running for his life and couldn't stay long. Well, that was some kind of progress. A long ways to go, though, he thought.

They rode into town and tied their mounts to the hitching post in front of the "station", that is, the Episcopal Church. It was a Friday morning and the area was relatively vacant.

"Well, Gabe, do you remember the place? How's it feel to be back?"

"I don't rightly know. Somethin' feels familiar. I never saw it in daylight. They took me out back and hid me in a crawl space under the back of the church. I was young and scared. An' I'd just killed a passel o' white men and pro'bly made a bunch o' others mad. Real mad. After runnin' and hidin' in the woods at night all th' way up here, it was a blessin' though, t' meet some folks weren't tryin' t' put irons on me or whip me or string me up. They fed me too, I remember. An' a further kindness, I thought, they didn' try t' preach t' me neither. They jus' tried to help me get t' Penns'vania."

"Hahaha! That was a blessing, Gabe. Sounds like some good people."

Gabe and Heck tried the front door. It was unlocked and they went in. They walked into the entryway slowly, respectfully, orienting themselves and looking at everything. There could be clues anywhere.

They poked their heads into the nave. "Smells like a church, too, doesn't it, Gabe?" Heck whispered. Even speaking in such a low tone, there was a slight echo. It wasn't a large church, but had a high ceiling and was darkened by its stained glass windows. "A little musty, maybe moldy, maybe a bit of candle wax. Surely, the smell of salvation!"

"Don't really know, Heck," I never got t' go t' church when I was little. Then, when I got older and went west, well, never was a place that was invitin' t' me."

"When I was growing up, I had to go every Sunday. I spent a lot of time in churches just like this," Heck said. They walked up the aisle to the altar and sanctuary, looking at the windows, listening for any indication of a human presence there. "Then I went to school and read books and learned to think for myself. You told me when you became a man. This was, at least, when I stopped being a child. There was no flash of light, just a gradual realization that it was more likely that man created God rather than the other way around."

"Well, now, those are some mighty strong words to be speaking in the house of the Lord, sir," came a booming voice from the entryway to the sanctuary off to the left side.

"Good morning, sir," Heck said in a voice a little louder than normal, but fully self-possessed and calm. "I hope you don't mind that my friend and I are enjoying your beautiful church this morning. And, as you have just heard, a little free speech while we're at it."

The man looked the pair of friends over. "I am Charles Dunbar, the rector of this church and parish. You gentlemen are welcome here for a brief visit so long as your intentions are honorable. And I would ask that you show respect for our beliefs while in this house," he said, emerging into the light. He was of average height, middle-aged, with a full head of dark hair and had a big, barrel chest that must have been the source of that resonant voice. Heck could imagine him inspiring his flock, arms outstretched, on Sunday mornings. He said to Heck, "Maybe I can be of assistance if you have any questions about the church."

"Thank-you, sir. I'm Heck McCabe, currently out of St. Louis, Missouri. My friend here is Gabriel Baker, Territory of Colorado." The Rev. Dunbar bowed slightly to Heck. Heck decided to test the waters. "We have been visiting some of the so-called underground railroad stations in these parts as a part of our work for the government. Gabe recalls that this place was important in that respect."

"I recall especially that it was important t' me, Reverend," Gabe said, without a smile. "But I never knew who was in charge here then. Them they called conductors wanted us 'passengers' t' 'ave as little contact as possible. This would o' been aroun' early summer, mebbe 1855."

"Well, the church has changed some now. I wasn't here yet. I don't know if I can answer any questions you gentlemen may have. My predecessor allowed the railroad operations to proceed, provided help in the way of church space and provisions, but was not involved in day-to-day operations. Today, I, uh, just try to keep the congregation together during these difficult times, you might say," Rev. Dunbar said, folding his hands together in front of him and looking down at the floor. He glanced back and forth at Gabe and Heck, eyebrows raised.

"Reverend Dunbar, I'd like t' thank your church for the part it took in me findin' my freedom. 'ave ya 'ad any other former slaves comin' by t' express their 'ppreciation?" Heck smiled at how Gabe was steering the conversation.

"Well, not recently anyway. There were a couple of Negro men came by here about a year ago. They were looking for a friend of theirs they said came through here about the time you did, Gabe."

"That's interesting, Reverend. I don't suppose you recall names or anything else about them?" Heck asked. "Please understand, this is government business." Heck drew his badge out of his coat pocket and held it so Dunbar could see."

"Hmmm. Secret Service, eh? Seems I've heard something about you men. But, in answer to your question, all I can recall is one was tall, one short, both scrawny and unkempt. I sent them out to the cemetery so they could speak to the new caretaker there. He was involved in the railroad operations. I never saw them again."

"Is that man still working there?" Heck asked.

"He is. They call him Old Henry. Henry Haymond. He's a good enough man, too, for a – well, I mean, he *is* a good caretaker. We're hoping he can bring the place back to its former glory. From before the war. I'm sure he'll help you any way he can."

"Thank-you, Rev'rend," Gabe managed, starting to tense up a bit.

"If you're still around come Sunday, I hope you'll join us," he said, looking at Heck.

Heck and Gabe took their leave, inspecting around the church grounds. There really wasn't much of a field behind the building. They then followed the directions the Rev. Dunbar had given them to the cemetery. It was only two miles away, but they rode slowly and talked. "So, our friends Nat and Dundee again, eh Gabe?"

"'ppears t' be. I didn' know 'em so good. Now, they're seein' my Mama and comin' t' this church. I don' reckon they jus' want t' share gold. Seem like they're thinkin' I can help 'em somehow. But how?"

"Yeah, that's right, that note even says you could help. So, when you didn't come, maybe they looked for help somewhere else. Or, tried something on their own. General Burke said there were those double eagles spent somewhere around Baltimore a few months back."

"Yeah, I been wonderin', Heck. Mebbe they found some gold. Mebbe just as easy as goin' back t' Fort Wagner an' diggin' some up - could do it at night. Why would those Gold Triangle varmints be out lookin' me up in

Colorado? You think Nat an' Dundee got lucky? They want me t' help find those two? I mean, I don't remember 'em bein' partic'larly smart."

"I don't know. But lately I've been thinking we're being followed, Gabe. Can't put my finger on it. Just a feeling. So, maybe . . ."

12

OLD HENRY

They rode in silence. There was a lot to think about. "There's th' buryin' ground, Heck, up ahead," Gabe said, pointing, as they approached.

"Well, good. Maybe Old Henry Haymond can clear up a few things for us," Heck said as they dismounted at the front gate. The Rockville Cemetery was well over a hundred years old and showing its age. It was obviously in need of the services of a caretaker. A jumble of bushes and long grass was taking over some of the stones near the borders. The many trees were mostly bare at this time in November.

The two looked around before they entered. There was what looked to be a caretaker's shack in the back on the right-hand side. They split apart a few yards and walked slowly and respectfully through the grounds. Each scanned from side to side, so that they were covering most of the area. They glanced at times at the stones, seeing many dated back to the 1700's. Heck turned and looked back a couple of times at the road they had ridden in on. Besides a lone raven watching them from the branches of an old elm, sending a shrill call of warning, there was no other sound.

They approached the back border, which was marked by an old iron fence, now rusting and sinking into fertile, black dirt close to the creek behind. A sudden clinking noise came from the vicinity of the shack. "Ho there, Mr. Haymond?" Gabe sang out. The two men stood and waited to hear a response.

There was a scraping and crashing, like metal on stone, and then a voice rang out loud and raspy, "Damn! Hold on out there, I'm a-comin'. Jus' hold your horses." Then the man emerged into the daylight, blinking and squinting.

"My friend and I are looking for a Mr. Henry Haymond. Might you be that gentleman?" Heck asked. Gabe came over to Heck's side for a better look.

"Might be," the old black man said, turning to the side and with a jerk of his head propelling a stream of tobacco juice into an arc that landed with a splurt six feet away. Heck and Gabe looked at each other, impressed. "Depends on who wants t' know." He peered suspiciously into the eyes of Heck McCabe, his head slightly cocked, hands on his hips. Then he gave Gabe a quick once-over. Old Henry was small. He was thin and bent over with a lifetime of hard work. He wore a permanent grimace on his face, but his dark, flashing eyes betrayed an underlying humor. He let out a "Hmmph! Who's askin', anyways?"

Heck looked to Gabe for help. "Well, sir, my name's Gabe Baker, originally from the Heavenly Hills of Maryland, lately out o' Territory o' Colorado. This here's m' friend, Heck McCabe. Well, I reckon, he's sort o' from all over."

Old Henry caught himself before his smile became too obvious, then, working a big wad of chew into his left cheek, said, "All right, then, Gabe – an' what's 'at – Heck – Heck-um? I never heard o' that one afore. Anyways, out with it, what y' want o' Old Henry, I got a passel o' work t' do, don't y' know?"

"My partner and I are lookin' for a couple o' young gents that mebbe come through this way a year or so back. Fought with 'em in th' 54th. One tall, one short. Names o' Nat an' Dundee."

"Hmmm. Mm-hmm. Well, now – that's Gabe, you say, young feller? Out o' Heavenly Hills?"

"'at's right, Mr. Haymond."

"I remember you, Gabe. I remember. You been through here afore, railroad times, ain't ya, boy?"

"I have, sir. An' I don't wonder if somethin' familiar 'bout you, too."

"Should be! Jus' mebbe I save your young black hide once back there 'round '55 or so. 'at's all. *Should be*, I say!"

"Then, yessir! I do remember you. I'm thinkin' you shoved me int' a hole back o' the church, kept me in there a long time, too. I like t' gone crazy down there. What you do that for, Henry?"

"Oh, 'Henry' is it now? No, 'at's all right. All right. You all growed up now, Gabe. Yeah, well, t' answer your fool question, I put you in there t' save your mis'able hide, 'at's what. An' then git you on up t' them Quakers 'cross the border. 'at was m' job and 'at's what I done." Heck watched, smiled, and crossed his arms. This wasn't his conversation. At least yet.

"Thanks for what you done, Henry. I reckon I could o' brought a bunch o' trouble comin' up behin' me after th' mess I left back at th' farm."

"Trouble. Hmmph. I reckon. Like a trouble *storm*. It was damn hot aroun' here fer some time after you gone, boy. But you with the 54th? Mebbe you make it all worthwhile. That bunch did make us proud. And, there *was* a couple o' your boys from your 54th 'round here last year, too, come t' think of it. Now. What you want with those boys?"

"We're thinkin' they might o' been stayin' aroun' here a while," Gabe said.

"That don't answer the question."

"Well, we're thinkin' – mebbe we're jus' thinkin' they bought themselves a heap o' trouble. Truth t' tell, Ol' Henry, those boys ain't th' most savvy ever come out o' the backwoods o' Maryland. Mebbe, jus' mebbe, even now, Heck an' I could save 'em a might o' misfortune."

"I seen your Nat an' Dundee hangin' 'round here'bouts fer some time. Didn' seem t' 'ave no work, nothin' t' do. Didn' seem t' care none either, wasn't worried 'bout gettin' fed. I tried t' git 'em some work, wasn't int'rested. They was campin' close by, come t' talk t' Ol' Henry time t' time. Then, one day some 'good ol' boys', sound like from way down th' river, come around. You know th' type I'm talkin' 'bout, Gabe. Anyways, them other two gone after that."

"What'd these southern gentlemen look like? You talk to 'em, Henry?"

"One, tall man in 'is fifties. Brown hair, a little gray. Scar tracin' right along 'is left jaw. Deep south talker. Other'n – diff'rent. This 'un 'ad a pock face and red hair. Look like 'e 'ad the pox mebbe, when 'e was a youngun. Sickly like. An' 'e was wearin' somethin' like cowboy's clothes."

"Thank-you, Mr. Haymond. Did you notice anything else about what these men were wearing?" Heck asked.

"I tell you what, there, uh, Hecka? Heck-um? Heck-um. Yeah. There was somethin' struck me up real peculiar." He gazed to the horizon. "Somethin'. Yessir! Yes! I do remember. They was both wearin' the same damn belt, ain't that funny? Only it wasn't like one you'd seen afore. An' 'at's why it stuck out like."

Heck and Gabe glanced at each other. Gabe let Heck keep the conversation going. "Well, that's interesting. Maybe helpful. Mr. Haymond, do you remember what it was that made those belts different?"

"Well, shore I do. They had a gold-colored shape. Like a arrowhead or somethin' like 'at."

"You mean like three-sided shape?" Heck asked.

"Well, now, dadgummit, 'at's what I jus' said – Heck-at? What's 'at - Heck-um? I don' know, don' make no nevermind."

"Just Heck, sir. Just Heck."

They suddenly heard a fluttering from above. It was the raven. It launched from its branch and disappeared.

"Wait. I know that ol' buzzard, somethin' goin' on. Listen," Henry croaked. He turned his head to better hear from different directions. Gabe and Heck squeezed the butts of their Colts, still in their holsters, and looked to the borders of the cemetery.

"Ol' man. Get down," Gabe loud-whispered to Henry.

Bang! Bang bang! Three shots. They came from the other side of the creek past the iron fence. One slug hit the top of the stone next to Heck and splattered granite into his face.

Each man was now crouched behind a grave marker. Gabe and Heck were beside each other, their Colts drawn. Henry was one row closer to the gunfire and in front of Heck. "Hey. Boys. I'm goin' t' th' shed t' git m' Spencer. Cover me."

"Don't do it, Henry. Stay down!" Gabe yelled.

Henry didn't listen. He scampered out from behind his stone, surprisingly spry for how he looked five minutes earlier. He dropped to his belly when he got to the shed, then crawled inside.

Heck saw movement from just behind the bushes closest to the fence and fired two rounds. "Ugh…uhhng…" they heard.

Henry poked his head out. "Ya got one, Heck! Ya got one!" he scrambled around to the side of the shed visible to Heck and Gabe and waved his arm. He then pointed the Spencer around the corner and waited.

"I reckon 'e's where he wants t' be, Heck," Gabe said, half-chuckling. "Crazy old man. What d' you think, Heck?"

"Only one or two left. I'd guess two, although I don't know if that first one is out of action yet or not. So, better assume three. I'd think there and there," he said, pointing.

"All right, listen, I'll move up a might," Gabe said.

"Good. I'll keep 'em busy. Then, if you can do the same for me, I'll go over to Henry, then around the back and see if I can get on their flank."

"Well, damn, what's 'at old coot doin' now?" Gabe whispered.

"Looks like he's one step ahead of us. He's going around the side. Whenever you're ready, Gabe."

Gabe nodded, cocked his Navy Colt and darted out from behind his stone. Heck poured fire into the bushes. He heard the Spencer go off too. Gabe landed on his belly, then nodded back at Heck. Heck ducked and ran over to the shed, drawing fire from in front of Gabe. The shooter made the mistake of showing himself to take his shot. Gabe aimed and hit his target twice, spinning him around and dropping him with a dull thud. The cemetery went quiet.

Heck called out softly, "Henry. You all right?"

Henry answered, "Shhh – shush now!"

Heck got down on his hands and knees and crawled over to the old man. He was in prone position, the rifle hard against his shoulder. "Shush now, Heck-um, I got a bead on 'im. Next time 'e breathes, I'll git 'im." The Spencer was cocked and ready. Henry knew how to hold it steady. Then there was a flash of color jumping from behind one elm towards another. He had his chance.

Boom! The Spencer .56 was loud. The man went backwards into the brush like he'd been hit with a board, the barrel of his gun glinting in the morning sun as his right arm went high and over his head. Henry had his man before he could reach the second tree.

Henry sat up. "See how I done that, young feller? Prob'ly save your hide, too. Good thing you 'ad ol' Henry aroun' t' take care o' things for ya, eh, Heck-a?"

"Good thing, pops. Good thing." Then Henry turned away and let fly with another big wad of juice. "See there, secret is, I git that t'baccy worked up all real nice an' fat, then I use m' cheek t' aim with. Works ever' time."

His big smile showed Heck that he was missing at least three teeth. Most of the rest were near black.

"All right, old timer, how about we check on Gabe," Heck said as he struggled to his feet. "Gabe! What do you say, all clear over there?"

"Come on over, but be careful. I ain't ready t' say yet."

Heck and Henry bent over and ran to where Gabe was crouched behind a stone while Gabe watched the bushes. They sat and leaned up against it while Heck and Henry caught their breath and reloaded.

"Well, boys, I didn' much 'ppreciate y' interruptin' m' work earlier but this 'as been somethin'. Things goin' better now. Weren't it a hoot? Glad y' 'appened by this mornin'. Ain't this much goin's on here'bouts since ol' lady Spindler shot 'er man down t' the feed store in town. 'Course, just like these fellers a-lyin' out in th' bushes yonder, I speckt ol' man Spindler needed shootin' too. 'e was a bad 'un. 'e's laid t' ground right over there," Henry said, pointing off to their left. "Nobody comes 'round with no flowers fer that one," he added, with a big nod. "I reckon there's some interestin' stories buried down deep with all these folks in here."

"Yeah, Henry, I'd think so," Gabe said. He turned to read the stone he was sitting against.

Don't grieve, I'm not really here –
I have gone to a better place

And then below that:

In Memoriam: Shemp Lee
Loyal and Brave Son of the South
1872

Gabe looked at Heck. Heck had a look of puzzlement on his face. Heck raised his eyebrows. "It was rumored there was a man working for the Rebs, Shemp Lee. You know, 'Lee', as in Robert E. It was said he was a bastard brother of the man himself. Our friend Deputy Chief Flynn in Washington was supposed to know something about him – he was talked about almost like a mythical figure. No one seemed to know what the man looked like. Or, even if he was real. But it was believed Shemp was head of the Triangle. You know, wanted to be successful where his brother wasn't."

"Them o' the Golden Triangle," Gabe said, looking over at Heck. "The 'Johnson Gang'." Henry scratched his head and listened.

"Well, Gabe – I just don't know about this. Henry, what do you know about this gentleman we're sitting on just now?"

"Two things I know, Heck-um. One. That ain't no gentleman. See right there? Says 'Son o' the South'. Second thing. We ain't sittin' on the son-of-a-bitch on account o' he ain't in there," Henry said, emphasizing by pointing straight down below them.

"Henry, what you mean, 'ain't in there'?" Gabe asked.

"I gotta spell it for ya, young feller? Not there. There ain't no Shemp Lee down there, an' I don' know who it is they put down there. I couldn' see it all, it was jus' a quarter moon when they come a-plantin'. But them two was talkin' 'bout one Shemp Lee tellin' 'em t' do that buryin'. Then, they was goin' t' visit 'im."

"Who? Who come a-plantin'?"

"Well, like I was tryin' t' tell ya afore – afore all that shootin' started – 'at scar man and 'at sick-lookin' man. It was all legal, I reckon. Anyways, I know they paid for that piece o' ground. But brung 'at box aroun' an' I was a–watchin' from over there by th' shed. I seen a body. Somebody in there, just not a Shemp. I told that Rector, he said leave it alone. It was some kind o' family thing. So, I figgered, it ain't none o' my bus'ness, some crazy white-man bus'ness, I jus' let it lay."

"Heck?" Gabe blurted out.

"Right. Well, maybe you and I are going to have to chase a ghost, Gabe. Not much to go on. He may or may not exist. No one knows what he looks like. But, at least we know someone is or was using the name."

"That don't say nothin' 'bout why Shemp's got a stone here in this bone-yard, Heck."

"No, it don't. I – I mean, doesn't. No. We've got a lot of work to do."

Gabe, Heck and Henry stood, nodded to each other, and guns pointed, slowly made their way to the fence. Just then, they heard a groan coming from back in the bushes. Henry cocked his head, and looked at Heck. "You want I should finish that one off, Heck-um? Put 'im outta 'is mis'ry like?"

"No, let's go see what we have out there," Heck said. They stepped over and followed the moaning. The man was half on his side, his hand gripped around the narrow part of the stock. He was gut-shot and rolling back and forth in pain. Heck put a boot under his arm and lifted. The man rolled onto his back. His face was contorted with agony.

"I know that man," Gabe said.

"Yeah. I know that man, too," Heck said. "Looks to be one Percy Briggs, lately of the Abilene, Kansas jailhouse.

"I know that man, too," Henry said. They looked at him. "That's the one come out here afore like I tol' ya. See what I mean? Sickly, with th' pox, see it, Gabe?"

"He shorely looks it. You described 'im real good. I reckon you just took care o' Wild Bill Hickok's bus'ness for 'im, Henry. This looks t' me jus' like a certain train robber we left off at 'is jailhouse a while back, doesn't it, Heck?"

"I heard o' that man. I help out Mr. Bill?" Henry asked, wide-eyed.

"You did," Heck said. "Mr. Hickok must have been pretty embarrassed when this owlhoot beat his lockup. Yessir. This jailbird is an outlaw named Percy Briggs. So this is one of those that planted Shemp over there?"

Henry nodded enthusiastically. "'at's, right. 'at's right, sir. You want I should finish 'im off now, don't ya, Heck-um?"

"No. Henry, you got a doctor in town? Can you get him?" Heck responded.

"I can git him," Henry said, disappointed.

Heck got down on his knees. "Briggs. Percy Briggs. Can you hear me?"

"I hear ya," Briggs wheezed, turning back into a fetal position.

"Listen, Briggs, we've sent a man for a doctor, do you hear me?"

"Yeah. Won't do any . . ." Briggs struggled. Heck got up and grabbed a canteen Henry had by the shed.

"Briggs, stay with me. I have a question," Heck said, holding the canteen so Briggs could see it. "Where's the gold? You can still do the right thing. You still got a chance. Tell me."

"Unghh. Uh – pull that cork. Give me some water. I'll tell ya, just give me that canteen."

"I'll help you pour this water right down your gullet, Briggs, or you'll watch me pour it on the ground. What'll it be?"

"I busted out. We've been following you, thought you'd help us . . ." Briggs fought for a breath, "find us those black boys." Briggs tried to hold up his hand.

"Here," Heck said. He pulled the cork out and held the canteen to Briggs' waiting mouth. "Percy. Open up a little. Take it easy." Briggs took a swallow, choked and coughed.

"Briggs, who or what is in that grave back there? Where's Shemp Lee?"

Percy Briggs smiled. He reached for Heck's hand and Heck helped him to another swig. "I'm just about done for now, McCabe. And with me the glory of the South." He coughed and spit up blood. "Might as well put *me* in that hole, it would be fittin'."

"Briggs! Are you – you're not . . .?"

But Briggs's reddish complexion had turned blue. He had the last laugh and he knew it. He smiled up at Heck and his head rolled slightly. He was gone. Heck threw the canteen on the ground next to him.

"Damn. Damn," was all Gabe could say, looking down at the man. "Mebbe we'd better check on those other 'gen'lemen'."

One of the other two gunmen wore the golden triangle buckle. The other one did not. Heck didn't recognize them. He searched their pockets and saddlebags. They had no identification with them except a telegram citing one of them for bravery under fire during battle. And a map. "Yeah, Gabe, the rebels didn't give out medals, but they had an honor roll after the war. Sometimes they were mentioned in telegrams or dispatches. It looks like this one here was proud of his record. His record's over now." He hesitated and handed the map to Gabe. "Can you make anything of this?"

"Could be. Could be. I mean, there're only two words on it, it says Davey Creek. There was a Davey Creek down by the Heavenly Hills." He pointed at the words on the map. The angle of this line here could make it a trail we used t' 'ave between two plantations down there. 'Course, most interestin' part is this 'X' right here." He looked up at Heck. "There used t' be an old shack in there, white folks would use it when they went huntin'."

"Well, maybe this bunch has been down to your shack and found nothing, or we distracted them and they hadn't got there yet."

"Well, Heck, we waitin' for local law here, or skedaddle out before they decide we might be some kind o' badmen, shootin' up these fine heroes here?"

"I think it would take too long to get us clear with the law here, Gabe. We best get on the trail, maybe we can find Nat and Dundee. There could even be others in the Triangle out tracking them down. When we get to a telegraph office, I'll have to report in about what happened here today. Maybe the Service can keep the locals off our trail."

"We got t' keep Ol' Henry out o' trouble, though, Heck. Anyone here'bouts thinks he shot a white man, 'is life ain't worth a nickel."

Just then, Henry came riding up to the gate on his mule, ahead of the doctor in his buggy. He dismounted, the doctor got down and the two of them walked around the fence to get to the trees behind the cemetery.

"Hello Doctor, I'm Heck McCabe, special agent with the United States Secret Service. I'm afraid you're too late," Heck said as he and Gabe joined them. "I've seen a lot in the war, and I don't believe the man had a chance anyway. I got him right in the breadbasket."

As Henry started to speak, Heck jerked his head to the side with a quick eyebrows-raised look that Henry understood immediately. Henry nodded.

The doctor was an older gentleman, wearing a dark broadcloth suit and a dimple-crowned fedora, slightly off-center, giving him a jaunty look. "McCabe," the doctor said, "I'm Doc Evers and I'd say you're right."

"There are two others over here, Doc," Heck said, pointing.

"Hmmph. You've been busy this morning, McCabe. You get all three?"

"Yessir. And lucky too. They were bad men and they meant to do bad things."

"Well, you say Secret Service. I don't know anything about this Secret Service. But I do have to report this to the law. The hole in this man here is bigger than you can make with that Colt you're carrying there. So, if either of these colored men here had anything to do with this, I'd just suggest you get them out of here and find yourself a different county in a big hurry. You hear me, McCabe?"

"I did the shooting, sir. And I'll report it to my chief. But, thanks for the warning."

"I'm sending our undertaker out here and will be going down to the jailhouse in a couple of hours."

"Thanks, Doc," Heck said.

Doc Evers rode off at a leisurely pace. "Thanks for what y' done, Heck-um , reckon I almos' opened m' damn mouth."

"We won't forget ya, Henry. Thanks for the help. Mebbe I'll be back this way someday," Gabe said.

"Where you fellers headed?" Henry asked.

"Best you don't know, Henry," Heck answered.

"I reckon," Henry said. He turned his head and spit. "You boys need some more shootin' done, I 'speckt you know who t' call on."

13

NAT AND DUNDEE

Gabe and Heck rode hard until they approached Prince George's County to the southeast. They didn't bother to stay out of sight. They wanted to get to the "X" on the map as soon as possible. They rode up close to the border of Heavenly Hills as the sun was going down. They camped along a creek Gabe knew from his childhood. Gabe's head was spinning as memories flooded his thoughts.

As they leaned against a log with their fire in front of them, Gabe became preoccupied with the mental images that invaded his mind and which he could not control. "I sure hope we catch up with those two boys, that Nat and Dundee tomorrow, Heck. Tell ya the truth this mission we're on is a bit wearin' on me now. Don' you worry, Heck, I ain't gonna quit on ya. I'm just wantin' t' get back t' normal livin'. You know, see my friends, get back t' work. An' ol Tex and John Henry, they're wonderin' if I'm *ever* comin' back, for sure."

Next morning, Gabe and Heck mounted up. Gabe was certain they could follow Davey Creek to the hunting shack. What he couldn't be certain of was what they would find there.

After a break to rest the horses and make coffee late in the morning, the two riders ran into what Gabe knew was Davey Creek. "Heck, I'd say we're within an hour's ride now. I gotta tell ya, my heart is poundin'. Just 'cause o' where we are, 'at's all. But if I seem a might jumpy that's th' only reason."

"I got your back, Gabe," Heck said.

"I know it, Heck."

After their break, they rode off, following the small meandering creek. The two riders now had a more concentrated awareness than usual. They listened to the noises coming out of the woods and continually looked from side to side. The horses perked up their ears and did the same. They came to a small clearing next to a bend in the creek. Gabe was in the lead. He signaled to Heck to stop behind him. They sat wordlessly, listening.

Gabe looked back at Heck, who came up alongside. "Do you smell it?" Gabe asked.

"Wood smoke. I don't see it, but I do smell it."

"That shack should be just yonder behind those trees," Gabe said, indicating. They looked at each other and sat, quietly.

"Gabe, how trigger-happy are these boys, Nat and Dundee?" Heck whispered.

"Couldn' say. Bein' on the run they might be a bit edgy."

"What do you think about calling out to them?"

"I'm not altogether convinced we might not find someone else over there, Heck. Mebbe not Nat or Dundee. How many o' those Triangle fellers are there?"

"Could be right, Gabe. Maybe we should get a closer look. We could leave the horses here and make our way over. Problem with those Knights is they are sneaky and well-led, so I just don't know how many."

"Plenty more than this ol' world needs," Gabe said, dismounting.

"That's a fact, sir." They picketed their horses, checked their guns and each grabbed an extra box of shells. Gabe led the way around the meadow through the trees. They stopped from time to time to listen. This being November, the cover wasn't good, so they made a wide trail around.

They stopped at a clump of bushes which partially hid a formation of rocks just high and wide enough to provide some cover. "Right there," whispered Gabe. "Right there in front of us. There's just a little rise in front of it, but you can see the upper half of the shack."

"I see it. Can we get closer and still have a good spot?" Heck asked.

"We can keep goin' aroun' where the tree cover'd be a might closer."

"Let's do it."

"But it sure seems unnatural quiet, don't it, Heck?"

"It does."

They started to move again. This time, they walked hunched over and stopped to listen every few paces. "There's where we'd want t' be, Heck," Gabe pointed. Heck nodded and they started off again. They settled in behind a large stump with some bramble and deadfall around it.

The little shack was now in sight. They sat quietly, watching. "Heck, over there, somethin' movin'," Gabe said, pointing at a pile of firewood beside it. Suddenly, a figure appeared from behind the wood. It appeared to be a tall man, but somewhat slumped over.

"Gabe?" Heck asked.

"Can't tell. Could be. If he'd take that beat up ol' hat off . . . all right, that ain't Nat an' it shore ain't Dundee, but it does 'ppear t' be a black man," Gabe said. "Time t' come out in the light?"

"Your call, Gabe."

"Hullo, the shack!" Gabe called out. "Hullo, the shack!"

The subject of their curiosity picked up an old musket off the ground and yelled out, "Who there? Show y'self!"

They didn't stand up yet. Gabe yelled back, "Name's Gabe. My friend here is Heck. We don't mean you no harm. Can we come in?"

"You come outta them bushes and show y'selves. Y' hear?"

"Hell, I don't know 'at old man can hit anything this far with that old antique he's holdin' there, eh, Heck?"

"No, I think we're pretty safe."

They stood and walked out into the clearing. Now, woodsmoke blew towards Gabe and Heck and partially obscured the figure who was holding tight to the old musket. The muzzle lowered a bit.

"Who you say?" the figure screeched.

"Gabe. Gabe, formerly of Heavenly Hills. Gabe and Heck. We just want t' talk."

The figure motioned with a lanky left arm for them to approach. When they had gotten within 50 feet, they saw a hand held out in a motion to stop. "Gabe?! That *you*, Gabe?"

Gabe squinted and held his hand above his eyes against the late morning sun. He gave his friend a quick glance and looked back at the person in front of them.

"Uh. Uh – Gran – Granny?"

"Hee-hee, well if it ain't m' own little Gabr'l!"

"Granny?!"

"Well, Gabe, don't you be gettin' me confused with some-un else now, like say, th' queen o' England. 'Course it's your ol' granny."

"Granny" was wearing shabby blue coveralls and big work boots. She had on a torn and misshapen straw hat that appeared one size too big. She was still tall, but slightly stooped over. When she smiled, she revealed that she was missing about half of her teeth. The smoke from her fire was now enveloping her as she stepped forward to embrace Gabe.

"Granny, it shorely is good t' see ya. But what're you doin' way out here in the woods like this? This your place?" he asked, indicating the cabin behind her.

"Hee-hee," she cackled, "Well, after we got done 'mancipatin' I needed t' find me a job, Gabe. Somethin' I could git paid fer. Come on back, I'll show ya."

As they walked behind the cabin, following the smoke as they went, Gabe introduced Heck to her. "I'm pleased to meet you, ma'am," Heck said, as she just nodded and chuckled.

They rounded the side of the cabin where the fire was. "There! Ain't she a beauty, boys?" she asked, indicating the gleaming pot with a coiled copper pipe coming out of the top. She had the fire blazing hot. An old axe lay against a stack of chopped wood next to it. Several jugs of various sizes and colors and a few glass jars were lined up on the other side. Granny had a side-shack just off the little clearing where the still stood.

Gabe stood in shock while Heck leaned in for a closer look. "She surely is a beauty," Heck said. "Looks like you're getting a good yield out of this set-up, Granny."

She smiled. "Well, ya wants t' try some, now don't ya, boys?"

"Yes, ma'am!" Heck said, convincingly. Gabe was searching for words.

"But, Gran – Granny, how'd you get int' *this* business anyways?" he asked.

"One o' those old field hands, you remember, Gabe – called 'im Scruffy – he used t' mind the works old master used to think he had hidden so good, back by the south woods. Well, he learned the trade and taught it t' me after we was set loose. An' there's a call fer it 'round these parts, too," she said with a smile. "Bus'ness real good right now." She poured the clear liquid into two tin cups for Gabe and Heck to try.

Heck took a sip. His eyes opened wide and he coughed a bit. Then his eyes started to water. He said in a husky voice, "Whoa, Granny, that is the real thing. That is some good 'shine."

"Whoa, now giddyup," Gabe said, tasting from the cup. "What you call this stuff, Granny?"

"Glad y' aksed that now, Gabr'l. That there is a special batch an' I calls it Granny's Mulekick. Ya like it?"

"Yeah, yep, Grans," Gabe said after struggling to get another sip down without coughing.

"Some mighty fine 'shine, Granny," Heck said. "Hey, Granny, you got a name, you want me to call you something else?"

"Just Granny D. That's all. You kin jus' call me Granny D, Mr. Heck. Here, now, drink up, there's plenty more where that come from," she said with a wink. She poured more into both men's cups. She nodded towards two larger logs rolled up close to the fire. "Here now, boys, jus' 'ave a sit, this where m' customers do their samplin'." They complied and took another sip.

"Now – what you boys doin' up in these parts? Last I hear o' you, Gabe, you went west after th' war. An' I heard you was doin' good."

"I was, Granny, 'til I got mixed up with this gentleman here," he said, pointing at Heck. "Now, I just go 'round th' countryside gettin' shot at. That's m' new job, I reckon." He took another sip. "Whew! Special batch you're sayin', eh, Granny?"

"Fact is, we're out here lookin' for a couple of ne'er-do-wells that go by the names of Nat and Dundee. Maybe we can even save their miserable hides while we're at it," Heck said with a slight slur. "Mulekick, huh? I'd say that's apropos."

"Apro – what say, Mr. Heck?"

"Fittin'. 'e jus' means fittin', I think ol' Heck 'as takin' a shine to your 'shine, Granny."

Heck lifted his cup to Granny and winked. "I have indeed, ma'am. My compliments." This time he took a bigger swig. "Kind of grows on ya, doesn't it Gabe?" Then he let out a big laugh and finished his cup. "Damn, Granny D, you are an artist, you are," he said, starting to list off to the side a bit. "But listen, you two have some catching up to do, so while I'm still able, I'm going to get the horses. I'll be right back."

Heck slowly raised himself up, found his balance, and sauntered off across the meadow. Gabe and his grandmother talked about what each of them had been doing since the night so many years before that Gabe had killed their master and escaped Heavenly Hills. Gabe told Granny all about meeting his Mother in Baltimore just a couple of weeks before. Granny was happy to hear about her and decided to plan a visit. They talked until the day started to warm with the afternoon sun. After a while, Gabe realized Heck had been gone longer than expected.

He stood up and grabbed his Henry. "Well, Granny, looks like I'm gonna 'ave t' go out an' find me a Heck McCabe now, 'e seems a bit tardy," he said, smiling down on the old woman. "It's not like the man t' get lost, but it is like 'im t' find trouble. I'll be back when I can." Just then Gabe saw a flash of color and some movement behind the trees on the other side of the shack.

"Granny, you expectin' customers right now?" he whispered.

"I seen it too, Gabe, don't know, sometimes folks just drop in," she said.

"Seems like they'd show themselves if they weren't up t' no good. I'm just gonna act like I don't see 'em, and start off th' other way. Then I'll wait or sneak up on 'em."

Gabe walked toward the edge of the meadow in the same direction Heck had gone. When he had disappeared in the trees, he stopped, crouched down and looked back towards Granny and her fire. He waited. He hadn't expected this. Heck came walking out of the woods where he and Granny had seen the movement among the trees. Then, right behind were two figures. One tall, one short. Nat and Dundee, holding their Springfield model 1861 rifles on him as they trudged out into the clearing.

Gabe noticed that the boys were not looking prosperous. Nat had on a torn checkered shirt under an open jacket that was too large for him and covered in stains. His pants didn't fit either. They sagged at the top and ended in tatters at the top of his ankles. Dundee had apparently fared no better. He had on a well-worn, buttoned-up work jacket and a pair of torn dungarees. Seeing them walking together, carrying their guns, brought back memories, but not good ones. But he did smile at Nat's big, goofy smile.

"Halloo, there, Granny D. Look what we all's caught hangin' 'round your doin's here. Got us a white man," Nat said, with a proud grin.

Granny looked up from the fire. "Hello Heck, come on in, looks like you found yourself a couple o' them scoundrels we was a-talkin' 'bout. Nat and Dundee, now you lower them fool rifle guns down and let th' man be. 'e's a friend o' mine. What's your bus'ness here today, anyways, boys? You gots th' money fer some o' Granny's sweet stuff? Or you just lookin' out fer some free hooch?"

"Well, we 'uns figgered that white man'd be worth somethin', Grans," Dundee muttered. "We did go t' some trouble a-catchin' 'im."

"You damn fools, you catched a friend o' mine," Granny said.

Heck hung his head. "Thanks, Granny, I'm afraid I was enjoying myself too much after sampling that sweet elixir of yours, let these boys come right up on me. And they haven't listened to a word I've said about who I am and what I'm doing here. Maybe they'll listen to Gabe but so far they don't believe he's with me."

"Sorry, Cap'n, we nevah met a white man we could trust," Dundee sneered.

"What the hell about Colonel Shaw?!" Heck bellowed.

"Yep. Right. There's one," Nat said, sniffling, wiping his kerchief across his nose. "But how you know 'bout Colonel Shaw, Cap'n?"

"I've told you. I am working with Gabe Baker. And I was in the war, too, Nat," Heck said, frustration in his voice. "And you can stop calling me 'captain'. Once again, my name's Heck McCabe."

Gabe decided to come out into the light. "And that Heck McCabe was an important man for the union in the war boys," he said as he strode over towards the group. "More so 'n you two mis'ble trigger pullers."

"Gabe!" Nat yelled out, and started to run towards him.

"Corp'ral Gabe!" Dundee shouted, following his friend Nat.

"Hello, boys," Gabe said, setting his Henry down and giving them a hug. "Good t' see ya. An' you're lookin' mighty good to an ol' 54th man. Although, mebbe you could use new uniforms," he added with a chuckle.

The whole group sat down by the fire. Heck secretly passed Granny some coins so the bunch could celebrate their meeting without leaning too hard on her good graces. They talked about what they had been doing in the seven years since they had received their discharge papers. Nat and Dundee had been inseparable. After April 1865 they were at a loss. They had been slaves. Then they had been soldiers. How could they learn to make their way in a new world? They started drifting, living off the land, taking odd jobs and trying to avoid trouble with the many white men who were living as if the South had won the war. With Reconstruction and equality efforts being so generally stifled, in institutional and violent ways, so that even the federal government was unable to change the slave culture in their world, many would say the South did win. Some wondered how much difference there was between a slave and a sharecropper. Nat and Dundee were creatures of an oppressive, bigoted society that did everything it could to prevent them and thousands of others like them from bettering themselves or even untethering themselves from dependence on whites.

And they looked it. Gabe was somewhat taken aback. He learned a new appreciation for what his move west had allowed him to do and to accomplish.

After a couple of hours of conversation and Mulekick, the afternoon November sky started to darken. Gabe finally put his hands on his knees, and leaning forward, said, "We saw my Mama in Baltimore. We saw your note. Why don't you boys tell ever'thing now. Mebbe, jus' mebbe, we can help. Heck and me."

"Them are some mean and lowdown white men doggin' us now long time," Nat said. He looked down at his feet as the flames lit his face. He spit. "Only matter o' time, they gonna git us, and lord – oh, lord, what they like to do." He took a deep breath and looked at his tired friend, sitting beside him. He hesitated. "Well, see it's jus' like this here. Dundee and me, we heard all th' talkin' jus' like ever'one else. Plus, turns out, Dundee here was holdin' out."

"Was not! No sir. Not holdin' out, Nat, an' you take it back," Dundee said, looking up into Nat's eyes. "Jus' didn' know what t' do with it. I was jus' scared, 'at's th' whole of it, an' you'd a-been too."

"It's just that Dundee was out cold for a while that long night at Fort Wagner," Nat continued. "Back in '63, it was," he said, as if clarifying for Heck. "He did take 'at rebel ball t' th' head, must o' knocked 'im clean out. Didn' do no damage though. Not much in there t' mess up anyways." Dundee smiled broadly and nodded. He took a short sip out of the tin cup he was working on.

"Well, seems like 'e's tryin' t' wake up, 'e's just a-clawin' and a-scrapin' in the dirt there, tryin' t' find a way up and git out. When 'e's clawin' up th' dirt like 'at 'e comes up with two pieces o' pure-d Confederate gold. Coins they was. Well, 'e kep' 'em and 'e kep' quiet about 'em all them years 'til a few months back. Him an' me was hungry. Our belly buttons was scrapin' up agin our backbones. 'e fin'lly tells me." Nat looked at Dundee for confirmation. Dundee nodded.

"We used one o' them coins t' buy us some food. Got a hunk o' bacon, some beans an' coffee, all for the one coin."

"Nat, what'd that coin look like?" Heck asked.

"It was real pretty. It 'ad a nice lookin' woman on one side and a shield with some stars on th' other. Shiny. Heavy. An' it 'ad some fancy-lookin' words on it, too."

Heck and Gabe looked at each other. "Yep, Confederate double-eagle. Twenty dollars," Heck said.

"Damn," was all Gabe could say.

14

BREAKFAST AT GRANNY'S

They made an early night of it. That was about all they could do. Gabe and Heck made camp at the edge of the woods, near where the creek flowed by. Nat and Dundee just curled up where they were, close to the fire and the still.

Early in the morning, Granny walked out onto her rough, little porch and stretched. She tried to shake off her usual morning stiffness as she hobbled over to the fire. Tending the still was always her first priority of the day. She'd have to build the fire up before she started. One of Nat's long legs was in her way as she brought an armload of wood over. She kicked at it. "C'mon now, y' good-fer-nothin's, time t' git yer mis'able hides up – an' at least out o' th' way. Lord knows I ain't like t' git 'ny help from yas."

Gabe and Heck strode over to the cabin as Granny worked the fire. "Granny, how about I chop some wood for you. Gabe here is volunteering to make us some breakfast. We got all the fixings and there isn't a man alive who can outdo him when it comes to camp grub."

"That'd be mighty fine, boys, mighty fine. Been long time since anyone made breakfast for ol' Granny," she said, standing up from the fire and showing all the gaps between her few remaining teeth. She looked off in thought for a moment. "No, sir, I don't believe 'at's *ever* happened - in all m' born days. Mighty fine."

As Heck and Gabe went to work, Nat started to stir. "Hey Heck, look here, ol' Rip van Winkle his own self is wakin' up to a whole new world. S'pose we should tell 'im what year it is?"

"Nah. Shock might be too much for him," Heck said between swings of the axe. Dundee continued to snore, oblivious to all the activity going on all around him. Nat struggled to stand.

"Ohh, Granny, I got a powerful bad head this mornin', 'ow 'bout just a bit o' th' ol' Mulekick, jus' medicinal-like, you know?" Nat said as Granny emerged again from the cabin. "Oh, an' that bacon smellin' good y' gots goin' there, Gabe. Can't wait for some o' that."

Gabe glared up at him and then went back to business. Granny turned towards Nat and put her hands on her hips. "Nat, how you gonna pay fer any more o' them squeezin's? Huh, boy?"

"Well, Granny, shore you must remember ol' Dundee here gots one more o' them, what they call, double-eagles?"

Heck dropped his axe. Gabe stood up from the cook fire. Heck nodded to Gabe and gave a go-ahead gesture with his left hand.

"The last thing Granny wants is t' spend that rebel gold and 'ave those white men you were talkin' 'bout comin' down 'ere askin' questions and prob'ly more, now ain't that right, Nat?" Gabe said.

"Oh, well, I reckon. I didn' think," Nat mumbled.

"But you knew they were trouble. That's why you waited until you were desperate to spend th' first one, ain't *that* right?"

Dundee started to stir a bit and moan. He blinked ragged sleep out of his eyes and looked at all the figures standing around where he was laid out on his dirty old Army blanket. "Yeah, they's right, Nat. 'at gold is trouble," he managed.

"It's trouble, all right," Gabe said. "So why don't you boys just tell us how you know those white men are after you?"

"We seen 'em! We seen 'em comin' up on us couple o' times, we give 'em th' slip. They ain't but a day or two back o' us right now. We jus' happen t' know the territory 'round here better, I reckon. Plus, we got some smarts. They start doggin' us right after we spent that gold. But it's gittin' mighty tiresome."

"In that note you left with my Mama, you said you could get more gold," Gabe said. "You just tryin' t' get me out here t' help you boys, weren't ya?"

"Well – now, no, you know, Dundee 'ere 'members jus' where 'e fell. We could go a-diggin'."

Gabe rolled his eyes, shook his head and let out an explosion of breath. "Really, Nat? With those southern white gen'lemen just breathin' down your necks?"

Nat slumped back down on his log and looked at his feet.

"How many you see – comin' after ya, I mean?" Gabe asked.

"We seen six or eight, I reckon, from time t' time," Nat said, looking at Dundee for confirmation. Dundee nodded.

"An' so I reckon you're bringin' 'em right on in 'ere t' Granny's fixin's 'less'n y' light a shuck outta 'ere and make some good tracks for 'em," Gabe said. Heck kept chopping.

Dundee sat up and rubbed his eyes. "You're right, Gabe. Ground's been hard with freezin' an' we come ridin' up the creek th' last mile or so, so shouldn't be too good a trail for 'em. They do 'ave some hound dogs with 'em." He looked up at Gabe like a child might. "You fellers gonna help us? They don' quit. Sooner or later they be gittin' us. Gabe, you know what kind o' men these are, what they gonna do t' us if they think we know any more 'bout their damn gold."

Gabe was sitting on his heels tending to breakfast at the fire. He stood up. "Well, Heck, 'e's right 'bout that. They 'ave special techniques o' persuadin'. Prob'ly handed down from father t' son."

"Our job was to find the gold and bring it back to the government. So far we have one double-eagle," Heck said, stretching his back. "I don't see how these jaspers here can help any. On the other hand, we can't leave them to the Knights. And, as far as we know, maybe the Knights have found gold, they just don't know how much these boys here know about it and they want to shut them up."

"What you mean, leave 'em to the nights?" Nat said.

"That's what those white boys call 'emselves, Nat. Knights o' th' Golden Triangle."

"Whoo-ee, 'at's a mighty fine name fer a bunch o' thievin' cutthroats," Nat said, pulling up his suspenders.

"We can mebbe use these boys as bait, too, but shore does sound like there's a passel o' those Knights," Gabe said.

"What you mean, bait?" Dundee asked, looking around for something to use as a plate.

"Yeah. Between you and me, Gabe, we can outthink the bunch of them, but I don't know if we can outshoot that many," Heck said. "Anybody got any more friends around here willing to shoot at some fine southern gentlemen? On behalf of the U.S. government, of course."

"I kin shoot!" Granny said, nodding at the rusty old gun leaning against her cabin.

Gabe smiled. "Granny you couldn't hit your cabin with that thing if'n you were standin' on the porch."

"Now don't you git smart with me, boy. I know that. If'n I 'ad a proper rifle gun is all I'm a-sayin.'"

"Granny's tellin' th' truth, Gabe. She kin shoot the ears off a gnat at 50 paces," Nat said, reaching for a strip of bacon.

"Plus, we read how you stood up in th' middle o' the street an kilt a whole gang o' them railroaders back in th' terr'tories, Gabe," Dundee said. "Single-handed. Saved your friend's life. Yeah, 'is name was Billy. See? We know somethin'." Gabe saw Nat give him a disapproving look. They had not admitted they had "read" the book yet.

"Don't believe ever'thing you read, boys. Those writers jus' tryin' t' make things excitin.' It wasn't like 'at. At all."

"But you done all them other things, though, didn' y' Gabe?" Dundee asked, wide-eyed, stuffing a piece of biscuit into his mouth.

"Yeah, 'at's right, an' killed me a dragon with this 'ere pigsticker I'm carr-yin,' too," he said, patting his Bowie knife.

"Whoa, 'at's a – wait now, what's 'at?" Dundee asked.

Gabe gave him a quizzical look. "What's 'at what?"

"What's 'at thing you kilt?"

"Oh, the dragon," Gabe said.

"Guess I never heard o' 'at one. You, Dundee?" Nat asked.

"No, don't know 'at one."

"A dragon. You know, a big lizard," Heck said, smiling.

"Oh, so you kilt a lizard with 'at blade there. All right. Yeah, 'at's good, Gabe. Guess they jus' fergot t' put 'at 'un in th' book, 'at's all." Gabe and Heck had a good laugh.

When they were done with breakfast, Granny ordered Nat and Dundee down to the creek to wash the dishes. Gabe stood talking with Heck. They were down to three possibilities, if there ever was a big cache of gold at Fort Wagner. It was still there, the Knights had found it by now or someone else had gotten away with it. Did the Knights think Nat and Dundee had found it or knew where to look? Or were they just covering their tracks and wanting to prevent the boys from talking about it? The likelihood that if it existed it was still there seemed small. The rumors of the lost Confederate gold had now been swirling for some time. And now, Gabe and Heck both felt some responsibility for the safety of Granny and the boys.

"I'm thinkin' th' best way t' that gold is right through that Triangle, Heck, much as I don't like sayin' it out loud," Gabe said.

"I'm thinking the same thing, Gabe. As much as I don't like hearing it. I could find a telegraph and ask for some men. But something tells me things are going to rip loose long before we could ever do that."

"Agreed. Somethin' tells me that bunch is even closer than Nat is sayin'."

15

HECK

Gabe pointed to a high ridge on the other side of Davey Creek. "I see five riders," he said to Heck. "I reckon we don't need much plannin' at this point. Looks like those Knights are goin' t' bring the excitement down here with 'em."

"I see them. Gabe, can you get Granny safe and those boys situated? I'll get all the guns and ammo and let the horses loose. I don't think we're going to ride out of this one," Heck said. "They should be given their own chance."

Gabe nodded. "I'm sure they see our smoke. They may be comin' in from diff'rent directions," he yelled out.

Nat and Dundee waited at a window in the shed. Gabe and Granny were in her cabin. Heck wanted to stay outside to move around and observe the riders' movement, and maybe get a better head count. Gabe was encouraged by how the boys got set without any fuss or fear. They had been soldiers. And Granny looked like she knew her way around the Henry .44 Gabe handed her.

"Granny, you got 'ny o' that Mulekick in the shed?" Gabe asked.

"Oh, yes, Gabr'l, gots a-plenty."

"Well, let's hope we can chase those Knights off afore Nat an' Dundee find it. I think they'll do good until they do," Gabe said with a slight smile. He had checked and they had a good stock of balls and paper cartridges.

Five riders approached Granny's little homestead across a clearing towards the creek. They rode at a leisurely pace, but Heck could see that this was a ruse. They all carried their long guns at the ready and were keeping a sharp lookout, from side to side as well as behind. Heck suspected their deception was meant to conceal the fact that other riders were being held back or were coming from other directions. He decided to play along. He called back to Gabe to keep an eye out. Then he sauntered out from behind the shed, holding nothing but Granny's axe. His Colt was tucked into his belt in the back. He had laid his Henry close by against the shed, out of sight.

"Good morning, gentlemen," he called out. "Anything I can do for you on this fine, beautiful day?"

The leader of the group was a tall, middle-aged man with broad shoulders and a spare frame. Underneath his open riding jacket Heck could see a shiny blue and maroon floral print vest. The high collar of an off-white shirt peaked up from behind. He wore a wide-brimmed hat with the right side turned upwards and attached to its crown with a gold-colored badge. A small plume stuck up from just behind. Heck couldn't help also noticing the ceremonial sword, complete with fancy etching, cross-guard and leather grip that hanged of the right side of his horse. It looked like something he'd seen a southern general carry.

He briefly took his hat off to wipe his brow with his arm, showing a full, thick head of brown hair, carefully brushed back to swirl around his ears. His bushy sideburns concealed much of his face, but his thin, cruel mouth was obvious. He started to step down from his horse, with his left hand on the butt of his sidearm.

"No sir!" Heck barked with an unambiguous tone. "I don't know where you're from there, sideburns, but I believe it to be the proper thing most anywhere to ask leave to dismount when you're in another man's camp."

Sideburns hadn't expected any kind of resistance, much less with this much mettle. He hesitated, and put his leg back over his saddle. "My name is William Fletcher. Most call me Colonel Fletcher. I'm sure you've heard of me, sir. I'll let those disrespectful words go just this once since you didn't know. These boys with me are, let's just say, my scoutin' party. Now, by your leave, sir, I'm gettin' down. Or, what were you goin' to do? Throw that axe at me?" he said looking back at his men to make sure they were laughing.

As soon as Fletcher got his second boot on the ground and was able to look up again at Heck, he saw that he was looking down the barrel of an Army Colt. "My name's McCabe. Heck McCabe. And I'm not much at axe throwing, but I can sure as hell put a piece of lead where it counts when I want," Heck said. "And, maybe you've heard by now, Colonel. The war's over. You boys out here just playing army, or maybe scouting for raccoons?"

Now that Fletcher was standing facing him, Heck saw the belt buckle. He glared at Heck. "Mister, pulling a gun on me was a big mistake. The only way I can forgive that is if you throw that Colt in the dirt right out in front of me right now, then offer up a real nice apology."

"Can't do it, Colonel. That's a rough looking bunch you've got there, and the last thing I'd want to do is face them all down with just one axe," he said, smiling. "Now, I don't recall giving you leave to dismount. I suggest you get back up and depart in peace. You've worn out your welcome, sir."

"You've got nerve, fat man, I'll give you that. But as you can see, there are five of us, and one of you. And you, sir, make a fine, big target. All I have to do is say the word." He looked back at his 'scouts'. "While we're at it, you boys get down and join me then, too." They did as they were told so that the five were standing together facing Heck.

"You say that word and it'll be your last, Fletcher. You'll hit the dirt before I do. Besides, I'm not as alone as you might think."

Gabe took that as his cue to make an appearance. He strolled out from the cabin like he was on a summer walk. He stopped at Heck's left side and stood, legs shoulder-width apart. He cradled his Henry in his left arm and his right hand brushed against the butt of his Navy Colt. He did not take his eyes off the men lined up in front of them, as he assessed who was the most impatient.

"Well, I'll be damned. I knew you had a funny accent, McCabe, but I didn't know you were from so far north you'd be consortin' with th' likes o' this," he snorted, throwing a wave of dismissal in Gabe's direction. He looked back again to make sure his men were admiring his sense of humor. They were dutifully chuckling and nodding.

Heck and Gabe glanced at each other. They understood each other implicitly. So Gabe spoke up. "Ya may be entertainin' t' these simple folk y' brought with ya, there, Colonel, but I b'lieve I can speak for Heck and me both, you're already startin' to bore us."

He looked at Heck. Heck nodded in agreement. That should do it, he thought. And it did. The five Knights went for their guns all at once. But they were eastern men. Not trained to a fast draw. Two of them still had their military holsters with flaps on them. Gabe pulled. Once his Navy Colt was level, he held it rock-steady. He started from his left to right. His gun barked three times in quick succession before any had gotten their guns clear. And three men were down. Heck shot the Colonel in his right shoulder and the man next to him in the midsection. Gabe lowered his pistol, smoke still wafting from the barrel. Then he saw. His third man had rolled onto his side and still had his gun in his hand, shaking. Gabe raised his Colt again. But the man got in his shot at Heck. A Springfield roared from the window of the shed and laid the man out before Gabe could pull his trigger. Gabe looked over at the window and smiled.

But something was wrong. Heck's posture started to slacken. Gabe thought he saw a spot of blood on his lip. "Damn! Damn, Heck," he stuttered. Heck's legs were starting to buckle as he slowly sank to his knees. The blood on his lip now started to trickle. He looked up at Gabe, trying to speak. The hole in Heck's shirt showed that he was hit just to the left of center in his chest. Gabe got on his knees in front of him and held him up by his shoulders. Heck started to lurch forward, leaning against his friend.

Now his head was on Gabe's shoulder. He whispered into Gabe's ear. "Gabe," he rasped, "my friend, the grave - " he coughed, "must be - " and Heck's eyes fluttered. One last, wet, raspy exhale. Gabe knew the sound all too well. Still holding his friend, now hugging him, he screamed a guttural scream that came from the deepest depths of Gabe's being. He cradled his friend in his arms and screamed and yelled and cursed. He hugged him as tears immediately filled his eyes. He slowly let him slip down beside him. He gently lowered his head to the ground. Then he sat. And he stayed by his friend on the cold dirt for an hour. No one bothered him. He stared into the distance.

Finally, Granny put down her Henry and came over to Gabe's side. "I'm so sorry, Gabr'l. I see this man was your true friend. So sorry."

"My friend. Granny," Gabe said looking up at her through blurry eyes. "He died good, didn' 'e Granny? 'e died well."

"Yes, Gabr'l, he done hisself proud and you, too, jus' fer bein' 'is true friend."

Nat and Dundee watched from the shed. When they finally scuffled out slowly, Nat said, "We seen it, Gabe. No human person ever died better, 'at's fer shore, ain't 'at right, Dundee?" Dundee nodded, looking down at Heck's rumpled form, a mournful look on his face. "Gabr'l," Dundee said, pointing across the meadow, the direction opposite of where the five Knights had come from, "Mebbe we ain't done jus' yet."

Three riders were coming fast. Each held a rifle in one hand and reins in the other. Gabe jumped up, grabbed Heck's Henry and ran over towards the Colonel's horse. He yelled at Nat as he kicked the Colonel's gun away. "Watch this 'un, he ain't done yet! Don't kill 'im." Gabe jumped on the horse, cocked the rifle and rode straight at the riders. He aimed and shot with his right hand. He dropped the reins and cocked again. He shot again, this time knocking a rider out of his saddle. He passed right between the other two, grabbed the reins again and spun the horse around, ready for another pass. Instead, though, he lifted the gun and shot one of the remaining two in the chest. His horse spooked, it took off, dragging the man behind. One to go.

This one decided he had seen enough. He kicked his horse hard and rode as fast as he could towards the creek. Nat took a shot at him and missed. Gabe dug his heels into the horse's flanks and he responded like a thoroughbred. Gabe cocked and shot. Again. Again. Finally, he had almost caught the man, and put a bullet into the middle of his back and through a lung. The man slumped over on his slowing mount. Gabe caught up to him and grabbed the horse's reins.

"You!" he sputtered. "Kilt by a goddamn nig- ." He choked before he could finish. Then he fell to the ground, his arms splayed out, only a dull shimmer left in his open eyes.

"I reckon, Johnny. Who can say? Mebbe y' 'ad it comin'." Gabe felt completely drained as he walked the Colonel's horse back to the cabin. "Mebbe we all 'ave it comin'," he muttered to himself.

He dismounted beside where the Colonel was still laying. Fletcher was lying on his side, holding his shoulder. "Well, Fletcher, your army's done for. For whatever you may've thought it worth. But your men did for my friend, too. What you think I should do about that, *Colonel?*" he said, in a mocking tone.

The Colonel half sat up, holding his left hand over his wound. "What are you goin' to do, uh – Gabe, was it? I need a doctor."

"Hahaha!" Gabe laughed. "Which one o' us black folks you think is gonna get you to a doctor without gettin' ourselves shot or lynched for our trouble?"

Granny stood by, listening. Nat and Dundee had half-carried, half-drug Heck off to the side of the shed and covered him with his blanket.

Gabe looked at her. "Granny, you got experience with this sort 'o thing," he said, with a devilish smile for Fletcher to see.

"Oh, yas-*sah*, Gabr'l. I ain't real good like a white doctor, but master had me fix up some o' us folks back t' Heavenly Hills after he lay on th' whip too much. Wouldn't do missin' a day in the fields jus' on account o' bein' beat most t' death." She looked at Fletcher. "Would it, Colonel?" she asked him. "I jus' bettin' you'd be a expert on 'at, right Colonel?"

"There y' go, Fletcher. Doc Granny'll fix you right up. Don't worry, she likes white folks. Hell, she was owned by one for more'n 50 years. An' 'e gave 'er steady work an' wholesome vittles th' whole time. Then, if'n you survive the fixin', we'll decide what t' do with ya."

"Wait a minute. Wait! You boys were in the war." He coughed, spit and looked down to the ground. He wasn't used to talking to a black man like an equal. It was hard for him. "You must know somethin' about gettin' a bullet out of a shoulder. Here, I'll make it worth your while. See this belt buckle? It's solid gold and you can have it if you patch me up right and let me ride."

"We can 'ave that damn buckle anyways, can't we Fletcher? But, oh, Sir Knight, we know it's gold. Just like all your 'scouts' are wearin', right, Fletcher?"

"Wha - " What? What do you know?" He let a big exhale as his head drooped.

16

COLONEL FLETCHER

G abe and the boys picked out a good spot for Heck. After hours with a pickaxe and shovels against the cold, hard ground, they had a grave. They wrapped Heck in a blanket and buried him. They put up a temporary marker. Gabe told Granny he'd have a stone made and when spring came he'd take him up to a permanent resting place in Rockville. He knew Old Henry would take good care of him. Or, depending on what the Service said, he might get a spot at Arlington. They read over him with Granny's old bible. Gabe felt like he had a hole in his heart he could never fill. The only thing keeping him going now was a case of red-hot anger. He knew he had to get control over himself. He had the memory of Heck McCabe to honor – he would continue their mission for him.

Much to Granny's disappointment and Fletcher's relief, Gabe dug the bullet out with his big knife while Nat and Dundee held him down. Gabe didn't bother being too careful but he did pour some Mulekick on the wound afterwards. They tied him and propped him up against the shed.

Then, Gabe spent a restless night, staring up at the stars. He remembered his friend from Heavenly Hills when he was still very young. Or, was the other boy his brother? The white folks wouldn't say. They used to lie on their backs outside of the shack where they sometimes slept and looked at the stars together. He told Gabe, "each one o' them stars . . . each a-one a whole other world, they gots t'be better'n what we got here." Gabe never knew what had given his friend such an idea, but he liked it. It had to be better up there than at Heavenly Hills. It was soon after that the slavedriver Sikes beat his little friend to death. Said it was because he looked at master's daughter too long. Of course, he was way too young to be "looking" at girls. Especially, those who could well have been his sister. That was the first time Gabe remembered being truly heartbroken. And there had been so many times since. It never got easier. And maybe this was the worst. And this night, Gabe was hoping his friend, his little brother, was right. There had to be somewhere better up there amongst the stars. Here, the struggle of life and death seemed too much to bear. Damn it, Heck . . .

No one spoke while they worked together to build up the fire again in the morning. Finally, Nat said, "Gabe, we seen what you an' your friend Heck done out here yesterday. All that stuff in th' book were true, weren't it? We seen it right here, live, in front of us. You was throwin' bolts o' blue lightnin' int' those poor white boys. Never seen somethin' so fast."

"Let's don't worry 'bout that right now, Nat," Gabe said, sipping his coffee. "I just have t' figure what t' do next. I have t' figure what Heck would do. Heck was some smart." He tried to cover his pain by keeping his mind busy. "We got t' do somethin' with all these 'scouts' layin' aroun' out here, dirtyin' up Granny's property. We'd be here 'til next year tryin' t' scratch holes in this hard ground for that bunch." He rubbed his chin and brightened up. "I know. Let's ask the Colonel." He knew that would shock the boys.

"Mornin', Fletcher," Gabe said, handing him a plate of food. "I'll take y' back t' the bushes there, y' can do your bus'ness, then leave one hand untied so's y' can eat. Then, I reckon you better start talkin' 'bout where I can find the rest o' your so-called Knights. I say 'so-called', on account o' I read 'bout the real knights in th' old days. Them like good ol' William Marshal? You hear o' him? They had honor and fought for what was good an' decent. Jus' th' opposite 'o your no-account rabble."

The Colonel was too weak to argue. After he was done eating, Gabe told him, "I'd just as soon leave that scum out there t' rot if it weren't for Granny. Buzzards got t' eat, same as maggots. Might leave a foul taste in their mouths, though. But Granny, she's got a wagon. I'm willin' t' tote 'em, an' let you go. Onliest way 'at's gonna happen though is this: you take me straight t' your commandin' officer an' 'e comes out an' talks t' me – alone, man to man, if 'e *is* a man. So, your choice, I leave you with 'im, or you stay with me – tied up, day and night, eat when I say, sleep when I say, ride when I say, 'til I get ya t' th' Secret Service. I reckon they'd 'ave you swing or spend th' rest o' your mis'ble life in th' fed'ral lock-up. See, Colonel. I know your type. You like to use respectable titles and respectable words. You like t' act like y' got some ed'cation and you're superior to th' rest o' folks. But you an' I both know, it's an act. You ain't nothin' but a lowdown, murderin' criminal, belong in jail, away from decent folks."

The Colonel looked up at Gabe, his cruel, thin lips blue with the cold. "I know who you are too, now, boy. My man Sweeney went west lookin' for a man who fought with the 54th. He never came back. At least, standin' and breathin'. But you're here. Must be you and this McCabe found him. And probably killed him."

"It was only because he did somethin' stupid, Fletcher. Like you did here yesterday. Like you plannin' t' do right now. And you don't start showin' some respect, things are jus' gonna get worse and worse for you. I can tie a tight rope or a loose rope. You can call me Mr. Baker or Gabe. And, no, your man Sweeney ain't never comin' back – at least, as y' say, standin' and breathin'. An' now we're all clear with each other, you must know I'm lookin' for the rest o' your boys and the gold you stole. That gold belongs to the gummint o' the United States."

Fletcher's head drooped as he weighed his options. "All right. I'll take you. But it's just so those fine boys out there get a proper burial," the Colonel said, wincing in pain. "And then you just ride on."

"Shore it is, Fletcher," Gabe said. "Now, I reckon you figure t' lead me into a trap, where you got a passel o' them play-soldiers ready t' shoot anybody come snoopin' 'round – 'specially a black man, eh, Colonel? So, we're gonna do it real careful. An' you're gonna do ever'thing I say when I say it. Or, it won't be good for you. No matter what goes wrong, you be the first man shot. Mebbe you saw yesterday. I do know how t' do some shootin'. Yeah, and m' friends Nat and Dundee are comin' along for the ride. Dundee's got one an' only one job this trip. That's shootin' you if'n y' make a wrong move."

The Colonel didn't respond. Gabe continued, "Your boys be gettin' ripe even in this weather, so we're startin' out first thing tomorrow. An' you're gonna help us load 'em up. Be good for that shoulder."

Nat and Dundee stripped the dead Knights of their belts, firearms and ammunition. They were happy to get some new guns. Granny was pleased with her new Henry and a horse. Gabe let her pick out what she wanted. She lent them her wagon and sent a couple of jugs along as well – for medicinal purposes. Granny let out a little sob when they left, wondering if she'd ever see her "Gabr'l" again. Gabe promised he would be back. "If for nothin' else, jus' a nip o' that Mulekick, Granny," he told her, winking.

"You be careful now, Gabr'l. Them boys you got with ya, I reckon they ain't much good for nothin'. 'Course, all in all, they is good boys. Mmm-hmm. An' first chance 'e gets, 'at 'Feltcher' fella stick a knife in yer back, Gabe. Oh, well, you know them things better'n me. I jus' needs t' act wise on account o' m' age, Gabr'l. Hell, you know 'at, too, I reckon. Hahaha! Oh, an' Gabe. I be takin' extra good care o' your friend, Heck, now don't you worry none."

They waved good-bye, Nat and Dundee on the buckboard, and the Colonel out front on one of his scout's horses, Gabe right behind, riding the Colonel's horse, the fastest of the bunch. His Henry was pointed at the middle of Fletcher's back.

Colonel Fletcher drooped in his saddle. Gabe rode up beside him from time to time to try to get as much information out of him as he could. Fletcher was weak, and Gabe thought he could get more out of him because of it. Much of what he said had a ring of truth to it, Gabe thought. Fletcher certainly wouldn't want to die with a black man's .44 slug in his back. Gabe knew how these "sons of the south" thought.

According to the Colonel, the Knights of the Golden Triangle were head-quartered in a remote cavern just across the border in Virginia. It was close to Fredericksburg where Burnside's Army of the Potomac had suffered so mightily at the hands of Lee's Confederates 11 years earlier. The little group rode for several days before Gabe sensed they were close. Gabe and Nat and Dundee were on high alert now, having crossed into Virginia. Every time they came across riders, they had to put on an act like they were working for Fletcher. Now, they were within a two-days' ride of the former capital of the Confederacy. Gabe and the Colonel had a tacit agreement. Fletcher cooper-ated when they met riders and Gabe used his "loose rope" on him at night. After they crossed the border, Gabe noticed that the Colonel seemed to sit up straighter in the saddle. He looked around more and sometimes behind. He was more animated and was getting stronger.

About mid-day, December 7, the Colonel stopped his horse. The buck-board came clunking and squeaking to a stop behind him and Gabe. "Whoa, whoa boys," Nat muttered at the horses, looking over at Gabe for direction.

Gabe rode up next to the Colonel. "Well, Gabe, we're within a mile," he said, looking Gabe in the eye. Gabe had noticed how steadily, but subtly Fletcher had been changing in his approach to him as they traveled. But Gabe had no illusions. This man would kill him and his friends at the first possible opportunity. And he had certainly been planning how he would direct them to the headquarters to his best advantage. Gabe knew the Knights didn't need him any more as he was sure Fletcher had figured out who Nat and Dundee were. But he was still unsure as to whether they wanted Nat and Dundee alive. It was still the same question. Were they seeking those boys out to silence them or did they need them to find the gold? He had to assume they would kill them all at this point.

Gabe turned in his saddle, and called out to Nat and Dundee, "You hear that boys? The man says we're within a mile. Within a mile of a nest o' white men who want nothin' more'n t' make us slaves all over again. Within a mile o' this dishon'rable trash that's too damn lazy t' make a livin' for their ownselves, gotta have some strong young bucks doin' th' work for 'em." He looked to see how Fletcher was taking this. Fletcher was just gazing up at the sky, trying to look bored. Gabe felt a rush of energy and kept talking.

"Only, you boys may recall, they did sometimes have t' work pretty hard, with th' lash or th' hick'ry stick. I saw poor ol' master plumb work up a sweat sev'ral times givin' out a beatin', always for good cause, o' course. Why, I saw a uppity black man once wanted a whole day off jus' 'cause 'is foot got broke an' 'e couldn' walk. An' one o' my aunties – you know she 'ad th' nerve t' push out a stillborn baby, could o' been a fine field hand one day. You know she deserved when master 'ad 'is slavedriver Sikes kick 'er in the stomach – 'ceptin' e' did it so many times she was laid up for a month. She got 'im back though, boys – never could 'ave 'nother baby after that. But you know, no need t' be livin' in th' past. What we gotta deal with 'ere is t' figger out 'ow ol' Fletcher figgers t' make us dead. What you think, boys?"

Nat and Dundee sat and listened, amazed. It seemed when Gabe spoke, he always spoke for them, too. Then, Fletcher spoke up, too. "Are you done, b--, I mean, *Gabe*? "I already told you I'll get the Knight Commander out to talk to you."

"The - " Gabe burst into an uncontrolled laugh. "The – the *what* now, Fletcher? Knight Commander? Oh, boy, oh ho . . . quite a fancy title for the boss o' a gang o' thievin', treasonous, belly-crawlin' crooks, I do say."

"I told you I'd do it. I'm a man of honor," Fletcher said.

"Your so-called honor'll only last up t' th' point where you think I can't put a hunk o' lead in your back, Fletcher. An' ya know I'll do it. So, keep 'at honor talk to y'self. I've seen too many really had it t' listen t' th' likes o' you."

Fletcher spit on the ground close to Gabe's horse. "Suit yourself, Gabe. You're in charge. So, what are we doin' now?" he challenged him.

"What we're doin' now is you're gonna sit quiet until I tell y' t' move," Gabe said. Then he dismounted and strode over to the buckboard out of the Colonel's hearing.

"Boys, listen careful, on account o' we can't be sure at all what's up ahead. I'm tyin' Fletcher up tight, but won't gag 'im. It might even help us if 'e tries t' yell out. I don't want 'im t' know, but you boys follow us – real quiet, on foot. Keep your eyes open an' keep lookin' up. Bring extra shells. If we're gettin' close, they're bound t' 'ave guards, some up high. You got those nice Henrys now, but don't use 'em 'less'n y' 'ave t'. Spread out a little, not too far. We're goin' into the worst nest o' snakes you ever saw, 'ceptin' mebbe at Fort Wagner. You hear shootin', go ahead 'long as you see somethin' t' shoot at." Then he smiled. "You 'ear me screamin' in pain, come on in an' shoot whoever's a-causin' it, all right?" Nat and Dundee just gave each other a quizzical look.

17

GENERAL LEE

" All right, Colonel, lead on, nice an' easy. Remember, you're just the colonel here, I'm the general. We start seein' your guards, you tell 'em, 'lower them barrels, we're comin' in together'. You do somethin' I don' like, don' worry, you'll die quick."

They proceeded slowly to a small, open field, where a recent cold snap had laid the natural grasses and wildflowers low. Gabe watched Fletcher closely and looked everywhere he looked. The colonel stopped to listen. "All right, Baker, let's go," he said without looking behind him.

"Slow and careful, Colonel. Slow and careful. And when I say stop, you do it now," Gabe replied. Gabe drew his Henry out of the scabbard and held it cross-saddle, at the ready. The Colonel's horse, which Gabe was still riding, started to dance around. He lifted his head and whinnied. Hearing that, the Colonel turned around and said, "See that, he knows he's home."

Gabe patted him on his neck. "Whoa, boy, whoa, take it easy now, we'll get you there, all right. Whoa."

Gabe was getting anxious about where Fletcher was headed, but when they reached the opposite end of the field, he could see the beginning of a well-hidden trail between a copse of yellow poplars to the right and a jumble of large rocks on the left. Before they re-entered the woods, Gabe looked back to see if Nat and Dundee were close. He didn't see them, but wasn't worried. They were supposed to stay out of sight.

Something about the country here reminded Gabe of the fighting at Honey Hill in late 1864. He had lost two friends there – soldiers who had fought gallantly for Colonel Shaw at Fort Wagner and survived that battle.

And then suddenly - he was there! Gabe's head swirled. He was overcome with the screams of fighting and wounded men. The acrid smell of gunsmoke filled his nostrils. He saw and smelled the ugliness of his friend's belly wound, as he twitched on the ground, yelling and grabbing at his intestines as if trying to shove them back inside where they belonged. It was a really bad time for this to happen. His heart raced and he broke out into a sweat. At least he was familiar with this experience. This was "soldier's heart". He knew it all too well. He was having a flashback. But he was unable to block it. Now, he was in trouble. What would Lin-Chi say? What must he do before the Colonel discovered he was no longer in control?

By sheer force of will, Gabe was able to tell Fletcher, "Don't move or make a sound," but his voice sounded other-worldly, like it was coming from somewhere else. Then, Gabe made himself remember Lin-Chi. "Mind state, only mind state," he would say. Gabe was never sure what he meant. But he also told him when the war came back into his head, "Not real, no deny, no avoid, just watch." Gabe tried to draw a deep breath. He stopped trying to block the madness that had taken over. Lin-Chi had sat with Harley and him when they were wounded and laid up in Doc Pierce's surgery back in Boulder. Something had happened there that he couldn't describe or explain. But Lin-Chi had helped him through a hard time just being there. He had sat in the corner, in the dark. There was something about his presence . . . And now, Gabe's mind rested on Lin-Chi for a moment. He thought of his beaming face and child-like smile, with those missing teeth. And in that brightness the darkness dissolved just as quickly as it had come. Here he was, back by the yellow poplars. He took a deep breath. Coming back that quickly gave him a lightness in his chest and a renewed sense of purpose. He felt no fear and he was ready to face anything. It was like a surge of manly energy, so much so that he had to calm himself before he spoke again.

"All right, Colonel, proceed," he said, regaining his normal voice. Just before they entered the trees, he saw a glint of gun metal from on top of a little overhang of rocks in front and to the left of them. They had been seen. He rode up beside Fletcher where the trail was just wide enough for two horses. "Colonel, your friends know we're here, now," he said. He drew his big Bowie knife out.

Fletcher's eyes got wide. "What are you goin' to do, Gabe? What are you doin' with that knife? I've done everything you said."

"Hold your hands out," Gabe ordered. He held the knife blade up between Fletcher's outstretched hands and cut through the rope with a jerk. "Wouldn't want your friends to think we're on unfriendly terms, I reckon," he said, slipping the knife back into its sheath. Fletcher stripped the remaining rope off his wrists and tried to rub the soreness out of them. Fletcher just glared at him. Gabe nodded and they continued through the trees.

Gabe whispered behind him, just loud enough for him to hear. "Colonel, this, right now, is where your life hangs by a thread. Make the right decisions." Fletcher didn't respond.

In a few minutes, they came to another clearing. But this time, they could see the opening of a cave about 100 feet away and 30 feet above them. The floor of the entrance was about 50 feet long. The irregular shape of the roof peaked out at about 15 feet. There was a narrow dirt trail with two switchbacks to the cave. It was well worn. Bushes helped obscure it from anyone passing by. As soon as Gabe started wondering where the guards were posted, four men stepped out from the cave into the daylight. It seemed like 1863 all over again. All four wore gray Confederate slouch hats, gray jackets with buttons down the front and brown trousers. The one who spoke also had the yellow crossed-sword design on the front of the crown of his hat and a yellow cord around it.

"Greetings, Colonel," he called out. "Good to see you again, sir. I trust your scouting party was successful. I see you brought a colored boy with you." He chuckled, "Did you have to get rough with the other one?"

"Good day, Captain. I'll get right to the point. Tell the General I'm here and I've got a package for him. This boy here has something to tell him," Fletcher said, looking over at Gabe to make sure he understood that he had to speak this way with his men.

The Captain produced a broad smile. "Excellent, sir. I'll be right back with instructions." The other four guards stayed put. The Colonel ordered them to be at ease and they stood down.

Gabe motioned to the Colonel to back up towards the bushes a bit. "Our only way in is you look like you got me under your gun, Colonel. I'm your prisoner. They haven't seen my guns yet. When we get leave, you walk me back. Here's my Henry," he said, jacking its shells onto the ground. "I want it back. You understand, Colonel? When I leave, under my own power, 'at's what I mean. I'm keepin' this Colt close t' hand and I'm keepin' you in my thoughts, Colonel." He threw the Henry to Fletcher. He tucked the Colt into the front of his pants. His jacket would keep it hidden. He kept his knife, too. And he didn't see any reason to mention the little .41 he kept as his hideaway.

Gabe saw that this was the best way in, although getting back out could be another matter. Maybe he'd have to rely on his crack team of sharpshooters to get out alive. He hoped not. Everything he and Heck had started out to do depended on what happened in that cave. He intended to leave here alive and with answers.

They waited, Gabe's horse getting edgy again. "Colonel, your horse is nervous as a cat. What's wrong with 'im?"

"He can sense danger. Can you?" Gabe couldn't help but notice the cheerless little grin that appeared on Fletcher's otherwise impassive face.

"There's danger here, all right. But just you remember, 'sir', it's as much t' you as it is t' me," Gabe said, returning the smile.

The captain of the guards came out into daylight after about 15 minutes. He stood, put his hands on his hips, while scanning the countryside. Then he called out, "All right Colonel, General Lee will see you and your friend now. You are to leave your horses, and walk on up."

Gabe peered at the Colonel and mouthed the words, "General Lee?" Fletcher smiled. Well, Gabe figured, even if I don't make it out of here alive, I'm bound t' find some interestin' facts. Just hope I get a chance to report 'em.

When Gabe and Fletcher made it to the top of the trail and the cave entrance, one of the guards saluted the Colonel, and said, "Sir, we'll have to check your prisoner for contraband." Fletcher saw a slight movement of Gabe's left hand towards his pistol butt.

"Sergeant, do you not suppose I de-fanged this snake days ago?" Fletcher scowled.

"Yessir, of course sir, it's just that - "

"That'll be sufficient, Sergeant, we don't have time to waste," Fletcher said. The Captain and two guards then led Gabe and Fletcher back into something of a great hall. Its ceiling was high and the open space under it large enough for 20 horses and men. At the far end, the space narrowed to a walkway back farther below the earth. It went back and slightly down. It had obviously been improved by human hands. Torches hanging from the walls on either side lit the way. Gabe knew Fletcher was walking a tightrope, pretending to have a prisoner, rather than actually being one.

After about 80 feet, the passageway widened again, this time into a large, central chamber with two paths, one continuing on straight, the other leading off to the left. The group continued straight. After another 50 feet or so, the passage opened up once more. This room was the same size as the last, cool, and a bit darker. It roughly described a circle, with large torches ringing the walls. It smelled of earth and acrid smoke. But there was also the slight, but unmistakable odor of cigar and whiskey.

This would be the men's destination. There was a desk at the far end. There were cabinets, files and a small bar near the desk. A small man sat in the outsized chair behind the desk. He was facing away from his visitors. The Captain announced their arrival. "General, sir, Colonel Fletcher and his darky." Gabe glared at the man but wasn't in a position to do much about his rudeness. The figure in the chair waved him off.

"All right, Captain, leave the Colonel and his charge alone with me," wheezed the man without turning. The Captain and guards gave a salute which was not returned and clunked in their boots back up the passageway.

Then the man turned in his swivel chair. He briefly looked at the Colonel, then studied Gabe for a moment. "Way-ell, Mr. Baker!" he drawled in an exaggerated accent. "It's been some time now. Glad to see you're still on the job. Reportin' in, are you?"

"Deputy Chief," Gabe said politely and without emotion. "I must say I wasn't expectin' t' see you 'round these parts. I do believe I like your other office a might better."

"Haha!" the General wheezed. He took a gulp of whiskey and coughed. He said to Fletcher, "You see, Colonel, your detainee and I happen to know each other, don't we Gabe Baker? Now, Colonel, what's your report? You got yourself one Gabe Baker, but it appears those two boys you were after got the slip on you. What happened?"

Gabe could see that Fletcher was now on the hotseat. "General, we came up on these boys' camp. There was a bunch of them," he lied. "We shot it out and I lost five good men. I brought them back for proper burial. But we accomplished our mission. We have Gabe here and although the other two are still free I know exactly where they are. I intend to use Gabe as bait and bring 'em in. I'd only need one good – let's say, two good men."

Gabe's mind was reeling. What was Fletcher up to? Did he really think Gabe would give up his two friends for his own freedom? Maybe so. These men were craven, down to their bony fingers.

The General scowled at Fletcher. "We'll talk more on that later, Colonel," he sneered.

Then he looked back at Gabe. "And, how may I ask, is our friend Heck McCabe?"

"He's dead. By the hands of a band o' ragtag cutthroats under the command o' this here Colonel o' yours. Seems they not done playin' soldier yet. Why don't you tell 'em, Deputy Chief Flynn? War's over some eight years now."

"Sorry to hear about Heck. I liked him. No, I truly did. Of course, he was a major pain in our rears for a while back there." The General coughed and cleared his throat. "Couple of things for you to understand, now, boy. I didn't know you were quite that thick-headed. First of all, the war isn't over – not to a pure and loyal southerner. Not to these fine men we have here and more further west just waitin' for my call to arms. Second, although I am Deputy Chief in your Secret Service, Flynn isn't my real name. I'm General Lee. Shemp Lee. Name sound familiar?"

Gabe wasn't ready for that. "What's a matter, boy, nothing smart to say 'bout that?" The General smiled broadly, poured himself a large whisky and took a gulp. Then he bent over laughing at his joke. He leaned forward and looked up at Gabe with his watery, blood-shot eyes.

"Nothin' smart, I reckon," Gabe said, regaining his composure, "just disappointed, I'd say. Was hopin' ol' Shemp Lee had been laid t' rest by now."

Shemp stood up and steadied himself against his desk with his left hand. He shook his bony right index finger at Gabe and rasped, "You killed Oliver Sweeney, a good man, boy. Sweeney did his share and more in the recent fightin'. Of course, you will pay for that indiscretion. We *will* take good care of you." He sat down hard and the squeak his chair made echoed in the room. "There's a way out for you though, Baker. Let's just see how smart you are. Heck thought you were. What's your way out, Baker? You tell me."

Gabe gave a sideways glance at the Colonel, as he furtively tapped the butt of his Colt under his shirt. "Well, sir. Mebbe I just run like 'at other General Lee did from Gettysburg. Only I do the reverse route. I cross th' Potomac and make it over t' Maryland way," Gabe said, with a big smile.

"Well, you impertinent scoundrel. How dare you even speak the name of my hero brother, and in such a way? Robert Lee's worth a hundred of your U.S. Grants. Don't forget you'self, boy. I can have you whipped any time I want."

"Figures. I notice how some folks run out o' somethin' smart t' say, all they *can* do is threaten a body. Happen all th' time like 'at back t' Heavenly Hills. I never heard - "

"What's that, boy? You say Heavenly Hills?" Lee interrupted.

Gabe ignored him and continued, "No one 'round those parts ever heard Lee had no brother name o' Shemp anyways. You makin' 'at up t' impress these soldier boys here, ain't ya? I guess y' need their help, y' gotta make some-thin' up, so's they think you got the, what they call, the 'bona fides'. Make up a fancy name – Knights o' the Golden Triangle. Land sakes. Sound even better all Frenchified. I think I heard it all." General Lee turned red and started to cough. Gabe kept at him. "Hell, General, I bet you got plans t' take all that Confederate gold for your ownself, leave these boys high and dry. That'd be just 'bout right for a white gen'leman from Virginnie."

"If I didn't need you, you'd be flogged and dead by now, Baker," he sput-tered, wiping his mouth with a silk handkerchief, regaining his composure. The Colonel stood by, listening, hearing things he'd never dared think before. But he was unable to do anything anyway. "But of course, you are wrong, boy. That is not your way out. And I don't need your blood. I'm going to tell you your only way out right now."

He reached for a match, leaned back in his chair and lit the half-smoked stogie he had been holding. He sucked on it and turned it until he had a good, full end burning. Your two friends, those two black boys the Colo-nel's got a bead on – well, if he does, I don't even need you – but it's easier this way and I don't want to lose any more men," he continued, frowning at Fletcher. "You just bring them in, leave them at the front door, we'll do the rest. You disappear into the woods. I'll throw in a little gold and you'll keep your mouth shut to the Service. Nobody'd believe you anyway whatever you think you could say."

"Well, General, sir," Gabe said, suddenly sounding deferential, "if'n you got gold t' give out, why you need them boys?"

"Hahaha! That's right. That's right. You call yourself a 'Secret Service agent', but you and Heck McCabe never figured it out."

"Uh, sir?"

"We got the gold, boy. All of it. Hahaha!"

"What? All right, General, I admit," Gabe hesitated, "that one's a surprise. Why you need them boys then?"

"'Them boys' know too much about us. 'Them boys' might know all about the gold, where it came from – sneaky sons-of-bitches, we caught them hangin' around, they might even know where we're heading and what we're doing. I doubt anyone would believe those two ignoramuses about us but we have to be careful."

"Really, General? And why would I believe you'd let me go? Hell, I'm drawin' pay from the Service right now. You know that – seein' as 'ow you're my boss an' all."

"Service already knows everything you do. Except where this hideout is – oh, and where the gold is. And we will be departin' soon as we take care of loose ends."

"What makes you think those boys didn't tell me everything?" Gabe asked, testing Lee again.

"Those boys needed you to help them. They tell you everything, you don't need them. And you aren't that good of an actor. You didn't know we are ready with stage two of our plan. Oh, and to show my good faith, I'll have the Colonel shoot you in the foot. That'll slow you down when you come after us." He puffed on his cigar, then looked at Fletcher.

"You're showin' your good faith by shootin' me?"

"That's right."

"All right Colonel, you heard me," the General said. "You know how to use that thing. Go ahead. Let's show our friend here our good faith. Then, if he doesn't reciprocate by bringing his boys in, you can complete the job." Gabe's hand went quietly to his belt.

The Colonel hesitated. He aimed the Henry at Gabe's foot, then lowered it. "General, you know how I feel about bein' underground. This whole place could come down with one shot. Gives me the jitters. If you don't mind, I'll take him outside."

"All right, Colonel," Lee sniffed. He took a gulp of whiskey. "If it bothers you that much. Just come back with those other two boys," he slurred loudly.

"Yessir," he said, saluting, and then, "Let's go, Baker." He pushed the barrel of the Henry into Gabe's back and they started back up the passageway.

18

FRESH AIR

Fletcher pushed Gabe out of the entrance into the daylight. Gabe stopped and blinked. "Whew! That fresh air fillin' your lungs shore do feel good, don't it, Colonel?" he said. He didn't wait for an answer.

As he took another step, Gabe realized he had made a mistake. This was Fletcher's chance and he took it. He caught the attention of two of the guards. "Put your guns on this boy and hand me some .44s," he ordered. "We're goin' coon huntin'." He loaded the Henry.

Damn, Gabe thought. I can't be making mistakes like this. "Hey, Colonel, y' know you was s'posed to give me that gun back," he said.

The two guards looked at each other, confused. "Don't mind this colored boy here," he said, "he sometimes gets mixed up, doesn't know if he's comin' or goin'. Now march, let's go."

Gabe looked back at the three of them as they started him walking towards the woods. "Really, boys, you buyin' that? Why you think that Henry was empty?" Then he raised his voice and said to all of them, "That Shemp Lee, he don't seem like th' type t' take it so good, you not comin' back with m' friends. Mebbe y' want me t' shoot you, make it look good, like I got th' better of ya? Hahaha! Leave three shells in there, I'll get y' all. Just nick y' in the liver a bit."

"We don't come up with those worthless sons-o'-bitches, that hole isn't goin' to be in your foot, Baker. Just you remember. Move."

"I don't reckon that's where y' expect t' put it anyways, Colonel. You know damn good 'n well 'at General Lee o' yours wants all three of us dead. Don't care what 'e said, 'e's just like th' rest o' you rebel scumbellies. Say one thing, do another. No honor, like with a real knight." Gabe stopped in the middle of the trail and looked back at them, putting his hands on his hips. "An' you call us black folk ignorant. You really b'lieve 'at bottlewash 'bout the gold bein' used t' get your rabble army marchin' again? Hahaha!"

"I never heard no black boy talkin' like that afore, did you, Albert?" one of the guards said, his thin mouth forming a frown.

"No Walter, never did back where I come from in Car'lina. 'Course, only the rich folks had 'em. I never was around 'em too much. My pa told me stay clear. You know, they got diseases an' such."

"Come on, boys, move," Fletcher said. "Don't worry, they don't have diseases we never saw durin' the war." Albert and Walter looked at each other in amazement. Weren't those bad enough?

Gabe started moving again. He tried to keep them talking while he looked around for Nat and Dundee. He was just looking for some kind of an opening. Maybe he could distract them and run off through the woods if the boys didn't show up. Maybe they wouldn't. After all, they hadn't been quite honest with him about the gold. He wished he had Heck with him. When Heck said he had his back, he knew he was covered.

He shuddered. Ah, Heck. He thought of Heck's outsized smile. He remembered the first time he met him, at his front door back in Boulder. How comical it was how he had that gunbelt up so high, resting on his fat stomach. He soon found out Heck knew how to use that gun, though. Nothin' funny about that.

Despite his efforts, thoughts of Heck lying on the cold ground with that hole in his belly started up – he'd better control those thoughts. He could feel the heat of the anger rising up through his body, up, up, to his neck and to his head, and he felt a hot flush. His heart raced. His jaw tensed. His hands clenched into fists as he walked along, listening, but now with a buzzing in his ears.

Walter and Albert weren't more than five feet behind. The Colonel was another five feet behind them. He moved his head slightly to get his bearings. Should he wait until they reached the spot where he left Nat and Dundee? He told himself, no, I can trust 'em, I can trust 'em. At heart, they're good boys. But . . . where are they? Mebbe they'd be back at the wagon.

It was late afternoon when the four men appeared in the clearing where Gabe and the Colonel had left Nat and Dundee. The wagon was standing off to the side near the thick trees of the forest. The Colonel's scouts were laid out, side by side, in the middle of the meadow.

"Colonel - " gasped Walter, pointing, "look!"

"I see it, son. We'll take care of them once we get those boys in chains. Keep an eye out, they're armed. And don't worry about hurtin' them." The three Confederates stood at the edge of the trees. "Baker, remember what you said? Well, now, I'm tellin' you. This, right now, is where your life hangs by a thread. Make the right decisions."

He motioned for Gabe to get in front of them. Gabe complied slowly. And he thought, the one advantage we have is these graybacks don't know how good my boys are with their long guns. They stood and listened. The shadows were getting long and the air chilly. Gabe could see that Walter and Albert were getting cold and impatient.

"Don't worry boys, we're not campin' out here all night," the Colonel said. After looking all around again, he called out, "All right, boys, come on out. We got Baker here and we will shoot him in the back of the head if you don't come out with your hands up. Then we will track you down and shoot you. You come out and we'll just talk."

Gabe didn't know if the boys had the gumption to start shooting, but, just in case, he started to move subtly to his right to expose the guards as much as he could. "Gabe, you tell them," the Colonel said, poking Gabe's Henry into his back. "Now."

"All right, boys, come on out," Gabe called out. He glanced at Fletcher. Then he yelled, "But talkin' ain't all they want t' do. So, come out shootin'.'"

The Colonel hesitated before he cocked his gun to shoot Gabe. Gabe used that split second to dive into the trees. He went head first, rolled, pulling his .41 to shoot the Colonel in the leg, and quickly found his feet in a run for his life. Just then, Nat and Dundee let loose with their Henrys. The forest crackled with gunfire as the guards kneeled and shot back. Gabe struggled with thick undergrowth a few yards into the woods. He looked back. Walter and Albert were down. Where was Fletcher? He stopped, trying to listen over the hard thumping of his heart. Then, a whoosh of someone brushing up against the scrub that lined the trail – he looked, holding his breath. Then he caught a glimpse of a figure, bent over, fast-walking back the way they had come. It had to be Fletcher. He was hit.

Gabe got on his hands and knees. He peered out from the edge of his cover. The boys were standing behind the wagon, rifles at the ready. He stood.

"Nat! Dundee!" he yelled out. "It's all right. It's over." He looked down at the crumpled forms of Walter and Albert. Albert was moaning and starting to stir. The Colonel had dropped the Henry. Gabe was happy to have it back. He picked up the other guns that lay on the ground and started to walk towards the boys. "At least for now," he said in a conversational tone as he approached the wagon.

"Good shootin', boys. An' I mostly 'ppreciate your bein' on time," Gabe said, breathing hard. He looked all around to make sure there was no more danger.

"Well, Corp'ral, we gettin' used t' havin' t' shoot bein' aroun' you again. Just like old days. 'ceptin' these here Henrys is a might bit better'n them ol' Springfields, eh Dundee?" Nat said, smiling at his friend.

"Hey, Gabe, you like our little collection here, we line these boys right up. Now, look like two more ready t' join 'em," Dundee said, wiping the side of his head with the back of his hand.

"Yeah, boys, right pretty, like a bouquet o' flowers. One o' those boys yonder ain't ready for th' bouquet yet, though. 'e's still twitchin' a might." Gabe said. "We'll leave 'im, they must 'ave a doc." Then he cocked his head at Dundee, "Look here, what y' doin' with your head there. You got blood. Let's see that," Gabe said, grabbing his chin and moving his head to the side for a better view. "Dundee. You have been *shot*. Did y' know that?"

"Oh, it ain't much," he said, wiping away more blood.

"Well, look, Gabe, it only got 'im in th' head. Dundee ain't known for usin' that much anyways," Nat said. Dundee responded with a gap-toothed smile.

"Mebbe, an' it looks like it jus' sideswiped 'im a bit, but 'e's still losin' blood." Gabe reached into the storage box under the seat of Granny's wagon and found the kerchief he was looking for. "Here, hold this up there. I'm gonna tear up one o' these boys' shirts and make a bandage," he said, walking out to where the guards fell. "But we gotta skedaddle. Get ready. Those soldier boys back at the cave ain't 'bout ready t' jus' let us be."

Gabe made a makeshift bandage for Dundee. Nat and Dundee drove the wagon and Gabe rode alongside, keeping an eye out in every direction for unwanted company. "Let's hurry them critters along a bit, boys. I've seen enough shootin' for th' day," Gabe said as they took the direct route back towards Granny's. "We need t' find a good spot to hole up in afore it gets too dark. An' get a better look at Dundee's noggin."

As they rattled along, Gabe thought of how to cover their tracks. But the ground was hard anyway. And the Knights would almost certainly return to Granny's, which is exactly where they were headed. He had promised to get her wagon back to her, but he also needed to make sure she wouldn't be in danger from those grayback coyotes coming up the backtrail. They would show up there sooner or later.

He wondered what kind of reception Fletcher was getting back at Golden Triangle headquarters. But the thought of it gave him no joy. Finally, he tried to think of what next step Heck would have had in store for them. At least he knew now that he was looking for gold that had already been dug up. He also knew he needed to send General Burke a report as soon as he could.

The three friends got an early start the next morning after spending the night in a cold camp. Gabe did allow them to have a fire for coffee at their first stop. He checked Dundee. He realized the wound was worse than he had thought. The bandage he had made was still wet. Dundee was unstable on his feet.

"Don't worry, Dundee, this here camp coffee gonna do y' a world o' good," Nat told him, offering a hot cup. He exchanged a worried glance with Gabe. Gabe made him a new, dry bandage. He cleaned the wound first with some of the Mulekick they still had in the wagon.

"Dundee, how's that feel?" Gabe asked, certain of the response.

"Oh, it ain't no problem, Corp'ral. I'll be good as new right soon now." Neither Gabe nor Nat had ever heard a word of complaint from the man.

"Well, bein' as how I'm actin' as your doc 'til we get to Granny's, I'm orderin' up a full dose o' the Mulekick for you."

Dundee's darkened face brightened up immediately. "Thanks, Doc, 'at's mighty fine – mighty fine."

Dundee held his own over the next two days, and early the third, the group pulled into Granny's meadow. They would settle here for the time being, with either Nat or Gabe on guard at all times, until Gabe decided on his next move. And, until Dundee looked like he was recovering. It was good to be "home".

19

GABE MAKES A DECISION

Gabe and Nat helped Granny around her place for two and a half days while Dundee snoozed, ate and sipped medicinal Mulekick. Gabe decided it was time to hide out and wait for the Knights to return. The three of them retreated to a spot on a ridge overlooking the woods where they could keep a close watch to see how they treated Granny. The timing was right. Just as they settled in behind a thick mass of log and rock, they heard the drumming of horses coming in fast.

Once again, there were five. Gabe wondered how many Shemp Lee had at his disposal. He didn't see the Colonel. As they approached, the leader put up his hand to stop his troops. Gabe chuckled at the sight of this rough bunch skidding their horses to a hard stop in front of a stooped-over old lady holding her Henry rifle across her skinny frame. Granny didn't flinch. She looked the leader in the eye.

"You boys look like you're in a awful hurry. What's goin' on there? You got 'ny gold?"

"What are you talkin' about, gold, Mammy?" the leader said. "What do you know about gold?"

"Just this, soldier boy. Gold is what I git fer m' Mulekick. You gots some gold, I gots some good 'shine. If'n y' think your boys can handle it, 'at is." She bent over, cackling at her own joke.

One of the men spoke up. "Cap'n, we been by here before. That is some good 'shine this here old granny's cookin' up. Maybe we should get us some for the road."

"You wants t' give it a try, Cap'n?" Granny asked. Without waiting for an answer she hobbled back to pour some out of a jug sitting by the still. She handed the mug up to the Captain. He threw it back in a single gulp, then coughed and choked a bit, his men laughing. He wiped his mouth with the back of his hand and swallowed.

"Yeah, Corporal, yeah," he rasped, trying to find his voice. "That is some good 'shine. First things first. Mammy, we know some black boys came through here real recent. You tell us where they are and we'll let you be. After we buy some of that good moonshine, of course."

"Why I wanna tell you where these boys are, Cap'n? What you want with 'em? You prob'ly jus' wanna shoot 'em, don't you now?"

"We don't mean you no harm, Mammy. An' all we want to do with those boys is talk to 'em and get some information. But we are serious. We want to know where they are."

Granny played along. She also kept a tight grip on her Henry. "Oh, well, suh, in 'at case I can tell ya." She turned slightly and pointed. "See 'at ridge up yonder? They was headed that way. Bought some o' my fine 'shine and took right off. No more'n a couple hours ago. Lookee here, you can see their trail on the ground over here. Now, how much you want, Cap'n?"

"Granny, I told you we were serious. We'll take a look and if you're not bein' straight with us, there'll be consequences," the Captain said. Granny looked up and gave him a hurt expression. He nudged at his horse with his spurs.

"Uh, Cap'n, we gonna get some o' that Mulekick before we go?" the Corporal asked.

"All right, all right, it has been cold out." Granny caught the gold coin he flipped at her and she turned to pick up two jugs.

"Here you go boys, I'm throwin' in a little extra for you brave soldiers, I do hope y' enjoy. And keep warm," she said, cackling and handing the jugs up to the Corporal. As soon as they were all headed away, she pointed up to the ridge to confirm for Gabe where she was sending them. She hoped he saw.

Gabe, Nat and Dundee were hidden behind a rock outcropping a third of the way up the slope when the Confederates rode by. The soldiers traveled slowly and deliberately, watching for sign along the trail. The boys had ridden to the crest, and when they found rock, circled back around, so at least the soldiers would see some evidence of their passing to the top. They had to hope they would assume they kept going in the same direction and would look for more sign ahead beyond the rocky top of the trail.

After the Captain and his boys went by and disappeared into the trees at the bottom of the ridge, Gabe spoke up. "Nat, this here is dangerous territory for you an' Dundee until those Knights pick up and head west, which I b'lieve is their plan. At least afore they go int' Mexico." Gabe scratched his chin, watching for any movement down below. "Granny's all right as long as they 'ave a taste for her 'shine, but it would be a comfort if you boys was around to watch over her. And Dundee's in no shape to ride anyways."

Nat and Dundee sat silently. Gabe scratched the stubble on his chin again. He looked off into the distance. He let out a deep sigh. "Boys, you know I gotta do what I signed up t' do and what I owe Heck t' do." He hesitated, searching for the right words. "And what's right for all o' us folk here an' all over th' south. Hell, th' whole country's the truth. Thing is boys, I gotta go it alone. Watch over those Knights and follow 'em until I find the gold. They got their boss with 'em now, I know they're leavin' soon. I'll just follow these boys that passed by and they're sure t' meet up."

"But – but - " Nat started to say, then looked down. "But Corp'ral. We'd be a might o' help. Mebbe they'd put us all in them dime books like they got you." Nat shook his head and continued, more sternly now, "Gabe, you know me an' Dundee's the best sharpshooters in this here whole county."

"County, hell! More'n likely, whole state o' Maryland. I know it, Nat, ain't no doubt. What I got t' do mebbe don't need no sharpshootin', but when I do, I'll send for ya. Fact is, I need ya here so's Dundee can heal up and you can watch over Granny. An' that ain't bad, she'll be needin' ya both, mebbe you can even learn th' trade." They were quiet for a couple of minutes. "An' if 'at dime novel man comes around again, I'll tell 'im 'bout your sharpshootin' savin' me from all them shiftless play-actin' soldier-boys by the cave."

Dundee lifted his head, and said in a weak voice, "Nat, me an' you can protect Granny an' 'er works and help out a might. Mebbe she need us t' sample from time t' time, too." Then his head slumped again.

"See there, Nat. I know it's a lot t' ask. But Granny and Dundee both need ya."

"I reckon, Corp'ral. I reckon."

20

GOING IT ALONE

Gabe knew his next move would depend on where those five riders led him. He wanted to contact General Burke as soon as he could, but knew he had little chance of getting service at a telegraph office in Virginia. He would keep a healthy distance and hope, first, that the riders would meet up with the rest of the gang from Knight headquarters, and second, that he could make his report. With Heck gone, every move he made would be more difficult simply because there was now no white man to make necessary contacts with the white world.

The Confederates were easy to follow. There was no need for them to cover their tracks, and as Gabe was finding, to hurry, either. They were going north. They generally followed the Potomac River and appeared to be riding for Washington, D.C. At some point they must have abandoned the idea of finding him or Nat and Dundee. They weren't watching the trails or road for sign anymore, and they looked to be riding with more of a purpose. Good. Maybe they had an appointment with Shemp Lee. Gabe followed the group into the city. They checked into the Willard Hotel, across the street from the White House. Here, Gabe could keep an eye on them. Meanwhile, he decided to look in on Deputy Chief Flynn's office to see if he could find any clues as to the Knights' travel plans. He chuckled to himself. Oh, yeah, he remembered, they were officially the "Johnson Gang".

As he climbed the stairs of the familiar government building he couldn't help but recall how he and Heck had solidified their friendship here, just a few short weeks earlier. He cautiously went in through the main entrance. He walked around the corner in the lobby until he came upon the office. The plaque was still there: "Hon. Hiram J. Flynn – Deputy Chief". Gabe started to feel the rise of anger build within him. He took two long, deep breaths.

The building was quiet. He stood by the door for a minute and listened. Then he tried the doorknob. Locked. He looked around for something, anything that might help him get in. Then, on the other side of the lobby, he noticed for the first time an elderly black man in the corner, quietly, deliberately swabbing a mop back and forth on the marble floor. A bucket sat beside him as he swooped the handle, left and right, in front of him. Gabe walked up to him.

"How do, sir?" Gabe asked, slightly bowing when the old man turned to address him.

"Heh-heh. Wondered where that 'sir' bus'ness come from," the man said, smiling slightly. He stood up to his full height, which couldn't have been more than just over five feet. He scratched the stubble on his cheek with one hand while he kept a hold of his mop with the other. "As t' how I do, well, fair t' midlin' as per most always. What can I do for ya, young feller?"

"I need t' get int' the Deputy Chief's office. Lookin' for papers. I would reckon you got a key t' every door in the buildin'," Gabe said.

"Sorry, you prob'ly know I can't do that – uh -?"

Gabe helped him out. "Gabe. Gabe Baker, of the United States Secret Service. Deputy Chief's my boss. Well, I should say, one o' my bosses, seem like I got a passel of 'em."

"Y – you? Secret Service? Well, I'll be damned. Haha! Someday, one o' our folks prob'ly be pres'dent!" he said, doubling himself over with laughter.

"Could be, uh, Caleb? I see your name on your badge there."

"Still, sorry, Gabe, I ain't supposed to let no one in the offices. I'd get fired, or worse, for sure."

"I'm sure you ain't. But this ain't reg'lar bus'ness neither. It's more important than reg'lar an' it 'as t' do with the Deputy Chief himself. Sometimes breakin' the rules is more important than keepin' 'em. This is one o' them times."

"Let's see your badge, Gabe," he said, looking up into his eyes. Gabe showed it to him. Without a further word, Caleb let his mop handle clunk against the wall, causing a sharp echo to bounce off the hard walls and ceiling. He led Gabe to the office as he fumbled with his keys. Without a further word, he opened the door and went back to work.

Gabe didn't know what he was looking for. He went through the Deputy Chief's desk, filing cabinet and shelves. He found a small safe hidden behind a stack of books on the floor, but it was open and empty. Frustrated, he sat down with a loud sigh. The Deputy Chief's chair creaked and groaned as he sat back and was forced to look up. Then he noticed. There was a small blemish in the ceiling medallion. It didn't look natural. It was perfectly square, and just a little off-color. Gabe scooted the heavy desk under it and stood on it so he could reach up. He pushed on it and it immediately gave way and fell, bouncing off the desk and onto the floor. Gabe quickly grabbed several books off the shelves and stacked them on the desk. Standing on those, he could reach his hand into the hole. He felt papers. He grabbed everything he could reach. Then he moved the desk back and sat down again.

It was a good find. Gabe found himself looking at a packet of cash and a small bundle of telegrams.

Before he could read them he heard Caleb's bucket clanking outside. Then he heard Caleb speaking in a loud voice that reverberated off the walls of the stark lobby. "No, *suh*," Caleb was saying, "Ain't nobody been 'round here all day, *suh*." Gabe shoved the telegrams into his pocket and snuck out the door away from the main entrance. There was nowhere to go but to a dark corner next to another office door and a statue of some long-dead patriot holding a large law book. He was also partially hidden by one of the building's many interior columns. He calmed his breathing and waited. Footsteps clattered along the polished, hard floor. They seemed to approach, then receded. Gabe waited. Then, more footsteps.

"You good now, Gabe," he heard Caleb saying in a lowered voice. "All clear."

Gabe came stepped out of the shadows. "Thanks, Caleb. I'm done here. You know who that was just came in?"

"No, I don' reckon. But I do know this. He was one o' them crackers from down piney-woods Georgia way, just as soon kill a man as spit on 'im. I can hear it in 'is twangy talk, and I can see it in 'is way o' dressin'."

"Way o' dressin', Caleb?"

"Yessir. Bunch of them good ol' boys hangin' 'round here recent-like, all wearin' them same ol' shinied-up belts. How can a man figger that, I'm askin' ya, Gabe?"

"With a gold buckle, Caleb?"

"Yep, 'at's right. You know 'em?"

"I do. Stay as far 'way as you can, my friend," Gabe said.

"But you ain't, are ya, Gabe? You're goin' after 'em, ain't ya?"

"That's right. And you already helped. Thank-you, Sir," Gabe said as he walked to the front door. Then, he thought for a moment. He reached into his pocket and walked back to Caleb. "For your troubles," he said, handing him a 20 dollar bank note. "Just probably don't want to spend it in this neighborhood." He bowed slightly, while Caleb's jaw dropped. Then he stepped outside into the sunshine.

Gabe knew of a place that would serve black folks. Heck had showed him. He found a table in a dark corner and ordered coffee. Then, he set to the task of reading the telegrams. Most appeared to be standard administrative messages. Gabe wondered why Shemp would hide them. Were they in some kind of code? Many of them were orders to the Deputy Chief from Secret Service headquarters in New York. After getting through most of them, Gabe came across several which were clipped together. They were messages between "Hiram J. Flynn" and William D. Fletcher. Ah, yes, our friend, Colonel Fancy Vest, Gabe thought.

Gabe found one that told Fletcher that Flynn expected to be at "HQ" in December. He told him to make preparations for travel. Then, he came across one that really caught his eye:

> WDF: find baker and friends (stop) important take
> care all (stop) take special care hm (stop) plan meet
> dc by january 10 (stop) make prep to pay respects
> shemp rockville HJF

Gabe sat with that one awhile. The Colonel had been ordered to kill Heck and him as well as Nat and Dundee. That was not a surprise. But, what about paying respects to Shemp? One thing was sure. If those Knights were going to Rockville, Gabe was going too. Maybe he could even beat them there. Looks like I'll get to see Ol' Henry again, Gabe thought. It would be nice to see a friend.

21

THE DISINTERMENT OF SHEMP LEE

Gabe rode north, back to Rockville. He had been watching the Willard Hotel. The Knights were up to something. More and more of them were checking in. They were in no hurry to leave. He decided to go ahead and wait for them. He wanted to keep Ol' Henry out of danger as much as he could, too. Before he left, he sent a telegram to General Burke. He told him the Johnson Gang appeared to be on the move. He asked for a response, but receiving none for a day and a half, left town.

The days were warming some in early March. It was 50 degrees as the sun lowered in the sky the afternoon Gabe rode slowly towards the Rockville Cemetery. He tied up near the gate in front and looked around. All was quiet. The old gate creaked as he pulled it open and walked in. "Henry?" he asked in a conversational tone. And then louder, "Henry Haymond. You here'bouts? It's Gabe. Come for a visit."

Ol' Henry stuck his head out of the tool shed door and squinted. "Gabe? Gabe, y' say?"

Gabe waved and started walking towards him. "'at's right, Gabe Baker. Y' remember me, don't ya, Henry?"

"Heh-heh, remember, 'e says. 'Course I remember, boy. Last time I seen you was the dadgumnest best day I had in a whole long time," Henry said as he dropped the shovel he was holding and walked out with his hand outstretched. "Good t' see ya, son."

"Good t' see you too, Pops," Gabe said, looking around. "'ppears like ya got it all under control here, Henry. I bet this here cemetery has never looked so good."

"Thank ya, Gabe. Say, where is that nice young feller you was up here with last time, uh, uh, that Heck-um, I b'lieve, ya called him, yeah, Heck-um?"

Gabe told Henry most of what had happened since he had seen him last. Afterwards, they sat in silence on a bench near the shed. "Yeah, I'm so sorry ya lost that boy, 'e was a real good 'un, weren't he?"

"Yessir, that 'e was."

"You been doin' up some kind o' high adventurin' though, sound like. You bringin' some o' that back here again?"

"Sorry t' say, looks like it's comin' whether I'm here or not, Henry. Them badmen are most certain on their way here - to your back yard."

"But why here – in partic'lar here, Gabr'l?"

"They're comin' t' dig up ol' Shemp Lee."

"Now, I done tol' ya afore, ain't no Shemp in that grave, Gabe."

"I believe that, Henry. One of 'em comin' is a real live Shemp Lee." Gabe scratched his head. "Or, least as far as I can figger. But I do believe they'll come diggin'. I can't be sure, but I think I know what they'll be diggin' *for*. And it ain't no Shemp or no other kind o' Lee. I think I'd like t' take a crack at doin' their work for 'em before they get here."

"Whoa, whoa now, Gabr'l. One rule here in th' boneyard is y' don't go diggin' up no dead folks. I don' even need 'at Rev'rend Dunbar tell me 'at ain't right."

"'Course you're right, Henry. In th' usual course o' things. This thing here is not in th' usual course."

"Why don't you talk plain t' me, Gabr'l? What you talkin' 'bout?"

"Well, you said somebody got themselves buried down there, now ain't that right, Henry?"

"That there is what I seen. Yessir."

"It wasn't Shemp. The stone says 'Shemp'. Now, you know them boys were up t' no good. It's my job now, even without Heck, t' get t' th' bottom o' that, y' might say. An' I mean t' the bottom o' that hole. Could be some Confederate plunder down there those boys'll fixin' t' use for no damn good. They don't know war's over. Want t' get it started up again. And it could be down below where that poor soul you saw before is laid out."

"Oh, Gabr'l. Now, Gabe. How come you gotta come 'round makin' things so – so troublesome like? Usual thing is I know what's right. Now here you are talkin' 'bout plunder an' a body in the hole. That body – that – well, it's a-restin' is what it is."

"Well, now, listen, old man. I ain't gonna wake 'im up, 'at's for sure. Mebbe 'e'll just keep a-restin'. And I ain't gonna mistreat 'im in any way. Hell, we find that plunder down there, ol' Shemp – or, whoever the gent may actual be – can jus' 'ave 'is hole back. See? An' more room down there for 'im, t' boot!"

"Hmmm. Well, mebbe make some sense. I don' think the gent needs no extra room, though. I reckon you're 'avin' a laugh on me too, jus' a little bit, huh, Gabr'l?"

"Mebbe. But I know you know it, too, Henry. An' mebbe th' gent 'as the last laugh an' he ain't hidin' nothin' down there but all the sins 'e racked up durin' a long an' murderin' life."

Henry sighed and looked off to the now-darkening sky to the west. "Well, I jus' want t' do what's right, Gabe, 'at's all." He looked at his feet and then over to the creek. "Like when me an' you an' 'at Heck took care o' them varmints over there t' the crick. 'at was right, *weren't* it Gabe?" He sounded like he needed some confirmation.

"Yessir. That was right."

"An' pretty damn invigoratin' too, Gabe." Silence again. "I jus' sure wish 'at friend o' yours, ol' Heck-um could be here now. Could be some more ruckus, couldn't there Gabr'l?"

"'at's a fact, Henry. Could be more excitement than even *we* want," he said smiling at his friend.

"Hmmm. What you want me t' do Gabe?"

"Lend me a good shovel. Then, you take 'at ol' mule an' go int' town. Go t' th' church, go downtown. Let them town folk see ya all over th' place. I'll be done here in, say three hours. Then come back, mebbe I'll be gone, mebbe not."

"Who you talkin' to, boy? I ain't leavin' you here and I ain't missin' out on the shootin' – if'n there is some, I mean. Now. What you want me t' *do*, I said?"

"Hmmm. All right. Get that sure-shot Spencer o' yours out an' loaded, put all your extras in your pockets. Keep a sharp eye out. Could be a whole passel o' them grayback soldiers comin' in. I'll do the diggin' an' th' sooner th' better. An' if ya got a lantern, might need 'at, too."

"Now you're talkin', Gabe. Now you're jus' a-talkin'." Henry whirled around and half-limped, half-swaggered to the shed. Gabe watched, shaking his head. There was no way he could keep the old man from staying. And there was no doubt he could be a big help with that .56 of his. Gabe hoped he wouldn't need it.

A half-moon gave the cemetery an eerie cast, but helped light Shemp's grave for the work to be done. Once he started, Gabe was committed. There would be no way to cover up what he was doing. His only chance was to recover any gold he found, and either get away with it or hide it somewhere else. He puzzled over his next move, but didn't know what he would find, or how much and how heavy it might be.

Henry was good company while he worked. They talked some. Henry brought water. After 30 minutes Gabe's shovel made the unmistakable sound of steel on wood. He redoubled his efforts. When he was ready, he said, "All right, Henry. I might need a bit - "

"I see ya, son, I'm comin'." He laid down his rifle and grabbed the rope handle at one end of the coffin. With one big effort the two men got the box out and set to the side.

Gabe stood up and stretched his back. There were four boards lining the hole. "Henry, I got t' look in the box afore I go down any deeper . . . would ya jus' keep a eye out?"

"I will, Gabe. I will. I ain't lookin' in that box." Henry grabbed his Spencer and moved off to the side.

Gabe used the shovel to pry the lid off. It made a loud, screeching noise. He was quiet as he looked inside.

"Oh, lord, oh, good lord," Henry half-whispered. "Well?! Dad-blame it, boy, what you got in there?" he squawked.

"Well, damn. Damn it all, Henry. I know this man. You're right, I don't 'ave a Shemp Lee in here. Damn! I got a gent called Sweeney."

"Wait. How you sayin'? How you know this?"

"Just this. On account o' I shot this man back in Colorado."

22

DEEPER AND DEEPER

Gabe used the shovel to pry the boards loose and threw them off to the side next to "Shemp's" box. He got down on his hands and knees and lowered the lantern into the hole. Sure enough. There were four large canvas sacks sitting at the bottom.

"Somethin' here, Henry. I'm jumpin' down in here and I need t' hand it up to ya, 'specially if it's as heavy as it looks. But keep an eye out, will ya?"

"Dadgum it, boy. I can't do two things at once no more," he sniffed. Then he thought better of it. "All right, all right, I'm a'comin'."

It took all of Gabe's strength to lift the first bag out. It took all of Henry's strength to drag it a couple of feet away from the hole. They got the next three bags out the same way. Gabe tested the dirt with the shovel for anything else deeper. He felt something another few inches down. He dug up a pair of saddle bags that were stuffed full, but not so heavy. Henry gave him a hand and he climbed out.

Gabe sat on his heels, breathing hard. He looked up at Henry. "Whoo, Gabe, I never saw them boys unload all this heap o' stuff in there. What you s'pose we got in here? Is it gold?"

"Yeah, but before we look, we'd best get it at least int' them trees over there. We took out so much I reckon we can get ol' Shemp Lee Sweeney back in an' still make a level grave. Never know when them grayback killers'll show up." He stretched his back again. "Oh, and Henry. When they do, they gon' be mad as hornets."

"Serves 'em right, Gabr'l, serves 'em right. An' me an' m' Spencer'll be ready."

The two men struggled with the sacks, finally covering them up with sticks and leaves in the ditch where the creek ran, but above the low, March water level. Gabe did his best to get Sweeney back in the hole and covered up, though the fresh digging would be obvious in daylight. Henry started his breakfast fire and Gabe kept a lookout.

They sat with their coffee after eating. Gabe tried to think of what Heck would say about now. Well, Heck might just ask him what his advice was. He had a duty to Heck and the Service. He had a duty to Henry now, too.

"Henry, you an' your Spencer are fit for duty, 'at's for sure. Downright dangerous. But there might be a whole army o' them snakes comin'. An' I need your wagon an' mule to haul this loot t' Washington. Shouldn't take more'n a couple days. I can leave ya here, you tell 'em ever'thing, they can see my tracks anyways with 'at heavy load. But I don't trust 'em. They still be mad enough just t' shoot ya anyways. Or, if they think you're holdin' out on 'em, ain't no limit t' how bad they can treat a man. An' I sure could use ya as a guard. I'm afraid I put you in a bad spot, old man."

"Hah! Bad spot, hell you say, boy. Where you think I been all my born days. I's born in a bad spot. Called Virginie. Then U.S.A. Then Confederates. Now, Maryland bein' better for me, but you know they still know how t' keep a black man down, don't ya, Gabr'l? I know that you do. So. You never put me in no bad spot," Henry's voice started to raise, "Now don't bein' sayin' 'at no mo', boy!"

Gabe put his hands in the air, palms forward and waggled them. "All right, all right, Henry. I hear ya," he said, defensively.

"Plus anyways, you an' 'at Heck-um o' yours, you put th' spark o' life back int' Ol' Henry. It's like some o' them happenin's back in th' railroad days. Adventuresome times back them days. Know what I'm sayin', Gabr'l?"

"I reckon I do, sir. Could be some too much 'venturesome times comin' our way now, though. We should get movin'. If'n you can get your mule hitched up and the wagon 'round back, I'll drag them bags out, we'll just hightail outta here. Leastwise quick as that critter can haul with all that weight back there."

"Sheba."

"What now?"

"Sheba. That's 'er name. From th' good book."

Gabe smiled and nodded, got up and went back to the creek bed. He made a small slit in one of the bags just to take a look. Confederate Double Eagles. They looked new enough that they had never reached circulation. As he started to drag the first sack up to road level, he thought he heard something. A rumbling, getting louder. It had to be riders, and lots of them. He pushed the sack back down and covered it with sticks.

"Henry! Henry, quick get a saddle on that mule, get your Spencer. They're comin'!" Gabe yelled. He got his horse loaded and cinched and went to help Henry. "You hear 'em? Sounds like the whole Confederate cavalry."

"Don't hear too much, Gabe, but 'at ol' buzzard up in th' tree, he's just a-flappin' and a-screechin' like never before. Yep. We gots t' light a shuck an' fast."

They took off towards a trail that climbed a ridge overlooking the town and cemetery. When they got to the top, they dismounted and watched to see how many there were and what they'd do. Gabe started counting right away. There were a few stragglers after he got to 25. General Shemp Lee was unmistakable at the head of the column. He was rail thin and slouched in his saddle. Next to him, Gabe recognized Colonel Fletcher, fully decked out in plume and shiny buttons. Gabe got his field glass out. He smiled when he saw that Fletcher's collar insignia had changed from three to two stars since he'd seen him last, bloody and limp-running through the woods.

What would Heck do? What would Billy and Harley do? Gabe's head swam with the possibilities and the risks. He knew two things. First, his primary responsibility was to get that gold back to the United States government. Second, there was a lot of gray down there. Gabe and Henry watched as they swarmed around Shemp's grave like a bunch of locusts. They were too far away to hear what was being said, but they could hear General Lee yelling and screaming as he waved his arms around.

"That man down there's gonna 'ave a stroke, he keep up like 'at, Gabe," Henry said.

"Well, if'n 'e did, 'e's in a good place for it. That there is one real Shemp Lee, an' the stone and the hole are all ready for 'im. 'Course, it might be a little crowded in there," Gabe said, smiling at Henry.

"Well, dadgum. Shemp Lee, y' don't say? Why all them boys wearin' gray uniforms, though, Gabe? War's been over some nine years now."

"I know it. You know it. Hell, Shemp's brother Robert Lee knows it. These damn fool hyenas, they don't know it. They wanna keep it goin' long as it takes t' put th' likes o' you and me back in chains and under th' whip. Seems like they never learned how t' do an honest day's work, ain't likely t' start now – 'at might be th' problem."

"They ain't like real men, are they Gabe?"

"No sir, they ain't. Somethin' wrong with 'em."

Henry shook his head. "I reckon you're the cap'n o' this outfit, Gabr'l. What's our next move?"

"I don' know nothin' 'bout a cap'n, Henry. Partner, mebbe. Anyways, we got t' watch 'em, make sure they find that booty and take off with it. It shouldn't be hard. All I know is we found that gold, we can't go losin' it now. They'll be lookin' for us, too. Mebbe got some riders already on th' job."

They stood and watched for a little while. Then, they saw two men down in the creek bed waving their arms. They could hear them yelling. Shemp Lee and Colonel Fletcher walked over to see what the commotion was about. Yeah, they had found the gold. Gabe and Henry waited again, this time to watch them load up their wagon and head out of town again. They organized into two columns and rode out at a slow, steady pace.

"Well, Henry, I guess we don't have a choice but t' follow, but from a long ways back."

"Sounds right t' me. Long ways. You was right, Gabr'l, there's a passel o' them varmints, all right."

23

THE WEST-BOUND SPECIAL

The gray caravan headed south. It appeared to be moving in a direct route to Washington, D.C. Gabe marveled at the audacity of the General. He was taking this load of war plunder right into the power center of the federal government. And most of his men were wearing gray. What could he be thinking?

As the group approached Arlington National Cemetery, it slowed and moved into a thicket of trees. From the distance Gabe and Henry were following, the riders seemed to disappear.

That night, Gabe and Henry kept a cold camp. They traded watch so one would be awake all night. But the Confederates got noisy. They had a huge bonfire going and hooped and hollered all night. The two friends were close enough to hear yelling, singing and shots fired, apparently into the air. It was enough to keep both of them awake most of the night. Before dawn, as first light approached, they crept up into the cemetery and found a good place from which to watch. The Knights were getting up and ready to move early. They had a couple of extra wagons with them that must have been scheduled to meet them. Some of the soldiers were milling around. Others were stripping off their uniforms. One of those wagons had brought civilian clothes that they were now changing into. They were also packing up the gold in travel trunks – lots of them.

"What're they doin', Cap'n?" Henry asked.

Gabe shook his head. He wasn't going to get Henry to stop calling him that. "Well, sir, I reckon they're plannin' a trip. A long trip with a lot o' heavy luggage. Can't be no other way, they must be takin' th' train."

"Train? Where they go, Cap'n?"

"West. But where west, we're gonna 'ave t' find out."

"I don' know, Gabe," Henry said. "On a train?" He looked down at his boots as he shifted his Spencer to his other hand. "I don' – well, th' fact is, I don' know how t' ride on no train. I - I don' know what t' do."

"Don't you worry, Henry. You'll be with me. It'll just be part o' th' adventure."

Henry nodded and looked back at the camp. General Lee had things well in hand and the packing and changing went quickly.

"Cap'n? Gabr'l? Uh – what I'm gon' do with my Sheba? She don't know 'ow t' get along without me. Ever' time I jus' go for couple hours, well, she get such a sad face on 'er. That mule, she *need* me, Gabe."

"We'll try t' get 'er on the stock car, Henry. Mebbe she can come with us. If not, I know a good liv'ry."

Gabe and Henry checked into a small hotel where they could continue to keep an eye on the Confederates, who had returned to the Willard. Gabe took his horse to the livery Heck had gotten him from and paid for Heck's. He convinced Henry that Sheba would not only be in good hands, but happy while they went west. Gabe tried nosing around a bit to find out why it was taking Shemp so long to get started. He went back to Caleb, who had over-heard much around the Deputy Chief's office. Shemp Lee had reserved an entire train for his men, their horses, and, of course, their baggage. Caleb had not learned where they were headed.

Gabe tried, but failed, to get in to see President Grant. If only he could get help convincing the President that he had the thieves and the plunder under surveillance right across the street from his office! Gabe was able to once again wire General Burke. He asked for men and help. And again, he received no response.

Gabe left their hotel every morning. He wanted to learn everything he could about the activities of the Triangle. Henry stayed close to "home". Gabe noticed that he seemed different, less certain of himself, than he was in Rockville. He figured out that Henry was not used to the city or being around so many people. After ten days in Washington, finally, one morning there was an abnormal amount of activity at the Willard Hotel. Men, horses and wagons queued up to leave together. Gabe and Henry sat in a nearby park, watching and waiting. Gabe made the decision that he would disguise himself as much as possible, go to the station, and find out where the train was going. There would be plenty of black porters with whom he could speak. There was too much chance that taking another train, which Gabe and Henry would have to do, could cause them to lose their quarry.

Gabe found a porter standing on the platform towards the end of the train. The engine huffed and sighed and spewed coal smoke as it sat there. It was obviously the right one. Even out of uniform General Lee and his "troops" were easy to spot. They were supervising a group of black men loading the luggage, some of it which appeared quite heavy.

Gabe approached the man, keeping the slouch hat he had borrowed from Henry, low over his eyes. "Suh!" he called out. "Cap'n!"

The man looked him over. "Who you callin' 'Cap'n', man? What you want?"

"Well, you, suh, y' gots th' fine uniform an' all. Ain't you a cap'n?"

"You are some kind o' ignorant backwoods hayseed, now ain't ya, boy? I ain't no captain."

"What are ya then, that fine blue uniform, them shiny buttons an' all?"

"I'm a porter. That's all, just a Pullman porter."

"Don't know what 'at is rightly. They do dress y' up right smart though."

"Don't let it fool ya, boy. Ain't like back in th' war. You could do a man's work then – if you were lucky. All I do is tote luggage and shine shoes for white folks, then serve 'em up a fine white-folks dinner. They don't let us do a conductor job or no other job. Just this."

"You in th' war, Cap'n?" Gabe asked.

The porter smiled. "Yep. 54th Massachusetts."

Gabe dropped his 'hayseed' talk. "Me too, my friend. Lost a lot o' good friends along with Colonel Shaw at Fort Wagner."

"I was there!" He stuck out his hand. "Glad t' meet you, soldier."

"Name's Gabe Baker. Company D."

"Name's Tom Watson. You boys took a beatin', for sure."

"I'm still kind o' fightin' the same war here, Tom. This train ain't all mebbe it seems. I came up to you to find out where it's headed. If you know."

"Yeah. Somethin' 'bout you didn' seem quite right, Gabe. You're too confident, lookin' a man in th' eye like – you know, t' be th' hillbilly you're pretendin'."

"Thanks for the advice, can y' tell me?"

"This here train is a 'Special'. It's supposed t' be a big secret. Even t' me an' I'm workin' this train. But most of us know already, she's headed t' St. Louie, an' then Denver. That's in the Colorado Territory. What you sayin', though, it ain't what it seems? It don't seem like nothin' yet, on account o' us porters, leastwise, don't know who's on it or why."

"You notice anythin' familiar 'bout some o' these white gents hangin' 'round, gettin' ready t' board?"

"Sure I do. They surely are 'sons o' th' south' like we were fightin' in th' war. I'm expectin' t' see my old owner anytime now. They all actin' th' same. Like th' war didn't change nothin'.'"

"You don't know how right you are, Tom. Let's leave it at that for now. But my partner and I will be followin' these boys, an' I hope to meet ya again somewhere down th' line."

"That'd be good. You know, sometimes, Gabe, I think it was better in th' war. At least we could be shootin' at these fellers 'stead o' wipin' their boots."

"I've 'ad th' same thoughts, friend. Believe me. I best be leavin', look like you got comp'ny comin', an' mebbe th' troublesome kind."

Gabe tucked into the collar of his coat and pulled the hat down again. As he walked away, he heard, "Boy! Boy! Get over here and start helping these gentlemen get settled into their cars. Move it."

Gabe thought he recognized the voice. He looked back briefly. He couldn't see a face but he did see that the man was fool enough to be wearing a gold buckle.

Gabe bought the tickets to St. Louis. Without Heck to get him past the color barrier he had to book seats in the "emigrant car". The hard wooden seats and crowded conditions would make for a long trip. But as long as Henry had a spittoon or a window, he would be all right. Gabe decided they should wait to see how things were going before they headed on to Denver. He would want to check in with General Burke.

Gabe was learning how limited Henry's experience was in dealing with the world at large. He didn't believe this would be a problem, but decided to keep it in mind, and help in any way he could. He had no doubt about Henry's courage or abilities under fire if it came to that. He chuckled to himself, remembering his times with Billy, Harley and White Crow. It always came to that!

Gabe and Henry would board early the next morning. His main concern now was how they would keep from losing that Special. Of course, keeping the gold in sight and figuring a way to get it back were two different problems.

24

NO MAN IN DENVER

There was no better way to cross the long distances between cities in this country in 1874 than by train. The two-month trip to St. Louis by wagon would take Gabe and Henry about 24 hours by train. It would not be the same trip being taken by the Confederates on their Special though. They were riding in Pullman "palace" cars that afforded them every luxury money could buy. They enjoyed plush, upholstered seats, a fine dining car and comfortable sleeping berths. The Pullman porters took their orders night and day. They spent most of their time drinking wine or whiskey, smoking cigars and playing cards. Passengers in the emigrant car sat on hard wooden benches. If they wanted to eat, they would have to bring their own food. There was no service and no other accommodations, other than a small "privy" at one end of the car that was no more than a closet with a bucket. It was up to the passengers to see that it didn't spill.

Still, the feeling of travel, and of the speed of the train, gave no end of delight to Henry. He marveled at the city sites as they trundled through Cincinnati. He watched the farms and natural landscapes roll by for hours on end. But when they reached St. Louis, the friends were bone-tired and sore.

Gabe decided that before they walked to their hotel, he would mine the porters for information. It had worked well in D.C. Sure enough, the Special was in town. It was sitting on a side track with no one around. Too bad he couldn't talk to his new friend Tom Watson again. No one he could find could tell him when it was scheduled to leave. Knowing the city well after his years of working for Mrs. Belcher, Gabe led Henry to a hotel that would accept them. It also had the advantage of being close to General Burke's offices and the river. Gabe knew Henry would love seeing the Mississippi. He'd heard about it and talked about it on the train. After they got settled, it was time to see the General. Gabe was anxious. Burke had not replied to his telegrams, at least that he knew of. And the Deputy Chief had turned out to be the head Knight. He was only sure of one man in the Secret Service, and he was dead. What else might happen? He wasn't sure he liked this kind of government work.

He would go to Avery Burke's office in the morning. He and Henry could use some time to recover from the bruising ride they'd just had. They spent the rest of the day eating and napping, and the night, sleeping. Gabe got up early. It was a fine, spring day in St. Louis. He walked around the neighborhood alone, thinking. He found a park bench to sit on in the early morning sun. He looked up at the sky.

What was he doing? Couldn't he just quit this job now? There would be no shame in it, it had always been his choice to stay with it or not. The only thing he couldn't get around, try as he might, was a feeling that he owed it to Heck to continue. Maybe a meeting with the General would help him decide. Maybe the General would want him to quit. After all, he could report that the Confederates were in town, and the gold was probably still on the train. Actually gaining possession of the gold and making arrests were jobs for law enforcement. The gold. Why hadn't he seen any guards around that train on the siding?

Gabe walked slowly towards the General's office building. The warm sun and light breeze had renewed his spirits. Gabe remembered what Heck had said about Burke. He was a man of habit and would be in his office by

7:00 a.m. Gabe climbed the stairs to the fourth floor, peeking out at the river every time he got a chance. He walked into the reception room where he was confronted with a familiar face.

"Good morning, Leonard," Gabe said with an enthusiastic smile as the door closed with a squeak behind him. But Leonard didn't seem his normal, introverted self. He was obviously agitated.

Leonard stood. "Ye – yes. Good morning, uh, Gabe? Gabe Baker?"

"Yeah, 'at's right, Gabe. It's been a while. It's after 7:00, Gen'ral must be in. Do ya think he'd see me now? It's kind o' important."

"Well, Gabe, I know it'd be important. The fact is, the General is not in yet. Strange, too. He has an appointment this morning. He's never missed an appointment before.

"Leonard, that's not good. There are some folks in town might prefer th' Gen'ral be missin'. Who was it the Gen'ral was meetin' today?"

"Well, uh, well, Gabe the General's schedule is confidential. I can't say - "

"Leonard! Did ya just hear me? This could be serious."

"Well, maybe I could tell Heck. Where's - "

"Heck is *dead*. Ain't you got any o' my telegrams, Leonard?"

"Oh. Oh, my, I - "

"Who was he seein'?"

"A – a Colonel Foster." Leonard looked down at the book on his desk. "A Colonel Warren Foster."

"What was the meetin' about?"

"I don't know. I never heard of the gentleman before."

"When was the meetin'?"

Leonard looked at the clock on the wall. "Well, right now. Supposed to be right now, 8:00 o'clock."

Gabe plunked himself down in the chair in front of Leonard's desk. That name. Something familiar. Colonel Warren Foster. A colonel. Maybe - Colonel William Fletcher?

"Damn," Gabe was now thinking out loud. "They set a meeting so they could grab him on the way to th' office. They don't know his schedule. Leonard, how many other Secret Service men you got here in St. Louie?"

"Well, it's just the General and me. Who? Who was going to grab him?"

"Those damn Confederates. The ones we been chasin'. Deputy Chief Flynn is one of 'em - hell, 'e's th' top dog. The 'Johnson' o' the Johnson Gang. The head Knight. Top o' the Triangle. An' 'at colonel works for 'im. I don' know if they want t' hold th' General for some reason, or jus' get 'im out of th' way."

"Flynn? One of them? What do you mean, Gabe?"

"I mean 'e prob'ly walked right up t' th' General this mornin', said 'is howdy-do's and took 'im prisoner. With the barrel of a gun stickin' in 'is back. They'll hold 'im, mebbe for protection, or t' barter with. Or just kill 'im, keep the Service out o' their bus'ness."

"Oh, Lord, oh, no," Leonard gasped. "Not the General. They can't - "

"Leonard. Stay with me, now. I need your help. Do you 'ave a man in Denver?"

"Wha – what?"

"The Service. Does it 'ave a man in Denver?"

"Well. Uh. Well, no, not exactly, that is - "

"Come on, man. Do we or don't we?"

"No!" He blurted out. "We have no man in Denver. We – we have an agent there."

Now it was Gabe's turn to be confused. "What? What does that mean, Leonard?"

"Our agent. She's not a man. I mean, she – she's a woman," he stammered. "A woman named Daisy. Daisy Wood."

"A woman. Daisy. Daisy Wood?" Gabe uttered, trying to grasp the situation.

"Yessir. *Miss* Wood. The General calls her 'Little Daisy'. She is small but she's right smart. And pretty. And I heard the General say she can draw her pearl-handled Colt 'faster'n a preacher can talk'. Yeah, that's the way he says. 'Faster'n a preacher can talk'," Leonard said, so pleased with himself he had forgotten the gravity of the situation.

"All good, I reckon. What kind of relationship does the Gen'ral 'ave with 'er?"

"What do you *mean*, relationship?" Leonard asked, defensively.

"Not that, Leonard. I mean, does 'e know her, does 'e trust her, 'as she been 'ere before?"

"Yes to all that. He confides in her. The General likes to say she's a real pistol and a real straight shooter. And then he laughs. Yeah, he respects her more than he does most." He hesitated. "Gabe, what are you – what are *we* – going to do?"

"Your Miss Wood may be good with 'er Colt, but even she can't stop some 30 o' those grayback vermin goin' to Denver plus however many other ones they got set up to meet 'em there, I don' know. My partner Henry and I couldn't do it neither. I know the U.S. Marshal for the Territory out there, even he don't have enough firepower. Who's left, Leonard?" Gabe asked, like a teacher to his student.

"The Army?" Leonard asked, clasping his hands together on top of his desk, smiling, because he knew he had the right answer.

"'at's right. They got the makin's of an army. We need one o' our own. I need t' go through the Gen'ral's office an' look for anything I can find. I'll write out a couple o' telegrams for ya to send, all right, Leonard? We'll be sendin' t' th' U.S. Marshal for Territory o' Colorado, the Chief, Miss Daisy Wood and

Sheriff Taylor in Boulder. Then, Henry and I will find where those scoundrels are. Mebbe we can help the Gen'ral afore they leave town or mebbe we just got t' follow th' whole lot of 'em t' Colorado. Wait for reinforcements. An' hope the Chief supports us an' the Marshal can get Army boys t' help out."

Gabe went through General Burke's office. He found nothing relevant to the case of the Confederate gold except a letter of encouragement from President Grant's office. And a golden belt buckle with a triangle in the middle of it. Gabe thought, well, at least he had caught one of those skunks.

Gabe wrote out the telegrams for Leonard to send. He reported his activities to the Chief, reiterating that the Deputy Chief was calling himself Shemp Lee, and was the head of the Golden Triangle, and telling him that Heck McCabe was dead and General Burke was missing. He briefly informed Miss Wood of the investigation and the fact that trouble was bound to be coming her way. He sent greetings to Sheriff Taylor and let him know what he was doing and that he hoped to see him and his friends in Colorado soon. And he asked U.S. Marshal Tompkins about mustering troops.

Now, it was time to find Henry and start trailing Shemp, Fletcher and their gang. As he headed out the door, he told Leonard, "You need to keep up on the telegrams. I need ya t' tell me what's goin' on with th' Service. You can reach me at the Boulder Sheriff, Sheriff Taylor, on account o' I know I can trust 'im. An' so can you."

Gabe felt alone again. He had Henry but he didn't have Heck. The only "boss" he knew about now was the Chief, with whom he'd never spoken. He didn't know anything about him except that he was reputed to be more of a politician than an executive. Plus, the Service was now busy moving its headquarters from New York to Washington. His focus was probably on that. This would be a good time for Gabe to quit. But, again, he thought about Heck. Heck had had confidence in him. He fingered the badge in his pocket. The one that General Burke had given him. It meant something. It was important, although Gabe had not given it a second thought until that moment. He sighed and shut the door.

25

A LAPSE OF ATTENTION

Gabe and Henry went back to the train station that evening when it was just getting dark. The Special was still there, still unguarded. Gabe decided they should sneak aboard and have a look. The Pullman cars were not locked. They searched through each one. They looked around the upholstered seats, walnut poker tables, and in the dining car, around the white linens and cabinets of silverware and cut glass. When they got to the last one, Henry finally said, "Whew, boy, Cap'n, them high-falutin' white boys shore did 'ave some plush ridin' out 'ere, didn' they?"

"Haha, yessir, m' friend, they did for sure," Gabe said, straightening up, putting his hands on his hips and looking around the ceiling of the car. They had found nothing but a few scraps of clothing, some well-used playing cards and three empty bottles of "Old Pepper".

"Too bad they wasn't thinkin' 'bout us poor workin' folk, they could o' left us a bit o' that 'Pepper', eh, Cap'n?"

"It was mighty thoughtless, Henry, wasn't it?"

It was getting dark, but they still had enough light to check the two last cars on the siding, the baggage car and the caboose. They jumped down to the train platform and walked back to the car. Gabe started to feel the hair on the back of his neck raise and prickle. He instinctively put his hand on Henry's shoulder. "Shhh . . ." Gabe whispered into his ear. "I don' think we're alone no more."

They crouched and looked around and then under the car. They didn't see anything. There was no lock on the sliding door of the baggage car, so Gabe pushed on it. It started sliding open with a loud creaking noise that sent a shiver up his spine. As he pushed, it gained momentum and came fully open, bumping hard on the end of its track. Without a word, Henry threw his Spencer up into the car and jumped in after it. He leaned over on his knees to give Gabe a hand up. Holding his rifle in one hand, he held out the other to Henry. But Gabe didn't make it.

"Hold it!" screeched the loud voice from behind Gabe. "Hold it right there, boy! Hands up or get shot!"

Another voice called out, "Look at that, Sarge, it ain't nothin' but a n___r. Hey, n___r, come on over here, so's I can get a look at you," he said to Gabe. Gabe gave a quick glance over his shoulder to see if Henry had made it into the dark of the car. He had his hands in the air, his right one still holding the Henry rifle. He strode confidently over to the two men who stood with pistols in their hands. He stopped six feet in front of them.

"Well?" he said, looking at one, then the other. They didn't seem to know what to do. So Gabe added, "Was there something that you 'gen'le-men' wanted?" He stressed the pronunciation so they would know he was being sarcastic.

The one called 'Sarge' said, "Grab his rifle, Rollie." Rollie stepped slowly towards Gabe, looking nervous and out of his element. He looked at Gabe and nodded. Gabe handed him his Henry and Rollie stiffly stepped back again.

"All right, Sarge, what'll we do with him? You want I should just shoot him. Cap'n won't mind."

"Thing is, I don't know about that, Rollie. Maybe he wants to talk to him first. You know, then shoot him."

"Tell you the truth, boys, I don' wanna get shot, you know, either now or later," Gabe said with a broadening smile. "Why don' we figger a way out like 'at?"

Gabe's attitude caused Rollie to snap. This black man was just not taking him seriously enough. He butted the stock of the Henry into Gabe's stomach, taking his breath away and doubling him over. Rollie was proud of his independent decisionmaking. "What'd ya think of that, Sarge?"

"Good one, Rollie. But don't hurt him too bad, we want him to be able to walk, so's we don't have to carry him. Then the Captain or maybe the Colonel can decide what to do with him."

The blow had brought Gabe to his hands and knees. He stayed down while trying to get his breath back. Before he could fully recover, the man called Rollie grabbed his left arm and raised him up to his feet. Gabe was still bent over and now put his hands on his knees. Rollie grabbed his arm and started trying to walk with him in tow.

"Hold it, now. Hold it," Gabe gasped. You want me under my own power, just give me a second y' damned fool." Gabe wasn't given to diplomacy in these kinds of situations.

"You hear what this black boy said, Sarge? To *me*? Let me stick this here knife right up under his ribs for that, Sarge. No black boy never talked to me like that."

"Stop messin' with that boy, Rollie," Sarge said, "and let's get goin'. We'll take him directly to see the Colonel. Then, maybe he'll let you stick him." They started walking, now Rollie behind, pushing the barrel of the Henry into Gabe's back at regular intervals. Gabe's mind was racing and he was stumbling, trying to get his equilibrium back. The Colonel? Gabe resigned himself to the probability of another meeting with Fletcher.

And what's Henry going to do? Gabe had given Henry plenty of cash in case they were split up. And he had told him the name of the building where General Burke's office was. But Gabe didn't know how to predict his thinking. Henry was smart enough but he had difficulty navigating the modern world, and especially, the city. He'd only been free for some nine years, and he was well over 60 years old. And even after emancipation, he'd led a cloistered life in Rockville. The race hatred he had lived with his whole life had kept his world small and narrow, and without reading or opportunity to travel he had had little chance to grow. In the end though, Gabe knew Henry would make the best decisions he knew how on Gabe's behalf. It was a comfort, at least, that he could depend on him to try.

Gabe waited for a chance to make a move as they walked along. He was gradually gaining back his breath. In the relative dark, those two grayback halfwits had not even noticed his Navy .36, plainly tied down in its holster on his right leg. Or, were they waiting for an excuse to kill him? No, they didn't need one. And, of course, he always had his hideaway – the little .41 Derringer he was carrying in his boot. They walked behind the train depot to a dark, one-story brick on the other side of it. A lamp was shining dimly behind one of the two front windows, both of which appeared cloudy with oil smoke. Sarge knocked on the heavy wooden door with the butt of his sidearm. One strike, a pause, two quick strikes. The door slowly came open about ten inches with a deep creaking noise. Sarge poked his head into the opening. "Is the Colonel here? We got a present for him."

"Let's see," came the response from inside. The door was now pushed close to wide open. Gabe kept his head down and his gun side away from the light flooding out onto the cut-stone plaza shared with the train station.

"Why do you think the Colonel would want to bother with this boy?" the man inside asked.

"Because we caught him trying to climb up into the baggage car."

"Hmmm. All right, probably just a bum looking for a place to sleep, but I'll get him. I know the Colonel's been tied up in knots looking for a couple of these darkies, but they were back east. Who knows?"

"Thanks, Cap'n," Sarge said. "We'll keep him right here."

"No, bring him in. Set him down. Keep your guns on him. If he moves, shoot him. It won't be any loss to us," the Captain said, heading back down a hallway towards the back.

The room was spare and dimly lit with the one lamp. Several high-back wooden chairs were strewn haphazardly around the room, with three of them situated around the rudimentary, bare wooden table pushed over towards the far wall and one on its side. There was a fine layer of greasy dust on everything. The place smelled of mildew, sweat and cigars. The ceiling was low and the air was bad. Gabe sat down and slumped over, feigning weakness and hiding his face and right side as much as possible. Should he pull the Colt and blast his way out? His friend Harley would. His friend Billy would probably wait to see how things developed. He was used to consulting them in his head on most matters of high risk. But that technique didn't help much if he thought they would disagree.

The Colonel stepped out of the dark hallway ahead of the Captain. He stopped when he entered the room and put his hands on his hips. "Well, well. What *do* we have here, then? A certain Gabe Baker, it appears," a joyless smile spreading across his lips. "You sure do have a talent for showin' up in the wrong places, don't you, Baker?"

Gabe slowly raised his eyes to look upon the face of a man who had already been disappointed in his desire to kill him twice. He was acutely aware of the fact that unless he could find a quick way out, things didn't look good for him. As always, he felt that keeping his enemy engaged was the best way to find an opening to escape a bad situation. So he responded. "Well, I was kind o' missin' ya, Colonel. I mean, after all we been through together."

"Still the funny man, I see, eh, Baker? Who knows, maybe I can plan something out for you you won't find so amusing."

"That don't sound like that famous southern hospitality, now does it, Colonel?"

"That hospitality doesn't apply to black folks and criminals. So, I wouldn't be expectin' too much in the way of pleasantries from here on out, Baker. But," and he hesitated, while he scratched the stubble under his chin, "we could make things a bit easier on you if you were to answer a couple of questions."

"Mebbe I can oblige, Colonel, what you got?"

"To start, who all was in on diggin' up Shemp Lee's grave? You know, grave robbin' is a serious felony in most states."

"Now, Colonel, what makes you think I would even know 'bout such a thing. Besides, last I heard, 'at Shemp Lee was alive and kickin'. Although," Gabe slowed a bit, "he never did look like a model o' health an' wellbein'. Mebbe drinks a might too much."

"I'm not in the mood, Baker," he glowered, moving his hand towards the holster on his hip.

"Well, I suppose it won't hurt none. It was me, Colonel. You already found out, I couldn't do nothin' with it. Too much for one man to tote around. I mean, look at you, you got wagons, livestock, a train and an' a whole passel o' good-for-nothin' trigger pullers who you got believin' are takin' part in a new uprisin' o' th' South." He conjured up a chuckle for effect. "I reckon you even selected 'em for their smarts, eh, Colonel?"

"I know *you* were there, boy. Now you tell me who else. There were tracks from two horses, maybe one a mule." Fletcher pulled out his gun. He pointed it at Gabe's head and cocked the hammer. Click click. Fletcher's mouth twitched nervously. And Gabe felt the nausea that he usually experienced with the sound of a gun cocking.

"Well, 'course there was mule tracks. They got an old, useless caretaker over there rides an old, useless mule. I don' know though, he don't seem t' be around no more. 'e certainly wouldn't o' done me much good."

Fletcher let the hammer down easily and holstered his gun. Looking at Sarge and Rollie, he said, "All right, you boys go get the cuffs and leg irons we got back in the caboose over there and bring 'em here. With the keys! We're going to show this boy some of our fine, southern hospitality he seems to be cravin' so much and then let the General decide how to dispose – er – I mean, what to do with him." He looked at Gabe and smiled again.

Just then the Colonel noticed Gabe's Colt. He pulled his gun out and aimed it at Gabe again. "You ignorant, dimwitted clods!" he yelled at the two men. Grab his Colt for chrissake. No wonder we lost the damn - I mean – we're still fightin' the damn war."

Gabe looked up at Fletcher innocently, and said, "Oh, Colonel, just a oversight on my part, I'm sure. I would o' handed it over if'n y' asked real nice."

Sarge and Rollie walked out into the dark. Fletcher glared down at Gabe, who had now turned in his chair to face him. Fletcher instinctively rubbed his lower back with the heel of his hand.

"What's a matter, Colonel? Sore back?"

"One more thing I owe you for, Baker. I've had two bullets pulled out of me on account of you. There won't be any more."

"Could be right, Colonel. Next one prob'ly go through an' through."

26

IN CHAINS

G abe struggled to keep his cool while Sarge and Rollie put the cuffs on him and he felt himself almost lose control when they clamped the leg irons tight. He watched closely as Sarge tucked the keys into the right front pocket of his dungarees. Then he looked at Fletcher, inquisitively. What brutish plan did this paragon of the South, this southern gentleman, have in store for him? He was having the same feelings he used to have as a boy when he knew the slave driver Sikes was coming for him with his whip and his stick. He felt sickish and his heart raced.

The Colonel answered Gabe's look with, "Throw him in the back room for now. Put a slop bucket in there, but he's to have no food, no water. You hear?"

"Yessir," Sarge said, sticking his gun into Gabe's ribs to get him up. "This way, boy."

The "back room" had a thick, heavy wooden door and a lock. When Sarge got it open, he pushed Gabe in, hard enough that he went down, landing on his elbow and hip on the hard floor. It was a small room, no bigger than Granny's tool shed had been. It had one window, up too high for Gabe to see out, but big enough that he could feel the cool air of evening coming in. He did what he could to investigate his surroundings. He went over whatever he could see or touch. There were no obvious weaknesses in the enclosure. Then, he sat against the wall under the window, opposite the door. Time to take stock. Maybe make some kind of escape plan.

Once again, what would Billy do? He'd think his way out. What would Harley do? He'd fight his way out. All right, no help there. What would Heck do? He didn't know, and he was too tired to think straight anyway. Yeah, tired. Best sleep while he had a chance. There was no telling what was coming or when. All he really knew was that he'd probably have one last meeting with Shemp Lee.

Gabe woke when he heard keys jingle and then the hollow sound of one of them in the lock. The door started with a jerk, then stopped as it scraped along the floor. There was cursing. Then it opened more to show, once again, Sarge and Rollie. Sarge was expressionless. Rollie had a broad, humorless smile on his face that Gabe read as a portent of bad things to come.

"Get up, slave boy," Sarge said with a rasp.

"Yeah, get up, boy. You gonna go meet up with yo' 'massah' now," Rollie said, hands on his hips and leaning forward so Gabe could see his malevolent grin better. He straightened up again. "Yeah, an' the good lord he'p ya, n_____r boy," he said, mocking Gabe with his version of how he had heard slaves talk.

The two "Knights" grabbed Gabe and lifted him to his feet. Gabe let his head loll downwards, once again affecting more weakness than he was actually experiencing. He walked down the hall as best he could with the irons on, Sarge in front, Rollie behind. The building was still dark, but early morning shadows were starting to appear in the main room when they pushed him down into a chair.

Rollie caught Gabe eyeing a pitcher of water on the table. "Now, you be a good boy and answer all the Gen'ral's questions real honest and polite-like and maybe I give you some o' that cold, fresh water." Rollie held it out in front of Gabe to taunt him. Gabe held out his palms, declining the faux invitation.

"Well, we'll just see, black boy. See if maybe you want some in a couple o' days. If'n ya last that long, that is. Maybe if y' beg. And you better stand when the Gen'ral comes in, I can tell ya that."

They waited five minutes. Then, the General came in. He wore his dress grays, long frock coat and blue-gray trousers with a blue stripe down each seam. He walked in a stilted and formal way, forcing an upright posture. He was preceded by Colonel Fletcher, resplendent in his formal uniform with ceremonial saber, and a guard. A sharp, spring wind followed them in. The air stirred up the dust in the room and stung Gabe's eyes. He squinted as he saw Shemp Lee, the first time since observing him through the spyglass at the cemetery. The man did not look well. His face was mottled with red blotches. His hands shook. Gabe watched him as he was offered, and accepted, a chair at the table. Gabe didn't stand. A third man walked in, wearing street clothes. He carried a satchel. He took it over to the General. He wiped off the table with a kerchief he pulled from his pocket and pulled a bottle of the Old Pepper and a glass from the satchel. He poured the glass nearly full, set the bottle down and stood back.

No one spoke while Shemp Lee took a minute to dramatically, silently pull off his embroidered officer's gloves and lay them in his lap. Then, he took a few tentative swigs of the whiskey. He swirled the liquid around in his mouth, swallowed and gave a half-hearted look of approbation. Colonel Fletcher started things off. "Well, here we are again, Gabe Baker. You're a lucky man. Well, er, you have been lucky anyway. You get your second audience now with the man who will bring the South back to its former glory. And more!"

Gabe couldn't help notice how much more obsequious Fletcher acted in the General's presence now. General Lee listened, nodding with approval while he finished his glass. The whiskey man quickly stepped forward to replenish Lee's glass. He lifted it in Gabe's direction and drank half of it down in one swig. "Ahhh. Yes. That's better," he said, holding his right hand straight out and admiring the steadiness he had just achieved. Only then did he look Gabe in the eye. He set the glass down with an authoritative thump. He put his elbows on the table and clasped his hands.

"Now. To business," he said.

Gabe looked back into Shemp Lee's eyes. Although he saw something strangely familiar there, all he could think was that he was looking at pure evil. This was a man who would kill as easily as he would spit. He would torture for the pleasure of watching someone else's pain. He remembered when he was a young boy and some of his elders at Heavenly Hills tried to teach him of the old ways, the Igbo ways, of his people in Africa. They had words and ceremonies to rid themselves of the devil. Gabe knew these words. But right now he would rather have his Colt.

He finally said, "Mr. Shemp Lee, I don' know of any poss'ble bus'ness I'd wanna be 'avin' with th' likes o' you." Sarge and Rollie both gasped at the audacity of this black man. They'd never seen the like. Colonel Fletcher pulled his pistol out and aimed it at him.

"Just say the word, Sir, and I'll finish the business for you," Fletcher said, peering over at Lee. Fortunately for Gabe, he had guessed right. Shemp wasn't ready for that yet.

"No, no," Shemp waved him off. "Let's call it a condemned man's prerogative. I just want to talk to the boy. After all, I am his boss," Shemp said, smacking the table with his free hand and laughing at his joke. The others chuckled nervously.

"Way you look, boss, better 'ave your say quick or you're liable t' beat me through t' th' gates o' hell. Truth is, an' you know I hate t' say it, you ain't lookin' so good." Gabe had a quick thought of pulling his .41 out and putting the General out of his misery. He might get away with it, but with his hands cuffed so close together, he probably wouldn't. And there were so many white men standing around who wanted to kill him, he thought better of it. Those two bullets might serve him better later – if there was a later.

"Haha!" the General slapped the table again. He was enjoying his exchange with Gabe. "I *can* guarantee you'll beat me there, Mr. Baker. We will see to that little detail before my men and I depart for Denver. Now, what I want to know from you is what you've done with the papers you stole from my office. A good employee wouldn't do that, but you may not have had a proper enough upbringing to know that." He held his glass out for the whiskey man again, who obediently filled it half full. "Oh – and by the way, you're fired."

"Fired? General, I don' believe you can do that. See, I was made a special agent by General Burke."

"Haha! Well, I thought you probably knew your General Burke has gone missing, Mr. Baker. I'm afraid the gentleman is, as they say, absent without leave. We used to call it, 'French leave'. So, see, Mr. Baker, you'll just have to take it from me. You're fired." Shemp raised his kerchief to his mouth as he coughed and spluttered. He motioned for another pour, which was again dutifully provided. Gabe stared at Shemp's every move. Something about his manner seemed disturbing. He didn't have time to think, though.

"Well, General, I ain't sure 'bout your, uh, negotiatin' skills. You want information but you say you're gonna kill me anyway. Ain't much motive for me even if I did know 'bout your damn papers. What's so interestin' 'bout them papers anyways?"

"Two things for you to think on, Gabe. First, there are many ways to die, some quick, some not. Second, see, the way this works is, I ask, you answer. You savvy that, boy?"

"We're back to 'boy' now, are we? I was startin' t' get used t' 'Mr. Baker'. Talk about upbringin', I'd say yours must o' been some lackin' for sure, 'least in the social graces, as they say." Gabe saw the color of anger rising in Shemp's face. So, he pushed further. "I guess ain't your fault, though, I heard tell you was a bastard, mebbe never even knew your real pa."

Shemp Lee controlled himself. He wasn't used to enjoying a conversation with another intelligent man like this, so he'd continue for sport for just a bit longer. "Pa? Ha! What kind of a worthless, ignorant darky field hand was your pa anyway? I wouldn't be trying to compare family stock, black boy."

Gabe glared at Shemp. He saw something. Something . . . He spoke up again, and even though he now knew better, said, "Well, General, I'd just bet you knew my pa. 'e was, after all, a respectable, white southern gentleman like yourself, an' from 'round your old neighborhood, too. My pa was a white southern gentleman, name o' James B. Haney, owner o' Heavenly Hills Plantations. A torturer of men, women and children. You'd o' prob'ly been proud t' be in 'is comp'ny."

"You impertinent son-of-a-bitch!" Lee yelled, standing up fast, his gloves dropping to the dirty floor. "How dare you impugn the good names of Haney and Lee?!"

"So, you did know 'bout ol' Massah Haney, eh, Shemp? You know what a 'respectable' man my pa was. I'm the product o' that respectable man rapin' my Ma. I reckon you and I 'ave somethin' in common. Both sons o' white, southern gentlemen, an' both bastards," Gabe said, nodding and revealing a broad smile of satisfaction.

Shemp Lee's face went blank. He appeared stunned for a moment. He stared at Gabe silently, with a combination of confusion and hate. Then he gathered his wits. He stumbled, kicking his chair back behind him. "Colonel, give me that Colt," he said, grabbing it from Fletcher's hand. Gabe thought, well, at least, I'm going down punching – and happy too, considering the circumstances. His last chance was his Derringer. He started to reach into his boot. It was too late. Shemp came down on his head hard with the butt of that Colt. Everything went dark.

27

HENRY'S BATTLE

Henry Haymond was a fighter. But he was also out of his element. Continually off balance, not knowing how to act in the city. He knew he had to take care about his usual temper, which tended to flare to conceal his discomfort with new experiences or unfamiliar surroundings. And St. Louis, Missouri was definitely new and unfamiliar. The only thing he could think to do now was get to General Burke's office as quickly as possible. He had waited in the baggage car until all the activity was over and it got dark. He walked furtively, staying in the shadows, confident that he could remember enough of Gabe's description that he could find the building. He would wait out the night and hope someone showed up to work in the morning.

His efforts were rewarded. Leonard came quick-marching down the street from the opposite direction soon after sun-up. Henry watched him enter the building, then poked his head inside to follow. Leonard sprang up the stairs and went into the office. Henry decided this had to be the Secret Service. The frosted glass on the door featured a five-pointed star that looked like the one he had seen on Gabe's badge.

He knocked, then opened and peered around the door. Leonard was just getting settled behind his desk. He looked up at his visitor.

"Mornin'," he announced hesitantly. "This here Secret Service?"

Leonard gave Henry a good, long once-over, and said slowly, "Yes. This is the Secret Service. I'm not sure - " he started.

"Good. 'at's what I wanted," Henry interrupted. "Name's Henry Haymond. Most recently outta Rockville, Maryland." Henry cautiously stuck out his hand. Leonard half stood and gave it a quick shake.

"My name's Leonard. Sir, I'm not sure you'd have any business with the Service. May I direct you to some other agency?"

"No sir. My bus'ness is with you. I'm a friend of Gabe Baker's and I - "

Now it was Leonard who interrupted. "Oh! Yes, please sit down, uh, Henry, right? That's right, Gabe mentioned you before. Do you have a message from Mr. Baker?"

Henry was impressed that Gabe seemed to have such respect from this white man, who although quite young, appeared to have a very important position, with his own desk and all. "Not exactly from 'im as much as about 'im. He's been took. By them Confederate scum down by the train station. I'm fearin' for 'im. An' if I can't get no help from this here Service, I'm goin' down to get 'im m'self."

Leonard stood and held out his hands in a 'stop' gesture. "No, no, Henry. I implore you not to do that."

"Well, then, 'ow soon can y' get some men together, I figger 'bout ten should be good?"

"I'm sorry, Henry, we don't have ten men, we - "

"Well, then, dadgummit, 'ow many y' got?"

"The General's been kidnapped. That leaves me," Leonard said, frowning.

"Y-you? Just you?" Henry wheezed in disbelief. He quickly stood up and then sat down again. "Uh – well, Leonard, you got a gun?"

"Henry, that isn't the way. We'd be killed and Gabe would be killed. And what I know of current law enforcement around here, they wouldn't be any help to us."

"Them belly-crawlin' sons-o'-bitches is gonna kill 'im. He knows all about 'em. He's killed several of 'em an' put lead int' others weren't obligin' enough t' die. And they're all white men. Um, no offense."

"No offense taken. I know what they are. I know *who* they are."

"I ain't a-gonna leave 'im t' them dogs. They is worst o' th' worst. What they can do to a man – all I can say is I'm goin' over there, with or without ya."

"Just wait a minute! Let me think. Maybe we can help get the General out of trouble, too. They might have him in there. Wouldn't that be something? But we can't go in there without a plan. Do you know where they all are?"

"Mebbe a couple in th' caboose on th' side track. Some in the buildin' other side where I saw 'em takin' 'im. After that, I don' know. But I figger Gabe's in that buildin' an' he ain't bein' treated good. He put 'is faith in me t' partner up with 'im. I'm gonna get 'im out if'n I can. And mebbe your General, too."

"I've got a couple of messages to send. A note to leave. Then, when it's getting dark I'll go down there with you, Henry. Just to get the lay of the land. Then, maybe we can make a plan. All right?"

"You bringin' your gun?"

"I'll bring it."

"Can you shoot it?"

"Well, I mean, I know how."

"All right, then. But I'm goin' in with or without ya after that," Henry said, rising. "I'll meet ya at that little park-like spot two blocks away come six o'clock."

Henry went to the train station. His rifle was at the hotel and he kept his Colt under his coat. He looked around. He stared at the little outbuilding for a long while waiting for something to happen. He was getting nervous. What was going on in there? He neither saw nor heard anything. He was finally run off by a station master's assistant who took him for a vagrant.

He was so anxious, he had to do something. He remembered Gabe telling him stories of St. Louis on their way west on the train. Gabe had talked about Bloody Island. It was nothing more than an overgrown sandbar in the middle of the Mississippi, but it had an interesting history. Gabe had told him about all the black folks who took refuge there at times as well as the duels the white folks fought. Including Abraham Lincoln. Gabe told Henry about the horror of 1841 when four Negroes had been hung after being condemned to death by a white jury. Tickets had been sold for $1.50 apiece so that a large audience of white folks could come out by steam packet to watch. Afterwards, the heads of the executed men were displayed in a downtown pharmacy.

Henry decided he would go. He would look for some kindred spirits who might be willing to help him. He was committed to attacking the Knights where they held Gabe. He would look for some extra guns. And he had money to pay for help.

Henry took the ferry out to the island, which at this time was starting to disappear. An army engineer by the name of Robert E. Lee had constructed two dikes back in 1838 to accelerate its erosion and movement in order to keep the city's harbors open. It was gradually washing over to the Illinois side of the river. Henry hoped some of the legacy of the island still existed, just not the hanging part.

Henry watched the ferry make its way back to the city before he started walking towards the tangle of brush and trees that covered the interior of the little land mass. He saw no signs of life other than a campfire ring and some empty bottles. He called out as loud as he could manage, "Hello out there! Hello! Can anyone hear me?"

He sat on a log by the long-cold campsite and listened. He had a funny feeling that he was being watched, but heard no one. For some reason, the memory of his old friend, the raven at the Rockville Cemetery came to mind. He looked up into the canopy of young maple and birch trees above him. Sure enough, a big old raven sitting just above him started to croak and flap its wings.

"Hello, mister, I know your cousin," he said out loud. "'e's a friend o' mine. Back home."

Then there was a rustling in the brush off to his right. He pulled his gun and held it barrel up while he waited. A young black man emerged. He wore a scraggly, torn white shirt and work pants with a hole in one knee.

"Hey, old man, you jus' talkin' t' that old crow up there?" the man asked.

"'at's right, sonny. 'e's related to a friend o' mine back east," Henry said.

"'Wha – what?" he stuttered, confused. He shook his head. "Um, Back east y' say? Hey, you ain't gonna shoot me, are ya?"

"Yeah, back east. And, no, I ain't gonna shoot ya. 'less'n y' give me cause, that is," Henry responded with a twinkle in his eye that the young man didn't catch.

"No sir. No sir, I ain't gonna give no cause." The man took off his gray Kepi hat and wiped his brow. "Where'bouts east? As far as Greenville, mebbe?"

"Don't know no Greenville. I'm from Maryland. Name's Henry."

"I'm from Greenville. Illinois. Name's Clem. Ain't seen ya here'bouts afore, Henry. An' don't know nothin' 'bout no Mar'land."

"You ain't seen me 'cuz I ain't been before. But here I am. And I'm a-lookin' for some men. Kind o' men have guns, know how t' use 'em for a righteous cause. And ain't afraid t' use 'em neither. You got any o' them out here, Clem?"

"Well, uh – not sure. What's 'at – righteous cause – what's 'at mean?"

"Means we're gonna shoot it out with a whole passel o' southern white boys t' save a good man."

"Whew! Whoa, Henry! You know what you're sayin'?"

"I know. You know any men I can talk to out here? Men! Shootin' starts tonight. You're invited if'n ya got sand. And a gun, o' course."

"But, old man. War's over! You gonna start it up again."

"Nope. Them scurvy grayback snakes startin' up again. You know any good men?"

"I can take you t' our camp. A couple got guns they toted in th' war. All I can do."

"Good. Then they aready know 'ow t' shoot an' what t' shoot at," Henry said, getting to his feet and sticking his Colt into his pants. "Let's go."

Clem walked ahead through the sand and brush until they reached an open spot with another, larger fire ring. Two older men were sitting on logs, smoking corncob pipes. Henry stood at the edge of the bushes for a moment regarding them before Clem spoke up. They appeared to Henry past their prime and broken down, maybe by the war, maybe by their current condition. Henry thought, "Yeah, well, just like me, I reckon."

Clem introduced the men as Josiah and Juba. "They's brothers. Boys, this here is Henry. 'e's lookin' for an army t' shoot up some white folks." Josiah looked to be the older brother. He was thin and taller. He had distinctive creases in his worn face and gray around his temples. Juba was thin, too, but a good four inches shorter. They did have a family resemblance in their friendly features. They wore matching, patched overalls and ragged shirts.

"That right, Henry?" the man called Josiah asked. "You gonna shoot some white folks?"

"Hopin' to, an' I need your help. On account o' there's a bunch of 'em. If'n ya gots th' guns, the know-how and the gumption, that is. Don't need ya otherwise. Pay be good."

"We gots a couple o' old pistols from th' war. Keep in good shape. Knows how t' use 'em," Juba said. "What about that other?" He looked up at Josiah, who was taller even sitting down. "We gots th' gumption?" Then he started laughing. They all laughed.

"Yeah, you in th' war I reckon you do. 'less'n it was shot, cut or beat out o' ya, like some," Henry said, walking in closer. One of the guns was sitting on the log by Juba. "This your .36? My friend Gabe carries a Navy .36 and he is why I'm here. Some southern gen'lmen in town want t' start up a new war. They're holdin' Gabe and 'e's th' man t' stop 'em if we can get 'im loose."

"I knew a Gabe afore. Used t' live right 'ere in St. Louie. He 'ad a .36 and knew 'ow t' use it, but didn' like comin' out 'ere much. A good man, 'e was, fought with th' 54th. Used t' be some white folks come out an' shoot up th' place, pullin' their guns out real quick an' shootin' bottles and such, too. Not so much no more." Juba scratched the stubble on his chin. "What kind o' pay?"

"Your Gabe an' my Gabe sound like th' same man. Now you know who you be shootin' for. I'd be payin' in greenback cash, $20.00 t' each man proves 'imself up and don't get hisself kilt."

"What 'appens he get kilt?" Juba asked.

"I don' know. I reckon you get your reward in th' hereafter. An' I'll see t' the buryin' my own self. I used t' work in th' boneyard, y' know."

"Seem fair. Fair," Juba said, looking off in the distance, now in a pensive mood. "What you think, Jos'?"

"Well, I don' know, Juba, us bein' so busy an' all. But - if'n 'at's *our* Gabe, I'd say it'd be a right good move," he said, sticking his pipe back into his mouth.

"Yeah. 'at's it. A right good move," Juba agreed. "An' fact is, we ain't got a *whole* lot o' prospects right now anyways," he said, looking up at Henry.

"Y' don't say. What *you* say, Clem?" Henry asked.

"Hmmm," Clem said, trying to appear as if he were seriously thinking about it. "But, well, I reckon not this time. Sound like righteous cause, but them rebels is th' kind folks is always gettin' kilt by. 'sides, I ain't no gun hand," he said, looking down at the ground where he was poking around with a stick. He looked at Josiah. "You fellers won't be thinkin' bad o' me I don't go, will ya?"

"Hahaha! You crazy, boy?" Josiah burst out laughing. He looked up at Henry and smiled, then over to Clem. "Chances us comin' back after shootin' white folks – 'specially th' southern gent kind – well, jus' ain't all that good. We won't be thinkin' nothin' 'bout nobody."

"An' you're laughin'," Clem said.

"I'm a sight older'n you, Clem, seen a lot. Also, knows what's important. 'at's all."

"Yep, you boys'll do," Henry said, digging a wad of spent chew out of his cheek and flinging it away. Then he gave the brothers their instructions. He told them to clean up as well as they could so they wouldn't attract too much attention, especially from the law. They were to ferry across the river in a couple of hours. He would meet them in the park close to the depot. He gave them spending money and promised them sandwiches and ammunition. Before he went back to the landing for another ferry, he helped them rig up some twine so they could hide their guns under their clothes.

Henry retrieved as much ammunition as he could carry from his hotel room and bought food for the boys. They hadn't looked too prosperous and Henry knew what it was to be hungry, and weak from hunger. He got to the park early and thought about how their attack on the train building might go. It would have to be fast as the gunfire would soon attract police officers. Officers who were more likely than not to shoot black men with guns before asking questions. But he figured he couldn't really plan more than attacking, breaking in and doing the best they could once inside. So, mostly, he thought about his friend Gabe. Gabe was the first man to show him respect in a long time. Whatever happened, he'd live up to that. Oh, sure, the Reverend Dunbar had tried to make a show of friendship, but he had difficulty hiding his true feelings, his contempt for those he obviously thought inherently inferior. Dunbar was the type who would never understand how the everyday attitude he demonstrated betrayed what was in his heart.

Henry sat, ate a ham sandwich, felt the sun on his face and contemplated all that was good about life. And how it all could end so soon. A few months ago Henry would say he didn't have all that much to lose, although he had learned to appreciate his responsibilities at the cemetery. And he loved his mule Sheba. He even thought of the raven in the tree as his friend. And he had his memories, many which came with a rush of fear and humiliation, but some, especially from his time working on the underground railroad, with warmth and satisfaction. He had done valuable and risky work and done it well. Even though he hadn't fought in the war officially as a soldier, he had done his part and he had taken a turn at shooting at rebels as well. No one could take that away from him.

He sat with his face raised to the sun, eyes closed, when he heard a nervously familiar voice. "He – hello, Henry." Leonard had not succumbed to his fears as Henry had believed he might. Henry felt a new-found respect for the young man right then and there. Here he was, shaking with dread, but he had come.

Henry tried to assure him. "Hello, Leonard, so glad y' could make it on this fine, beautiful day. Please, sit down, we 'ave time. An' I got good news for ya, too. I found two fightin' men t' throw in with us. They should be comin' any time."

Leonard sat on the bench hesitantly. "Um, two fighting men, Henry? We didn't talk about anyone else joining in."

"No sir. But I figger the more th' better so long 's they're good men an' I b'lieve 'em t' be that."

"Uh, Henry. Are they – are they, well, black men?"

"Yessir," he answered quickly. "An' they seem t' know our Gabe, too. You know, from when 'e used t' live 'ere in St. Louie."

Henry reached into his satchel. "Here, Leonard, I brought sandwiches. Have one," he said gesturing.

Leonard was pale as a ghost. "I couldn't eat a thing, Henry. I'm a bit nervous, you know."

"Oh, you are? Well, I figgered mebbe you was an old hand at this sort o' thing – bein' in that Secret Service an' all," Henry lied.

"Henry! I'm an assistant in an office. I file papers and do for the General. In the war, I worked for the quartermaster, never saw the front lines or any fighting at all."

"But you're here now. You brought your gun. You got sand, Leonard," he said, looking him in the eye.

Leonard gave him a weak smile. Just then, Josiah and Juba came marching around the corner in the shadows of the late afternoon light. Leonard jerked his head towards Henry, his mouth opened in shock, then looked back at the approaching figures. "Henry! These? These two? Oh, no . . ." his voice trailed off.

"Now, now, Henry, I know they look a bit ragged, but they can prob'ly shoot, an' if'n you want somebody t' shoot at some southern gen'lemen, these here are jus' what you want. We do good enough shootin' an' mebbe you get your Gen'ral back an' I get m' Gabe."

Henry stood up and greeted the brothers. They both looked stiff and out of place. It was obviously unusual for them to leave the island and come into the city. Josiah appeared slightly joyful, with a smile of anticipation. Juba stood, looking anxiously from side to side. Henry wondered what he was getting himself into, but knowing he was doing the best he could for Gabe was enough to ease his doubts. He didn't want to die, but he was ready to die. But what about the younger men, Leonard and Juba? Was it fair to ask them to help? Well, they were men. They had decided for themselves. Just as Clem had.

"I ain't no general, but I figger we need Leonard t' check on that Special if it's still on th' side track. See if anyone's around, or even in th' caboose, where some were holed up afore. Any train folk there'bouts see a black man snoopin' aroun' might just start shootin' right then and there. We get close t' the depot, we gonna spread out a little and wait for Leonard to tell us what's what. We be hangin' around, jus' like the loafers an' layabouts they figger us t' be."

"Me an' Jos' can do that, can't we, Jos'?"

"Born to it, Juba."

Leonard smiled. Leonard had never been around a group of free black men before. Or any group of men intending to use guns. He felt a sense of camaraderie with them. And even with the fear, he liked the feeling.

"Then, when it's all clear, I'll go to the front door o' that shed. I'll knock. When they open you all can come up an' start t' shootin' when y' see one o' them varmints. Shoot our way in, grab our friends, shoot our way out if we has t'. Nothin' to it."

"That's the whole plan, Henry?"

"Like our cap'n used t' say, plan's only good until the shootin' starts. After that, it's just shootin' an' gettin' shot *at*. Plan don't matter much," Josiah said. Juba nodded in agreement. Even Leonard looked satisfied. Yeah, don't make it too complicated.

The group walked down to the depot, Leonard in front. If he had walked with them, it would appear suspicious.

They turned the corner to the block where the depot stood. Leonard looked back at Henry and spread his arms out in a questioning gesture. "Henry?" he said.

The Special was gone. Henry saw a Pullman porter off by himself pushing a luggage cart. He held up his hand for the others to wait. "Hello porter," he called out. The man straightened up and looked at him.

"Name's Edward. What can I do for you, sir?" he said, showing deference to the older man. Henry gave him a quick once-over and decided he should be careful, but he needed some answers.

"Name's Henry. I was int'rested in 'at Special was on the side 'ere before."

"Why you care 'bout that?"

"Got m' reasons an' they're good 'uns. You know where it is?"

"I s'pose mebbe you got reasons, jus' by th' looks of ya, anyways." He was eyeing the Colt peeking from behind Henry's coat. "Took off last night, middle o' night. Curious, it was," Edward said,

"Curious? What's 'at?"

"Means a bunch o' no good - " Edward stopped and looked around to see if anyone else was around within hearing distance. "Those hill boys over there with you, Henry?"

"They are."

"Hmmm. Anyways – well, what they doin' down here, an' you too, Henry?"

"We come down t' shoot th' place up, if you gotta know, Edward," Henry said, without smiling. "I figger those no-goods on that Special 'ave a friend o' mine an' mean 'im no good."

Henry felt relieved that he had just showed Edward his trust.

"Well, y' got that right. No-goods. Sorry y' didn' get a crack at 'em. They was actin' mighty suspicious, they was."

"Edward, you see 'em pushin' around any prisoners? Anyone, black or white, in cuffs or irons?"

"No sir."

"You know where they headed?"

"Talk was, to Denver City, out Colorado way."

"Any more talk?"

"No sir."

"Damn. I'm feelin' a might fearsome for m' friend. I'm gonna 'ave t' check that shack out for 'im."

"Careful. Don' know they all gone."

"Thanks, Edward. The barrel o' this here Colt will go through that door afore I do."

No one else was out on the platform. Henry gestured to the others to follow him. They went to the shack. Henry tried the door. It was unlocked. He eased his Colt around the door and then they walked in. It was a scene of chaos and wreckage. The table was still there, but the chairs were broken, most into small pieces. Henry held his gun out in front of him as he slowly crept down the dark hallway. Nothing in the room to the left. The door to the room to the right seemed stuck. He pushed on it and it wouldn't give. Josiah helped him and it gave a little. Henry looked in. They shoved harder until they could get through.

Henry took his hat off and ran his fingers through his hair. "Damn. What 'appened in here?" A pair of leg irons were thrown into a far corner. Juba brought a lit oil lamp in. There was blood on the irons and on the floor. They kicked remnants of broken furniture and debris around, looking for anything that might shed light on what had happened.

"Oh, damn, oh, lordy. Mercy, mercy. What 'appened here?!" Henry put his palms to his eyes, rubbed them as if to make the scene disappear, and looked again. He got down on his knees and looked at the rubble more closely. There were pieces of furniture, old clothing and spent shells.

Leonard watched while the other three investigated. Then, Josiah picked something up, and shouted, "Henry! Look at this!" It was a .41 Derringer. Gabe's Derringer. Henry cracked it open. It hadn't been fired.

"That's Gabe's," he said, holding it tight and waving it up and down like he had found treasure. "Josiah," he said looking up at the man he now thought of as a kindred spirit and friend, "what you think happened to our friend Gabe?"

"I think like you say, they treat him bad. But they don't kill him. Them rednecks has got some use for 'im yet mebbe. Else, they'd leave 'im 'ere an' never mind th' law. White man's law 'round 'ere you don' get slapped int' jail for killin' a black man; y' get slapped on the back with a free whiskey t' boot."

"Lookee here, lookee here, Henry," Juba said, picking up a piece of cloth with a blood stain on it."

"Damn. A piece o' Gabe's shirt."

"I figger them savages whipped the poor man, then broke up all these here chairs beatin' 'im, th' way we all know 'bout. For the entertainment of it, 'til it ain't no fun no more 'cuz 'e's knocked senseless," Josiah said.

Leonard was listening outside the door. He was seeing something with fresh eyes. He knew he came from a family that was just as guilty as were the ugly cowards who had done this low business here. And he knew at once his own people - friendly, god-fearing, upstanding citizens – were in fact, savages to these men. He shuddered and quickly wiped a tear away. Then he heard something else. He poked his head into the room where the others were still standing.

"Shhh. Shush. Everybody, quiet. Listen. What was that?" he asked. It sounded like a moan.

"I heard it. I heard it, too," Juba whispered. "Like a moan. Was 'at real? Where that come from?"

"Listen," Leonard said. Everyone stood still, turning their heads, trying to locate the faint sound.

"I'm going out back," Leonard announced. His speech had become more decisive and his posture more confident. He held his gun out in front of him. "Maybe something's out there."

Juba stayed with him, then the rest followed until they were all outside. Again, they stood silent. Again, the moaning sound.

"There!" Leonard said, excitedly. He pointed to a bunch of old railroad ties leaning next to the corner of the building. They were next to a mound of trash that smelled of rotten food and feces.

Leonard and Henry started to look deeper into the corner. The moan was louder now. "Gabe. Gabe. You in there, Gabe?" Henry stuttered and looked at Leonard. How could a man be in here, in this place?'

"Gabe!" Henry said louder. "Gabe, you in there?" The pile of trash was heavy and thick. It appeared to have been there for a long time, with newer additions made just recently. It was as tall as a man, and a good 12 feet across at the bottom. Henry became frantic. He started digging with his hands. Leonard did the same. Soon, Josiah and Juba were digging on the other side, closest to the shack.

"I found him!" Henry called out. "I think it's 'im. I see a eye. Careful. Help over here. Careful."

"Oh, my god, who could put a man in here? Why?" Henry's digging started to reveal the side of a face and a shoulder. The group dug quicker until they were startled to see the source of the moaning. It looked something like Gabe and something like something else. It was – he was - ghastly. It was Gabe all right. He was naked. His face was battered almost beyond recognition. His jaw was broken so badly it appeared to be unhinged. His tongue was swollen and lolled out between broken teeth. One eye was swollen shut. His ribs on one side were caved in. He was caked in blood from head to foot. At least one arm and one leg were broken. He was bruised badly from his lower back down. Everywhere. The telltale signs of a brutal whipping were all over his chest and back.

28

THE NEXT TRAIN WEST

Gabe had told Henry of his time living and working in St. Louis. Gabe and Mrs. Belcher had become friends during the time that he worked at Belcher's Boarding House and afterwards. When Gabe rode to Colorado with his new friends Billy and Harley, the two of them became regular correspondents. In this way, they had become even closer.

Finding Gabe naked and unconscious, near death, in the middle of a trash heap behind the railroad building, was a shock to all, but especially Leonard. Whereas the other two had seen such things before, Leonard had not. But he was a great help in getting Gabe wrapped in a blanket and transported to Mrs. Belcher's. Without his help they could be near certain to have been arrested and Gabe never would have been heard from again.

Mrs. Belcher saw to it that Gabe was washed and put into a clean bed in a room which he would share with Henry. She knew a young doctor who would be willing to work on a black man. His wounds were cleaned and his broken bones set. Doctor Crabbe gave Mrs. Belcher instructions on how to care for Gabe and began sending his nurse over for regular visits. After two weeks Gabe had not spoken yet. Henry tended to chatter and sometimes sing when he was with him. Henry imagined Gabe's part in any conversation he started and kept it going by himself.

Henry had paid for a month's room and board for the two of them based on Dr. Crabbe's prediction of how long before Gabe might be able to move. But Henry had worked regularly his whole life. He needed something to do. After a few days, he found it in helping Mrs. Belcher around the house. At first, he did odd jobs. Mrs. Belcher took notice that Henry could handle anything she asked of him, and so, one day, handed him a list of needed repairs that had been growing for some time. Gabe and Henry's stay at Mrs. Belcher's turned out to be of great advantage to her as Henry fixed every item of delayed maintenance on the list. Among other things, he fixed and painted the sagging front porch, rebuilt one of the supply sheds in the back and repaired the water pump in the kitchen. He made quick work of mending and refinishing several chairs and a guest room bed. He made her weather-beaten shutters work and look like new. He scrubbed and cleaned everything in the kitchen to such a shine that when she saw it all, she gasped with delight and hugged him. Afterwards, she had gone about her business, but he just stood, his arms hanging down at his sides, in shock. He had never been touched, let alone hugged, by a white woman. When he regained his composure, he thought, well, nothing wrong with that!

Mrs. Belcher and Nurse Rebekah sat Gabe up twice a day and spooned hot broth and laudanum into him. He wouldn't be able to eat solid food for a while anyway. He looked at them with wide, shining eyes, but no other expression. When Leonard visited every couple of days, he would nervously pace around. Gabe followed him around the room with his eyes, but showed no emotion then either.

After a month, with no apparent improvement, Henry and Mrs. Belcher both were becoming increasingly concerned. The nurse told them that there was just no way to predict, after the extreme trauma he had suffered, when he might come out of it.

"'When', she said," Mrs. Belcher encouraged Henry, "Not 'if', but 'when'."

"I know, ma'am," he said. They sat at the kitchen table having coffee as had become their custom. "Gabe went through so much as a slave, then in th' war, I just can't help worry if they fin'lly broke him. Any man can get broke, I reckon. It all jus' adds up, more an' more 'til mebbe somethin' inside jus' dies. I seen it before. Durin' slave days."

"The best we can do for him is what we are doing, though," Mrs. Belcher said. "We don't want him to see us worried. And as far as that goes, you and Gabe are welcome to stay as long as he needs."

"Thank-ya kindly, Mrs. Belcher. Fact is, I ain't got much else t' fix up 'round here, though."

"That's got nothing to do with it!" she protested, hurt at the inference.

"Hold on now, hold on," Henry said, defensively. "I didn't mean nothin' like 'at. It's just, well, I don' know, we don' want t' wear out our welcome. An' I wonder if some kind o' change'd do some good for 'im anyways."

"You cannot wear out your welcome here, Henry. And as for change? Well, I don't want to see you leave, but it is something we should put to the doctor, I suppose."

"If I could get 'im back t' Colorado, seein' 'is old friends, 'is house, even them old house varmints 'e sets so much store by – well – mebbe that could turn th' tide. I'm afeared 'e's been gone so long, mebbe 'e ain't comin' back. Heard 'bout that and seen it m'self."

"I heard about it, too, Henry. They called it 'soldier's heart'."

"Good name for it, I 'speckt."

The next day when Nurse Rebekah came, Henry and Mrs. Belcher talked to her about making the move. Two days later, Rebekah and Doctor Crabbe came to look at Gabe. There was no change. Gabe's breathing and heart rate were normal. His many wounds were fading some, at least they appeared less gruesome. His eyes were open most of the time, but he was not responsive to light, or sound, most notably, voices. He did look at people, but didn't appear to recognize anyone.

After an examination, Dr. Crabbe and Rebekah sat down in the parlor with Mrs. Belcher and Henry for tea. "I'm no specialist in cases like this," the doctor said, "but I've heard some stories about soldiers with Gabe's kind of symptoms. We've tried bed rest, and of course he needed it for his many injuries, but more of the same may produce more of the same – that is, yes, I think the best thing to try now is to expose him to a different set of stimuli."

"Uh, Doc - ?" Henry asked. "What is 'at stimu – stim - ?"

"Oh, yes, Henry. It means I agree with your proposed course of treatment. It couldn't hurt, in any case, so long as his physical injuries continue to be cared for, and someone takes responsibility to keep giving him the broth and other fluids. And, that includes the laudanum, as well, for a little while yet, anyway. So, yes, if he can be carefully moved, a new environment could help."

Henry's elbows were resting on his chair's arms. He put his face into his open hands and sighed. Then, he looked up at the doctor. "Doc, I want t' take 'im to 'is home. In Colorado. Can 'e travel by train?"

"You'd need sleeping car accommodations. Keep him sedated. Then, yes. And I think taking him home is a good idea. If his memories are sparked, good ones that is, that could bring about a positive change. Gabe could come back. Slowly, or even in an instant. I've heard of these things too." He paused. "You'll need a wheelchair."

Henry had to rely on Leonard to help him with tickets, boarding and accommodations. Before they left, Mrs. Belcher kissed Gabe on his cheek and whispered in his ear. Then, she kissed Henry on his cheek and he blushed. And she told him if he ever needed a job in St. Louis, she would have one for him. They took the next train west. Once again, it was just Gabe and Henry. But Henry was no longer looking for the Golden Triangle. He was just looking out for his friend.

29

DAISY WOOD

When Henry reached Denver in late summer 1874, his mission had changed from tracking down Confederate insurrectionists to bringing Gabe back into the world. But really, it had always been just about helping Gabe. Henry stayed awake the 36 hours it took to ride to Denver and watched over him. He knew that Leonard had wired ahead, but didn't really know what to expect. If nothing else, he would arrange for a wagon to take Gabe to his home in Boulder.

As he struggled to lift Gabe out of the car at the platform in Denver, he heard his name being called. Surprised, he almost dropped Gabe into the wheelchair a porter had brought for him. He looked around, but saw only a very pretty, young white girl, waving and walking briskly in his direction. This couldn't be . . . the Daisy Wood he'd heard about? Well, it had to be.

It *was* Daisy Wood. Her parents had come west with a wagon train in 1850. She was born in the back of a "prairie schooner" on the Santa Fe Trail. She came into the world a hard way and her mother paid the ultimate price for it. Her pa did his best bringing up his little girl on his own on a hardscrabble 80-acre ranch in the southeast part of what would later become Montana Territory. She grew up watching him work himself near to death in freezing and in scorching weather alike, to scratch out a living and make things better for her. She watched and learned as he became friends with both Lakota and Crow. She saw that it was because of his simple, but tough and respectful ways. He taught her tolerance of different people and lifestyles, the value of books and how to shoot quick and straight.

The one thing she refused to learn was how to slaughter the cows, pigs and chickens her pa kept on the ranch. It was just after she turned 15 that she announced to her pa she was quitting eating meat. Her pa tried to understand, but all she could say was that when she looked into the eyes of a cow or a pig he was about to butcher, she saw the fear. She felt the fear. She had been taught that animals had no feelings. She had come to believe otherwise. And she thought it should be obvious to everyone. When her pa took a calf away from its mother, the mother would cry and bellow. The calf would make all kinds of harsh, loud noises. They both would appear to be looking for each other for days after the separation. She knew why, why didn't others?

Daisy soon started collecting a wide array of creatures she found on the prairie that were injured or orphaned. She took in a variety of birds, some of which she nursed to adulthood. She fixed the wing of a young great horned owl. She cared for osprey, eagles and herons, but also for smaller birds she found in any kind of distress. From time to time she came across larger creatures needing help. Her pa objected when she brought a pair of orphaned wolf pups home, but she kept them until they were older and strong, returning them to an area where she knew a pack regularly hunted. She did the best she could to help any creature out and was heartbroken when she was unsuccessful.

At some point her pa gave up on her as a future rancher and decided his kind of life wasn't for her. He had wanted her to get a more formal education anyway. He sent her off to complete her schooling in Denver City, Territory of Colorado. It was there, after she finished, that she applied for the new position with the Secret Service. She had applied as D. Wood. She had been hired before the Chief knew she was a woman, but by the time he discovered the truth, General Burke's reliance on her as an indispensable asset to the Service in the west saved her job.

Now, Daisy's natural inclinations would be of great benefit to Gabe Baker. She would take him in and do everything she could to make him better. Leonard's telegram was necessarily brief, and she had no idea Gabe would be as bad as he was. She gasped when she saw him, thin and slumped over in the chair, with the marks of an extreme beating visible on every exposed part of him. Henry didn't want to let go as primary caregiver, but immediately saw in Daisy a special and caring woman who could maybe give Gabe the best chance he had to improve. Henry would stay close enough to make sure things were done right.

The care she showed for Gabe caused Henry to befriend her right away. The feeling was mutual. She had a room ready to take him in just two blocks from the depot. They were able to wheel him there in the chair and get him settled. Gabe looked around from time to time but his stare was vacant and his face blank.

Henry was aware that they were only about a two hours' ride from Gabe's home and friends. He planned on taking him there as soon as he thought Gabe was ready for more travel. Now, of course, he would want Daisy's agreement on that move as well.

After they got Gabe into his bed at the rooming house, Henry and Daisy sat talking and drinking coffee. "Part of th' reason for gettin' 'im all th' way out 'ere is to bring 'im home. Get 'im a stimuli, the doc said. You know, uh, a positive one."

"Yes, I think he has friends or family in Boulder? That's a good idea. When he's ready for it. He needs some rest before he moves again. For right now, I'll be taking care of him. When the time is right I have a wagon we can use."

They went back into the room where Gabe was lying. Daisy wrung out the cloth she had in a bowl of water and patted Gabe's face with it. She wiped his forehead, his face and around his neck.

"All right, ma'am. I reckon I'll go on t' Boulder an' meet with some o' his people, mebbe get 'em t' come visit. Somethin' else I'm wonderin' on account o' Gabe an' me was workin' on it. And I figger I got a score t' settle anyways. You get any word on where them gold-thievin' scoundrels are?"

She brushed her long brown hair from in front of her eyes and turned to look at Henry. She looked down again and was quiet for a minute. "I alerted law enforcement in the area that they were coming." She went back to her work, but continued, "I've been trying to round up some help. I found out when their train got in, but that was about five weeks ago. It was in the middle of the night and they slipped away quickly. Our Chief wired me not to go after them without help and he promised some men, but I don't know how many or when they might show up. I don't know where those murdering fools are now and I'm afraid the trail has grown cold. And they may still have our General Burke."

"Miss Wood, I aim t' find 'em no matter what else 'appens." He looked down at Gabe. "They done this t' my friend and I won't let it lie."

"Henry, I think we're going to be friends. Please call me Daisy. And please, at least, let me know before you go off after those sons-of-bitches, so maybe we can coordinate. And I certainly wouldn't want to think of you going by yourself!"

Henry thought, she just said 'sons-o'-bitches'. I do like this girl. "Thanks, Miss Daisy. I reckon I'll go out an' find a room now. I'll stop t' see how our patient is doin' tomorrow mornin' afore I ride int' Boulder. You know where a black man can stay aroun' these parts?"

"Yes, Henry, I know. Right here. I got an extra room for you next door. Come on, I'll show you."

"Why – ," he stammered. "Uh, th - thank-you, Miss Daisy, 'at's plumb good o' ya."

"Daisy. Not Miss Daisy."

"Daisy. Thank-ya, Miss Daisy, ma'am."

She just looked at him, smiled and rolled her eyes.

30

HENRY VISITS BOULDER

After coffee with Daisy at first light, Henry took off for Boulder on her piebald mare, Magic. Henry was used to Sheba, who, although cantankerous at times, could be brought to heel with a few stern words. He had never been on such a spirited horse, and struggled for the first mile to get her used to him. Once they started to get along better, Henry enjoyed the ride, marveling at the sight of the mountains as they got closer to town. Now he knew what Gabe had been talking about.

As he came to the final overlook into the Boulder Valley he stopped to wonder at the mountains, the impressive rock formations above the town and even the town Itself. It looked so small and insignificant under the shadows of the foothills that marked the end of the Great Plains.

"Let's go, Magic! Let's get 'er done!" he yelped with a new surge of energy, touching his heels into her ribs. He was excited to find out what this new country was like. And to meet Gabe's friends. Magic galloped down into the valley and they followed an obvious trail that would take them to the center of town.

Magic and Henry slowed as they approached 12th Street and Pearl from the south. Henry turned right onto Pearl. He knew this would be the place to find people, but he figured he should just go to the Sheriff's office first. He tied Magic out front. He'd been working on a chew most of the morning and finally spit that out before he went in. Sheriff Taylor was at his desk, having a coffee and looking at "wanted" posters. He looked up at Henry. Henry looked down at him. There was a moment of silence.

"Well, you mus' be th' sheriff, then?" Henry said.

"Must be, I guess, on account of no one else wants the job," Taylor said.

"Well, I don' know 'bout that. I never talked t' no sheriff afore. This here – first time."

"All right, fair enough. I'm Sheriff Taylor. How am I doin' so far?"

"Good, I'd reckon. I am one Henry Haymond, most recently out o' Rockville, Maryland," he said, attempting formality.

"Hmmm. Makes me wonder if you might know a friend of mine, comes from that neck of the woods. Name's Gabe Baker."

"Damn! You are good. Yessir. I'm proud t' say Gabe Baker is a friend o' mine, too."

"Please, Henry, sit down. I'd like to hear everything about how Gabe is doin'. I hope we'll be seein' him soon? Cup of coffee?"

"Thank-ya, Sheriff. A cup o' good black coffee'd do me just fine, sir."

"Now, hold on there, Henry. I never said anything about 'good'."

"All right. I'll jus' take it black then."

Sheriff Taylor set the steaming mug in front of Henry, sat down in his swivel chair with a loud squeak, and looked Henry in the eyes. Henry responded, "Gabe's a friend o' mine, too. I brought him with me. To Denver. He been beaten within a inch o' his life over in St. Louie. Right now, 'e's in good 'ands, with Miss Daisy Wood o' the Secret Service. I come here lookin' for any friends o' his I can find. Doc in St. Louie say he needin' a stimuli. A pos'tive one. Friends would be good for 'im is what 'e was sayin'. I'd be sayin' it, too."

"Damn. Damn. I got a telegram from a man named Leonard, and so we were expecting to see Gabe soon. But not in that condition. When can we get him over here, Henry? I know Miss Daisy Wood. She would be the one to take good care of him. But this right here, in Boulder, this is where everybody knows him. And where those confounded critters he seems to admire so much are. They both took sips of their coffee. There was so much to say neither knew how to continue. Then, the door rattled open.

"Oh, hey Sheriff," Harley Cobb said as he stepped in. "Didn't know you was busy, I just came by for a free cup, I can come later," he said, turning to go.

"No, no, Harley," Sheriff Taylor said, "This conversation here maybe has as much to do with you as anyone else in town. Sit down." Harley sat in the chair next to Henry, held out his hand and the two shook. Harley raised his eyebrows.

"Harley, this gentleman here is Henry Haymond of – uh, that was Rockville? Yeah, Rockville, Maryland." He turned to Henry and said, "Henry, this is Harley Cobb, I'd guess Gabe's best friend in town."

"You got news o' Gabe?!" Harley screeched, standing up so quickly he knocked his chair over.

"Harley, give the man a chance," Taylor said, trying to calm him down. "Henry, you should tell it."

"I'm mighty pleased t' meet ya, Harley, Gabe's said a lot o' good things about ya."

"*Good* things? Well, them's all true, I reckon."

"Haha. Well, 'e did say you was a might funny, too, Mr. Harley," Henry said. Then Henry told briefly of their encounters with the Knights and in more detail, Gabe's current condition, including how Henry and the others had found him. "And them sons-o'-bitches killed Gabe's partner, a man name o' Heck or Heck-um or some – some-such. Gabe set a lot o' store by that man, an' what I seen a-fightin' with 'im, I know he'd o' died good."

Harley and Sheriff Taylor looked at each other and nodded.

"Henry, I know Daisy Wood must be good for Gabe, we all heard real good things about 'er. But what you're sayin', I mean, well, I think we gotta bring the man home. We got Billy an' me. We got Dr. Pierce and Melissa. We got ol' Red, them house critters o' his, an' mebbe most of all, we got Lin-Chi and Mai-Ling. They got somethin' 'splicable. You know," Harley nodded deeply to Henry with clenched fists, as if that gesture would explain all, "'*splic*-ables," he emphasized. "Sound like he'd be needin' some o' that. I know, I got experience."

"I don' know 'bout a – what's 'at, a '*splic*-able – Gabe said somethin', didn't understand. Miss Daisy ain't agin' 'is comin' over here. She just say, Gabe needin' a rest afore 'e come a-rattlin' and a-rollin' over in 'er buckboard."

"I'm gonna talk t' Lin-Chi, then Doc Pierce," Harley said, "and well, I guess Billy's still down in Colorado City?" he said, leaning forward to pick up his mug and looking at Sheriff Taylor.

Sheriff Taylor nodded. "Yeah, long trial down there. Important, too, for the whole territory. And Harley, Doc Pierce is out around Valmont birthin' up a couple babies."

Harley took a swig and scowled. "Damn, Sheriff. Why don' you hire a deputy can make coffee? Anyways, Henry, I'd take it kindly if ya went with me, then mebbe we can all decide together on gettin' Gabe back home. I got a real strong feelin' we should go see Lin-Chi now."

"I'm proud t' go with ya, Mr. Harley," Henry said.

"There ain't no 'mister' to it, *Mister* Haymond," Harley told him with a sly smirk.

The two talked more about Gabe and finding the gold in the grave in Rockville. And how Henry had recruited the help in St. Louis to get Gabe out of a jam. They walked west on Pearl Street until they came to the sign, "Chinese Laundry".

Harley stopped in front of the modest little house that served as Lin-Chi's business and home. He became serious. "I don't know what all Gabe told you about this man. Mebbe you'd be thinkin' 'e was a bit funny or somethin'?" Harley said. "Well, mebbe 'e is. But mebbe 'e's the smartest man you ever met in your whole life, too. Oh, 'e's got the 'splicables like you never seen."

"Smart and funny?" Henry asked. "Sound like a good combination." Harley nodded, realizing he couldn't make Henry understand. Then, they opened the door, the little tinkle bell announcing their arrival.

Lin-Chi immediately appeared from the back room to regard his two visitors. He bowed to each, beaming with his unguarded, gap-toothed smile. "So good to see, friend Harley. And you bring other friend. Gabr'el's friend? I'm thinking of friend Gabe lately. A lot. Much pain he having, I think. What to do?"

Henry's jaw dropped a bit as he looked in disbelief at Harley. Harley just smiled, knowingly. "Lin-Chi, yes, this is a friend o' Gabe's, name o' Henry. This man brought Gabe with 'im t' Denver. An' you're right, sir. Gabe's in bad shape, needs help."

"Good meetin' you sir," Henry said to Lin-Chi, holding out his hand. Lin-Chi shook it, then bowed again. Henry tried to make a bow back, smiling, and Lin-Chi laughed out loud and slapped his knee.

"Yes, I already ask Mae-Ling come look over store. I will go Denver tomorrow," Lin-Chi said.

"Wha - ? Mr. Chi, how you - you know?" Henry stuttered.

"Hahaha," Lin-Chi doubled over giggling. "Sheriff tell about telegram, maybe Gabe come soon. I see you come to town. On Miss Daisy Wood Secret Service horse. You don't look like horse thief."

Henry scratched his chin. "Hmmm. Yeah. I reckon, yeah." Harley gave Henry another big smile that said, "See, what'd I tell you?"

Harley and Henry rode to Denver. With his new horse ranch starting to thrive, Harley had his pick of some fine mounts. But he still preferred to ride his old bay, Cedric, who had adventured with him across the midwest and to Colorado eight years before with Billy and Gabe. Daisy's horse kept Cedric challenged most of the way. They arrived late afternoon.

31

GABE GOES HOME

"Shh-shhh," Daisy said, with her right index finger to her lips as she met Harley and Henry at the front door to her rooms.

"Miss Daisy, this here's Gabe's friend, Harley," Henry half-whispered.

"So pleased t' meet ya, Miss Wood. I've heard you're takin' real good care o' my friend."

"Good to meet any friend of Gabe's, Harley. Especially you. You see, now I think I know what Gabe's been trying to say. He's been saying your name. I know it!"

"Miss Daisy! He's done woke up then?!" Henry asked.

"Yes. He comes around, briefly, then goes again. He's saying something else, though, that I can't make out. It almost sounds like - something horrible."

"Can you try, Miss Wood?" Harley asked.

"Well, I can try, but it doesn't make sense. See, it's something like a lynch, a lynching? Henry, did they try to lynch him? I looked and didn't see rope burns, well, fresh ones, anyway."

Harley rubbed the stubble on his chin and sat on the hard wood chair at the little table in the front of the room. Henry and Daisy watched him as he thought.

"Gentlemen, I'm going to make us some coffee while you think," Daisy finally said. "You can look in on Gabe, but please don't wake him. Not just yet." She turned to go.

"You know, Henry, I know all about Gabe's time at Heavenly Hills and with the 54th. He never said nothin' 'bout no lynchin'. Lynchin'. Lynch. Henry! I know what it is!" Harley crossed his arms and gave a self-satisfied smile.

"Well. You gonna tell it, or am I gon' 'ave t' go ask the man hisself?"

"Hahaha! Not lynch-*in*'. It's Lin-Chi. Don't ya see? Lin-Chi been there with 'im. In 'is troubles."

"What? What you talkin' 'bout Harley? That old man ain't seen Gabe since 'e left 'ere months ago."

"No, no, 'at's right. You're right, Henry. But e's been in Gabe's mind. For sure, 'e 'as."

"What's 'at mean, Harley? In 'is mind. What you mean?"

"Gabe's been thinkin' or dreamin' or somethin' like 'at. An' Lin-Chi's been there, with 'im. I mean, at least, Gabe's been *thinkin'* 'bout Lin-Chi. Like, mebbe, adventure journey or somethin'.'"

Daisy brought in two coffees. "Miss Daisy, do you know what the man's talkin' 'bout?"

"I'm not certain I do. But I don't know that he's wrong, either. I'm sure I remember you now, Harley Cobb. It was in the papers. About the horrible thing that happened to you and your wife, that is. I remember. Isabelle, is that right? Everybody said she was so beautiful. And Dr. Moreau from here in Denver was called in on your case. And he said wonderful things about this Lin-Chi. It must have been your friend, Lin-Chi. Was that you, Harley?"

"Yeah, me," Harley hung his head.

"Sorry, Harley, I guess it's still painful."

"Yeah, but I was out – gone somewheres, like Gabe is now. An' ever' time I woke up, Lin-Chi was sittin' in the corner o' old Doc Pierce's surgery, like in the dark. With that crazy grin 'e 'as. An 'e was lookin' right inside o' me, I could feel it. Got me through it alright. Later, 'e said we 'ad 'adventure journey', and we did. But still, I was never really sure what 'e was talkin' about."

"Hmmm, what was it Dr. Moreau called him? I remember, because it had such a good sound to it: a man of tender heart and humble mind! That's it. Well I've heard of strange things before," Daisy said, crinkling her nose and looking back and forth between Henry and Harley. And I never knew Doc Moreau to be wrong about anything."

"Well, that's 'ow those 'splicables are, I reckon," Harley said. "You just don't know."

"The what now, Harley?"

"Well, you know, what they call the 'splicables."

"The – um, you mean *in*explicable?"

"I reckon 'at's it, ma'am."

She looked into her cup and thought in silence for a minute. "And, this Lin-Chi, he's coming soon?"

"Should be 'round tomorrow, Miss Daisy," Harley answered, looking off into a distance he couldn't see.

She set her cup down and slapped her knees, before she stood up. "Excellent," she proclaimed. "Now, why don't we go in and see if Gabe can tell if you're here, both of you? Henry, you already know, but Harley, please just don't expect too much."

Harley walked into the dark room. His friend Gabe was on his back in bed with blankets covering him up to his chin. He appeared weak, skinny and broken. Harley immediately felt a tear start its way down his right cheek. And then the anger welled up. He stood and took three brisk strides out to the front room, breathing hard. He was shaking violently as he tried to speak, "Miss Daisy - " he gasped. "Miss Daisy," he tried again, trying to spit the words out.

She faced him, put her hands on his shoulders and helped him sit. "Harley, Harley, I'm so sorry. Take your time."

Harley's heart was pounding, his breathing staggered and heavy. "Miss Daisy," he screeched. "I'm gonna kill ever' last man had anythin' t' do with this!" He pounded his knees and yanked himself up again, looking to his left, then to his right like a man who was trapped. "You hear me, ma'am?! I'm gonna kill 'em! I'm gonna – ah! Ah! I'm gonna . . ." Harley caught himself. He stood breathing hard with his hands on his knees. "Miss Daisy – I'm so sorry. I'm sor - " He stopped.

Daisy put her hands on his shoulders again and her forehead against his, then eased him back down into the chair. Harley hung his head, his heart hurting with the intense beating. Daisy got on her knees, reached out and lifted his chin. "I know, Harley. I know. Your time may come, but it's not now, it's not today. Right now, Gabe needs you here. Here, in his room. Here, for him to look at next time he opens his eyes." She took a couple of breaths. "Here, with your mind here, too, not out on the trail. Not yet."

Henry sat by, nodding. Not smiling, but moving his head up and down, taking in words like he'd never heard before. He thought, these are good words. They have a special sound. They are wise words. Harley looked at him for something – for what? Neither knew. Maybe he wanted to see some sign of agreement. Maybe if Henry could wait, he could wait.

He looked into Daisy's big green eyes and got lost, but just for a moment. For that moment it felt like Isabelle was with him again. He shook his head and looked away. Daisy gave him a confused, but not hurt, look. "Harley!" she cried out. And then, calmly, "Harley, your friend needs you." Harley nodded and went back in. He pulled up the chair as close to Gabe as he could get.

He put his hand on his shoulder, gently. He felt bone, where once there was muscle, but not now. He squeezed just a little bit. He started to talk. So just Gabe could hear. "Hey, Gabe, you know what your varmints 'ave been up to? 'Cuz I could tell ya." He turned away to sniff and wipe his eyes. Then, he continued. "You know 'at fat one, 'at big, fat one - John Henry? He is always gettin' int' some trouble out at th' ranch an' 'e's blamin' it on Tex. Ever' time. John Henry'll do somethin' bad and then skedaddle an' leave ol' Tex at the scene o' the crime. That Tex, 'e's such a innocent, 'e just sits there an' looks up at ya. Well, John Henry just loves t' get some o' the new mustangs all hurried up and stompin' in the stalls. When 'e hears me comin' out 'e takes off under the porch. I throw some meat out for the crows, who gets it most o' time? John Henry. I put the bird seed out. You know who's sittin' and waitin' for 'is chance? They both been just a-waitin' for ya Gabe, like th' rest of us, I reckon. An' Lin-Chi – he'll be out tomorrow and we'll jus' get ya home."

Harley hung his head. He looked on Gabe's face and could barely recognize him. He couldn't continue. He walked out of the room feeling his own shame. He had failed his friend. How? He didn't know. He just had.

Early next morning, Mae-Ling and Lin-Chi rode up to the rooming house on the Laundry's buckboard. They had blankets and pillows in the back. Mae-Ling helped her father as he struggled to climb down off the seat.

They were met outside by Harley and Henry. Father and daughter bowed low and slowly to Harley and Henry, without speaking. The two men took their cues from Lin-Chi and did the same. Lin-Chi burst out laughing. "Oh, very good! Very nice from two such honorable gentlemen. Do so good for American man." Mae-Ling stood by smiling and shaking her head at the old man.

Lin-Chi was small, thin and stooped with age. His white hair was gathered into a pony tail in back. He wore a long, brown tunic that went to his knees. His short black pants were gathered and tied at his ankles just above the sandals he wore. He stood looking around. He didn't get to Denver much.

"OK, Papa, let's go see Gabriel," she said, grabbing onto his left elbow to help him navigate the uneven curb and walkway. They walked slowly up the four steps onto the porch and into the house. They entered the bright front room and stood for a moment waiting to be invited in or greeted. Henry and Harley came in after.

Henry called out, "Miss Daisy, our visitors are here." She was happy to meet them both. She didn't have much female companionship and she took to Mae-Ling right away. And she was exceptionally curious about Lin-Chi. Who was this strange little man from another world who was deemed so special, so different? So "'splicable", she smiled to herself. She tried not to be judgmental. After all, she had never heard a bad word spoken about him. Daisy wasn't used to company at all, except for business purposes once in a while. She tried to be a good hostess and offered tea. But Lin-Chi wanted to see Gabe.

"Of course, Lin-Chi," she said, rising from her seat. She reached out her hand to help him up. He smiled at her and the two of them went into the bedroom. Lin-Chi stood for a moment to adapt to the relative darkness of the room. Then he sat in the chair by the bed and gazed at Gabe. He put his old, bony fingers on Gabe's arm and squeezed gently. He looked into Gabe's eyes, which were open but vacant. He felt Gabe's chest with the palm of his hand. He used two fingers to feel Gabe's wrist. He breathed in deeply. By the time he looked up at Daisy to say something a tear was already trickling down his face. He opened his mouth to speak, said nothing and put his forehead down on Gabe's shoulder. He moved slightly and gently put his head against Gabe's head and whispered. Using the index and middle fingers of his left hand, he touched Gabe on his left cheek and temple.

Then he lifted his head again. He looked directly into Daisy's green eyes. She was immediately drawn deep into his gray eyes. She was amazed at how comfortable it was – she did not feel compelled to speak or look away. She felt a strong wave of bittersweet warmth wash over her. And she cried. But felt no shame in it as she had when she was a little girl. She didn't care what her hands were doing. They just hung at her sides. Then, she took a step towards Lin-Chi, leaned over and buried her head into his wrinkled old neck. And she sobbed. As she wept, she realized she wasn't just crying for Gabe anymore. It was for the horror of what had happened to him, yes. For the first time, she was really feeling it. But it was also for the horror of men doing such things to other men. It was for all the horror in all the world. Somehow Lin-Chi being there had allowed her this release. Or, was it because he wasn't there? It was so powerful as to be overwhelming.

When she could, she lifted her head and looked at Lin-Chi again. "Lin-Chi. Can you say? How can such things happen? How can men - ?"

"Daisy Wood - desire, anger, ignorance. Ignorance is worst - keep men craving, attached to things craved. All in service of desire, then bigger world forgot. Ignorance mean seek to satisfy craving, not knowing only cause more. Bigger and bigger hole made. Then, more and more bad things done. Hole not filled, just deeper. All come from same thing – not knowing - ignorance. Live in world but not see world."

Daisy kissed the top of Lin-Chi's head. "What can we do for Gabe? Can he come back to his friends?"

"Gabe still far away from friends. No one can say. We do best for him we can. I must take him. You can let him go, Daisy Wood?"

"Yes, Lin-Chi."

Henry, Harley, Lin-Chi and Mae-Ling settled Gabe into the back of the Laundry wagon. Daisy Wood said good-bye and immediately felt profoundly lonely. But she felt a curious new strength as well. She would go to Boulder as much as she could. She would talk more with Lin-Chi and she would learn, oh, she had so much to learn. And she would do whatever she could for Gabe. That was her plan.

But, of course, there was also work. So, she would also check in with the Chief and Leonard. And she would follow up on any new leads about the Triangle that had come into her office.

32

THE BEST CARE ANYWHERE

G abe's friends got him settled into his house. Doc Pierce and his daughter Melissa, Harley, Sheriff Taylor and Mae-Ling visited regularly. Henry moved in and became Gabe's primary caregiver. Lin-Chi spent most of his time sitting with Gabe. Then came the day that Harley brought Gabe's family back home to stay. Red, the redbone hound, John Henry and Tex all came into town on Harley's ranch wagon. Red sat on the seat next to Harley. John Henry and Tex were heard howling from inside a wooden box in back. Henry came out front when he heard the wagon roll up.

"Howdy, Henry," Harley called out as he reined in and set the brake. "I brought ya a whole new set o' problems t' deal with. 'course mebbe they'll turn out t' be the good kind."

Red started barking and jumped down. With tail wagging furiously, he headed straight for the open front door. Harley handed the wooden box down to Henry, who set it down and lifted the lid slightly.

"So, these here are the famous house varmints the man's so attached to. Hmmm. Well, I reckon ever'body's got t' 'ave somebody, even if they is furry little ones," Henry remarked. He gave a quick thought to his "buzzard" back at the cemetery.

Harley jumped down. "Yessir. Henry, these here are some precious cargo t' hear Gabe tell it, and so, I reckon they must be. And 'at ol' redbone is somethin' too. Fact is, I'm gonna miss th' lot of 'em, so I'll 'ave t' keep comin' by. These here might jus' be th' answer, you know. Even ol' Lin-Chi can't say it ain't."

The cats must have sensed they were home. They started to cry and whine until Harley stepped inside with the box and opened it up. When he got the top off, they sat there looking around, wildly sniffing the air.

"Well, I'll be damned, Henry. You'd a thought I was stranglin' these critters half t' death all the way int' town th' way they was kickin' up a fuss. Sounded like some kind o' death wail. Now look at 'em. They don't even get out! Gabe's only one has figgered these crazy things out. Or, jus' as likely, he gave up an' quit tryin'."

Tex sniffed the air again, then suddenly jumped out of the box and ran into the bedroom where Gabe lay in the bed. Lin-Chi sat in his usual spot, the far, dark corner. John Henry followed. But Red was already there, pushing on one of Gabe's limp hands with his wet muzzle.

"So happy see help coming," Lin-Chi said. He smiled broadly and reached down to pet Tex who was running in circles around the room. John Henry jumped up on the bed and landed on Gabe's stomach. Red started licking Gabe's face. Lin-Chi stood up and put his right hand on top of Gabe's head and petted John Henry with his left. Red was still licking and started to whine. His tail was wagging fast. Harley and Henry stood in the doorway.

Lin-Chi spoke quietly, "All right, Gabe. Time come home."

Gabe's eyes closed. They fluttered open and shut. They came open and even in the darkness of the room, all could see they were trying to focus – to focus and see.

Lin-Chi looked back at Henry. "Maybe have water, please." Henry disappeared into the kitchen and quickly brought back a glass full.

Gabe's eyes fluttered again. He looked into Lin-Chi's face. Then, he opened his mouth as if to speak. He croaked a barely audible, "Lin-Chi – whe - . . .?"

"Gabe, we home now. Your home. All house creature here. Friend here. No need speak." Lin-Chi nodded at Henry who handed him the glass. He motioned with his head to Harley, who came around the other side of the bed. He and Henry slowly, carefully lifted Gabe up on his pillows. Only then did Lin-Chi put the glass to Gabe's lips. "Here, you try, just little-little." Harley and Henry looked at each other and smiled. Gabe took a sip and Henry sighed with relief. The water dribbled down Gabe's chin and Red stuck his big tongue out and caught it before it could go any further.

"Red," Gabe rasped. "Red."

"Gabe, 'at's right, ol' Red 'ere at your service," Harley said.

"Ha – Harley," Gabe said. "Hi. Hi - Henry," he said. Every syllable was a struggle. John Henry stared at Gabe's face from his perch on his stomach, while Tex started to snuggle into Gabe's right ankle. "My - critters," Gabe said softly, showing the slightest glimmer of a smile. Just then, in a case of perfect timing, Melissa Pierce appeared in the doorway holding a tureen of hot broth.

Melissa and Harley shared a knowing smile as it was Melissa who woke Harley up from his dark space while trying to get him to take broth just a couple of years before. "Well, good. Good to see you up and ready for a little of my special cure-all broth, Gabriel. My father can only do so much," she said, looking around at all the men in the room, "and after that, it's up to me. Right, Harley?" she said, with a wink. Harley nodded in gratitude.

"With your permission, of course, Lin-Chi?"

"Oh, yes. Lin-Chi know special power Melissa broth," he bowed, smiling. Lin-Chi stood so she could sit next to Gabe. She carefully tested the temperature of the fine, brown liquid, then held a spoonful to Gabe's lips. He tried to slurp it. It went down onto the top of his bedclothes. Then, she held the back of his head up a little and told him, "Just open a very little bit, Gabe. I will spoon it in slowly, and you won't choke." They figured out how to do it and Gabe took in several spoonsful before he looked too exhausted to continue.

This was the start of Gabe's return. It would be painfully slow. But, at least, it was a start. As Gabe started to re-enter into his consciousness, he understood, even in his feeble and confused state, that he had a fine group of friends who he didn't want to let down. It was this care that helped offset in his mind the unspeakable horrors he endured at the hands of the Knights of the Golden Triangle.

33

DAISY COMES CALLING

Two weeks after Red and the cats came home, Dr. Pierce visited with the specific purpose of getting Gabe out of bed. When he entered the house, Gabe was sitting in his favorite chair by the fireplace. Red was by his side on the floor with his tail perilously close to the back of one of the rockers. John Henry purred in his lap. Gabe stroked the back of the big cat's head.

"Please – come in, Doc," Gabe said in his halting voice. He was still hoarse and hesitant in his speaking but had come a long way.

"Hi, Gabe, how're you feeling today?" Dr. Pierce asked, as he did every visit.

"Fine, Doc, fine," Gabe answered, as he always did.

"Well, Gabe I came to see if I could get you on your feet. It looks like Henry has already taken care of that detail. Can I see how you're doing standing and walking?"

"Henry and Lin-Chi, Doc. They insisted. Henry said - if I could make it - here, he might - pour me - rye."

"Ah, the power of motivation. Gabe, and I think you are out of laudanum. Do you need more?"

"No, Doc. Think – Lin-Chi help – with pain. No need."

"I think Dr. Lin-Chi is very good. Glad to have him on the case. Is there anything I can do at all?"

"Maybe Melissa – with – broth?"

"Good. Good. Yes. I will send her. She likes coming over here to see you, Gabe."

"Melissa broth – better than – Henry broth."

"Haha! Don't worry, your secret is safe with me," Dr. Pierce said, pleased that Gabe was regaining his old humor.

Gabe's days were spent laboring to get up, walking a short way and resting after the effort. And sitting with Lin-Chi or Henry and Red and the cats. But this day he had a new visitor. Daisy Wood came calling.

"Good morning, Gabe," she said through the half-open front door to announce herself. She used a sing-song, carefree voice that made Gabe smile. He called to her to come back into the bedroom where he was once again resting.

"And, finally, I get to meet the famous herd," she said, smiling and picking Tex up for a squeeze and a kiss. Gabe smiled.

"And – this one – here – John Henry," he said, indicating the cat snoozing on his belly. Old redbone – here," he said, pointing to the floor just beside the bed. "Thanks, Miss Daisy – for – coming to – see me."

"Gabe. You know me, don't you? I didn't know if you would. Coming to see you is my pleasure, Gabe. And I know with the care you're getting here, you'll be up and ready to work when it comes time. This is not just a social call. I have been getting telegrams indicating where those – what did Henry call them, scumbellies? – where they have been seen recently. And Avery Burke may have been sighted with them, too."

"Good," Gabe said, raising himself up on one elbow and dislodging the cat. Tex hit the floor with a thump. "Mebbe General Burke - survived then.

I think – I'm – ready – soon. Can't talk good – but – think I can – shoot. I – haven't finished job – it was important – to – Heck. And they - killed him. And Heck was my friend. Damn good friend."

They both noticed that Gabe lost his hesitancy when he spoke about Heck. Neither said anything. Gabe pushed himself up on his pillows. All of a sudden, he realized he was feeling self-conscious having a woman in his room. A white woman! Daisy noticed his nervousness. She asked him playfully, dipping her head to her right shoulder, "What's the matter, Gabe, don't you like having a woman in the house?"

Now he was hesitant again. Perhaps for - different reason. "Um, well, I don't know, Miss Daisy, I never – I mean, I guess - I never . . .'"

She laughed. "Oh, please, Gabe. What is it you don't know? You don't remember, do you? When you first came to see me in Denver, you were in bad shape. Oh, and dirty, too. Whew! Really dirty, actually, and still caked with old blood. Well, the first thing I had to do was give you a bath."

"What. I mean, a bath. Well, o' course - I reckon." He hesitated and his eyes widened. "You washed - face and arms. They were cut up some."

"Oh, now Gabe, you were dirty everywhere. Needed washing *everywhere*. Don't worry, Henry was there to help get you into the tub. And to make sure everything was done – you know, just right and proper, you might say."

"The - the tub?! Well, Miss Daisy, you mean t' tell me that you – you . . .?" He didn't know how to finish. Daisy burst out laughing.

"Hahaha! Gabe, I guess I saw as much as your Mama ever did. Hahaha! *And* scrubbed it all clean, too." She laughed again. Then, she settled into a giggle, seeing how shy and embarrassed this raw, tough man was. She had seen all his wounds as well as the old scars from whippings and beatings he was given as a child. She had gasped when she first saw his back. She had an idea of how tough his young life must have been. And now she was having fun at his expense. But only because she wanted to break down his tough veneer and get him to feel easier with her. "See now? I guess you shouldn't call me 'Miss Daisy' anymore, should you, Gabe? I know you too well. I'm just Daisy."

Gabe did feel like a heavy load of some kind had been lifted off him. He let out a long exhale. He let his eyes narrow just a bit. He smiled at her, openly and without reservation. Not as a black man to a white woman, but as a man to a woman. He felt that. He hoped she did, too.

"Daisy, I see you're totin' a new Army Colt. A .45? You like it?" Gabe asked, now feeling pleased with the conversation, but thinking it was time to change the subject, so he could avoid further embarrassment. He wanted to take everything slowly.

"I do, Gabe. I liked the seven and a half inch barrel, but I figured it might take a bit too long to pull out compared to my old one. This one's shorter. They're calling it a 'Peacemaker'. It shoots true and straight." She pulled it out quickly and smoothly and handed it to him butt first. He took it. "I hope we can go shooting soon and I can show you."

"I'd like that, Daisy. This gun feels good. Nice weight. And it's much prettier, I will admit, than m' trusty ol' .36."

"It's a good gun for sure. Depending on the man – or woman - ," she said with a big smile, "holding it. That Navy Colt may be a bit big for me. It would still be interesting to try it though. Now. How about I get you up into the chair out front? I brought sandwiches."

Gabe smiled. He hadn't felt this happy for, well, he couldn't remember. The feeling was familiar, but only in a nostalgic way, from something or someone in his dim and murky past. But for this moment at least, right now, he *was* happy. He had almost forgotten the feeling. And he didn't feel guilty about it either. Gabe would not soon forget this day.

As it turned out, it was the first of many happy days. Daisy started visiting Boulder every week. The two of them shared meals, talked about their lives, and when Gabe was able, took short rides into the countryside. At first, they went to shoot. After a while, they would sometimes just ride or walk and talk. It didn't take long before they each became acutely aware of how much joy they felt in each other's company. They had gradually and inadvertently become closer to each other than either was to anyone else. They both came to understood this. But it seemed like it had to remain unspoken. No matter how much they might try to deny it, they carried with them the intolerance of their culture in ways that did not even rise to the level of consciousness. Neither tried to predict where their relationship would take them. There was just a vague hope that somehow it could last in a dangerous and intolerant world.

34

EMERGENCE

When Gabe was finally able, in the Spring of 1875, he started riding to Denver. And since Gabe was getting out more, and it didn't look to others like he needed daily nursing, people started to talk. The people of Boulder were like many who had come west at that time. They were escaping from their past or were trying to imagine a new future. They believed everyone should mind his or her own business and folks could prosper together. As long as they were not hurting anyone, the West was a place to grow, be yourself and live your own life – the best way you could.

But there would always be a noisy minority. People who did meddle in other people's business, maybe because they wanted to forget their own failures, or because they figured they could make up for their disappointments by bringing others down to their level. And so, Gabe started to hear rumors. Believing it was in Gabe's best interest, Henry reported on things he was hearing, too. That way, Henry thought, Gabe could be ready for trouble. Based on the life Henry had lived and the affliction he'd seen, he always expected trouble. It was for that reason he always carried a clean, loaded gun.

Gabe had come to rely on carrying a sidearm as far back as the war. Of course, he couldn't get away with that when he was living in St. Louis. Like he had told Billy and Harley when he first met them, "Funny, most folks aroun' here don't cotton t' colored folks totin' guns aroun'."

He had renewed his practice of keeping his Colt with him as soon as he and Harley and Billy headed west. More recently, shooting with Daisy had not only brought back his old ability but had caused him to decide to order a new pistol. He received his new seven and a half inch Army Colt .45 by freight delivery in April. By that time Billy was back in town, and just like in the "old days", Gabe, Billy and Harley rode out into the countryside, exploring and camping.

But Gabe wanted to be ready for the trouble he felt was inevitable. So, now they also practiced shooting like they used to do, so he could get used to the new gun. Billy, who had learned fast-draw gunfighting from the great Jeb Baker, from whom Gabe had adopted his last name, worked with Gabe. Gabe and Harley could shoot better than anyone he'd ever come across with the long gun, but Billy was the fastest with the Colt. Gabe had heard multiple times of how after Billy had blamed himself for his friend getting shot in West Virginia, he had decided to learn. Billy's first idea was that if he just drew his gun 10,000 times, he would get fast. He drew and counted, without actually firing, over the course of several weeks. But then, when they arrived in St. Louis in 1866, Billy and Harley took lessons from Jeb Baker out on Bloody Island. And so, like some nine years earlier, on some of the friends' trips into the countryside, they would take bottles. After several such trips Gabe had managed the trick that Jeb had told Billy meant he was ready to head west. Harley held the empty bottle at arm's length, waist high, and dropped it. Gabe drew and shot it before it hit the ground.

"And with that big, long Peacemaker o' yours, too, Gabe," Harley said, with a smile. "Damn!"

"Your namesake would be proud, Gabe," Billy told him. "The fact is, I hope you never have to use that draw. Eventually, we'll have enough law around here we won't even have to carry these damn things around with us."

"For now, I reckon it's a good idea," Harley chimed in.

"Yessir. I believe you're right," Billy said.

"But I do hope t' see th' day, Billy," Gabe said.

Gabe bided his time. He knew he was not ready yet to get back out on the trail and complete Heck's mission, which he also considered to be his now. Daisy updated him on all reported sightings of the Confederates. So, he was also waiting on some solid information upon which he could rely to pack up and leave. Meantime, his old boss at the Red Rock Flour Mill welcomed him back for as much work as he could manage.

On a Friday afternoon in May, Gabe met Billy and Harley at O'Neill's for an after-work whiskey. They stood at the bar talking and laughing. It was like old times, the three "desperadoes" together. Only now, Billy Forest was a respectable attorney, Harley Cobb a thriving horse rancher and Gabe Baker a "secret service agent", though just now on hiatus.

As they settled into their drinks, Billy started to regale his friends with a story of his recent trial in Colorado City. But soon enough, he couldn't help but notice, Gabe was no longer listening. Gabe had thrown down a shot and set his glass on the bar when he started staring at two men who had just walked into the dark saloon.

One of the men was younger, of medium build and height and wore a Confederate kepi. The other was Colonel William Fletcher, formerly of the Confederate Army and currently a Knight of the Golden Triangle.

As soon as they entered the room, they both glared at Gabe. Colonel Fletcher looked like he wanted to speak. But he stood still, clearly shaken by what he saw before him. Gabe was surprised, too, but automatically put his hand on the butt of his Colt and squeezed while his eyes locked onto those of Colonel Fletcher.

"What's th' matter, Fletcher, you look like you seen a ghost?" Gabe asked.

"Colonel, you know this boy?" the younger one asked. Fletcher gave a slight nod, still trying to assess the situation.

Harley and Billy had no way of knowing the history between Gabe and Fletcher, but it was obvious to Billy that he should find an opening to de-escalate. Harley, being Harley, didn't do that. He just drew his gun and pointed it at the newcomers. Gabe looked sideways at his friends. "No, boys. This is mine. You can see it's mine."

Billy looked at Harley, who nodded and said, "All right," as they moved farther down the bar. Harley holstered his gun, but kept his hand close to it.

"Your white friend there's a little short on conversation, ain't he, boy? Glad to see you got some sense, though," the younger man said. Gabe kept his right elbow on the bar, in a relaxed fashion in spite of his pounding heart. Harley looked at Billy when he heard that word "boy", like he was about to explode. Billy made a palms-down gesture to him, wanting to keep him out of it for as long as he could.

The two men squared up next to each other, facing Gabe. Colonel Fletcher glanced over to his shorter friend, and said, "You know somethin', Beau, I bet Gabe here's the one's takin' up with that pretty little white gal down in Denver. You hear 'bout that? Everybody's talkin'. I don't think that's legal. It *sure* ain't right."

"I'm almost sure of it, Colonel," Beau said, with a slimy, sideways smile. "Maybe we should make a citizen's arrest."

"You two rabble got bus'ness with me, state it," Gabe said, "otherwise, let it be so's I can continue on with more important bus'ness – like whiskey drinkin' with m' friends here."

"See now, Beau, he always was a sassy one," the Colonel said. Then he looked back at Gabe, "Well, Mister, here's our business. We don't allow black boys takin' up with white women down where we're from. And so now we figure to do somethin' about that up here, don't we Beau?" the Colonel said.

"Do it," Gabe said. "But just remember last time, Fletcher."

Beau drew his gun with a rough, jerking motion. Gabe pulled his Peacemaker out and cocked it in one smooth, quiet motion. He fired twice before

Beau was able to clear leather. Two .45 slugs slammed into the middle of his chest, his gun dropping back into its holster. He fell backwards in a heap, one leg at an awkward angle. Gabe was able to fire twice because Fletcher was even slower. So slow, in fact, that Gabe stood with his Peacemaker aimed at the Colonel's face while the Colonel still struggled to get his pistol out. The Colonel sighed and didn't bother raising it once he got it out. He stood with it in his hand hanging by his side while he blinked at Gabe and looked down on the floor at his dead partner. His shoulders slumped, but he still glared at Gabe.

"Well," Gabe said in a relaxed tone, "are you gonna raise that pistol up or drop it an' sing us a verse o' 'Marchin' through Georgia'? You got experience with this sort o' thing. I jus' bet you know what the smart thing'd be."

The Colonel let go and the heavy gun hit the wooden floor with a thud. He slowly raised his hands. "Now what, Gabe? You just gonna shoot me down here in front of all these people?"

"Thinkin' on it." Gabe held the Colt steady. He looked over his shoulder at his friends and Isaac the barkeeper, who was now standing with them at the other end of the room, and said, "What d' you think, boys? You gonna complain t' the law if'n I put a hole in this – uh, this here - "

"Skunk?" Harley pitched in.

"Yellowbelly?" Isaac offered.

"Miscreant!" Billy added.

"Yeah, 'at's right. All them, an' 'specially 'at last one, 'at 'mis-*cre*-ant'," Gabe said. "I like th' sound o' that one."

"No, I reckon you should do what comes nat'ral, Gabe. I mean, 'e's yours now," Harley said.

Gabe nodded and turned his attention back to Fletcher. "I'd be wantin' some straight answers from you, Fletcher. Or you gon' be a *ex*-Knight. You know what I'm sayin'? Such as, the where'bouts of our ol' friend Shemp Lee."

"I'm sure I don't know."

"You damn fool enough t' come walkin' in here with 'at belt buckle and kepi boy here an' then tell me you don't know nothin'?" Gabe growled. He cocked his gun and glared.

"All right, all right, I'm just goin' to put my hands down," the Colonel said, now regaining his composure. Gabe let the hammer down slowly on his Colt and let the gun slip back into its holster. He crossed his arms.

"All right, Colonel. We're gon' be all friendly like now, is 'at it? Go ahead. Shemp Lee?" Gabe said, with a quick nod.

"Well, I guess I might know where they were some time back," he started. He held his hands out, palms up, apparently trying to be convincing. "I do think I - " and as he appeared to be gesturing he stuck his right hand behind his vest, drew and cocked a Derringer. Gabe pulled his Colt out again and shot him in his right shoulder, knocking him down and sending the little gun skittering across the floor towards the front door.

"Damn," the Colonel muttered, as he lay on his side and put his left hand over the new hole in his shoulder. "Damn."

Gabe stood over him with his Colt still smoking. "How many damn times I gotta put lead in you, you don't stop shootin' at me, Fletcher? You wanna talk now?"

"You dirty son-of-a-bitch. I don't have to say anything to the likes of you. And you don't you have the guts to shoot me again – not in front of all these people here."

"Well, I reckon you're right, that's where we're diff'rent," Gabe said. "'course, I could give you some o' what your boys gave me over in St. Louie." Fletcher's eyes widened. "No, no, you just turn me over to the law. You got law here, right?"

"Don' worry, Fletcher, wouldn' wanna muss up your hair none," Gabe said. He holstered his gun. Billy walked over beside him, Harley following.

"Let's take this poor fool down to Sheriff Taylor's. He can give him over to the U.S. Marshal if he wants," Billy said. "The federals will definitely want him. Could be on a treason charge, too, an' 'at's a hangin' offense, right, Billy?"

"Yep, shouldn't be too hard to make, from what you've told me," Billy answered.

"All right, Billy," Gabe said, now in a somber mood. "An' then I'll let Agent Wood know we got one of 'em in jail here – another one down t' Mr. Dankworth's."

35

THE COLONEL IN JAIL

Daisy Wood and U.S. Marshal Tompkins met Gabe and Sheriff Taylor at the Boulder jailhouse mid-morning two days later.

"Well, here he is," Sheriff Taylor said to Daisy and Tompkins, showing them back to the cells. "A little worse for the wear, you might say, after Gabe was done with him, but good enough he can answer questions. If he's of a mind to, of course."

"And he's not of a mind to," the prisoner said, as they walked in. The Colonel was sitting on his bunk leaning against the cell's brick wall. He looked up at Gabe, who was bringing up the rear of the group. "And keep that black son-of-a-bitch away from me."

"Why, Colonel Fletcher, that's no way t' speak t' the man who saved your life, is it?" Gabe said.

"Saved my – what are you talkin' about boy, save my life? You shot me!"

"Colonel, I shot you in the shoulder. Good thing you're so slow, I had time t' pick my spot. That way you can finally be of use t' somebody. Just talk to the nice lady and the Marshal. 'Course, you don't wanna talk, you ain't much use. I can always finish the job."

"Keep that son-of-a-bitch away from me!" the Colonel said again, pushing back up against the wall.

"Well, Colonel," Daisy said with the sweetest smile, "I don't know if we *can* keep that son-of-a-bitch away from you. Or you from him. How many times has he shot you now? You're luckier than you are smart. You just keep coming back for more. Maybe if you answer some questions . . . and the answers sound right. Maybe we can do something." She looked at Gabe and winked.

"You'd do best to listen to the lady, Colonel. If she's satisfied with your information, I'll let the U.S. Attorney know and he may give you a break. Maybe even a choice. Jail or rope," Marshal Tompkins said with a slight Texas drawl. The U.S. Marshal was an imposing figure, some six inches taller than the average man, with broad shoulders, swept-back black hair and moustache, impeccably dressed. He wore a beige, wide-brimmed cattleman's hat that made him seem even larger. The Colonel seemed to take note of what he was saying.

"Maybe I can do you one better, Marshal. You let me out of here, I can get back to my boys. Then they won't come in here to this nice, friendly little town and turn it completely upside down bustin' me out of here. I can assure you they have the firepower to do it. How's that?"

"Sounds like a threat, Marshal," Daisy said, smiling at him and crossing her arms.

"Mebbe empty one at that. This jasper an' 'is part-, er, former partner, put together don't look like much t' be comin' after," Gabe said.

"I believe you may be right, Gabe," the Marshal said.

"All right, then, Marshal. Maybe the Secret Service wants its General Burke back. How about that?"

"A trade? Sounds like an admission to a kidnapping, too," the Marshal said, glancing over at Daisy. "Just what makes you so important that that gang of thieves of yours would want to trade Burke for you?"

"Yeah, a healthy general for a banged-up colonel with a hole in him? Don't hardly seem fair," Gabe said. Daisy and the Marshal smiled.

"Don't be too sure about 'healthy' there, Mister. And they'd do anything to him if I told 'em," Fletcher said. "And as for my value? Fact is, and Gabe knows it, General Lee is not in the best of health. We could make a deal."

"And what are you proposing, exactly, Colonel?" Daisy asked.

"Easy. You send the telegram I dictate, using my exact words, to where I tell you, and wait for a response. We'll just have a couple of the boys bring the General along and make the trade right here, maybe just outside of town," Fletcher said, rubbing his sore shoulder. "You just send me walkin', they send Burke walkin', I'm under your guns until we make the switch. You try to follow us after, maybe I'll have some more boys waitin' on the trail for you. You don't try to follow, and you've got nothin' to lose."

"Well, Colonel, I doubt it. You see, we just don't have much reason to trust you," Daisy said. She turned away from the prisoner. "Are we done here?" she asked of her friends. Not another word was spoken. They walked out, Sheriff Taylor shutting the big wooden door to the cells with a heavy thud.

Daisy Wood sent a telegram to the Chief, now located in Washington, D.C. Avery Burke was important to the Service as well as a good boss to her. But she wanted approval for a trade. Thinking ahead, she also inquired into the possibility of getting some backup from the Army. Fort Wallace in Kansas looked like a good source. While she was thinking of how to use the trade to catch the whole lot of the Knights and recover the gold, Fletcher was thinking how to use it to kill as many lawmen and Yankees as possible. Daisy and Gabe knew that. It would be nice to have the Army on their side.

After agreeing on the language, Fletcher had Daisy send the telegram to Cheyenne. It simply requested that General Lee send two soldiers with Avery Burke to a field some two miles out of town. If they were willing to make the trade, it would have to be done within four weeks. When they arrived with Burke, one would ride into town to alert the Sheriff. The Sheriff and one other rider would be allowed to go back out to the field to make the exchange.

The Secret Service knew enough of the Knights' intentions to believe they were headed to Mexico to execute the first stage of their plan. They would establish a base of operations somewhere along the east coast, taking advantage of the instability of Mexico's Lerdo government, at that time being constantly harassed by rival Porfirio Diaz. It appeared that Fletcher directing that his message be sent north to Cheyenne was a ruse to keep the Service off the scent of the Triangle. Still, Fletcher wanted out, so his message must have been calculated to reach someone he could trust to send it along to Shemp Lee. The telegram was addressed to "Jeff Davis".

Gabe and Harley would ride to Cheyenne before the telegram was sent, and then stake out the telegraph shop to see who retrieved the message. When they reached the city, Harley's mind wasn't so much on their mission as it was on seeing the young woman with whom he had fallen in love some three years earlier. He knew she would still be waiting for him. He knew she was allowing him all the time he needed to get over the trauma of the murder of his beloved young wife, Isabelle. But Harley also knew he was there, in Cheyenne, for Gabe this time. And the telegraph operator remembered how Harley had gunned down Jake McConnell and Black Bear Parker back then, three years earlier. That made him eager to help.

The two friends found a convenient, if shabby, room across the street from the shop. The operator agreed to signal them from his front window. One would be watching at all times. Mid-morning, their second full day in Cheyenne, Gabe saw a lantern being placed in the window. The two of them walked out the front door of their boarding house as nonchalantly as they could manage. Such was the arrogance of the Golden Triangle that the young man collecting the telegram wore a Confederate forage cap and the golden triangle on his belt buckle.

Harley walked into the office, while Gabe kept an eye on the Knight. "Mornin' Hans," he said, as he looked around to see if they were alone.

"Goot morgan, Harley. Ja, that was your man, just leafing. He takes der telegram but does not send der response. I tink he low level man. Needs talking mit somevon else. He comes each day, never gets telegram. Today he is excited."

"I think you're right, Hans, thank-you, see y' soon," Harley said as he stepped outside, breathing deeply of the sweet early summer air.

"He just walked up that way towards the depot," Gabe said. "'ppeared to be in a hurry." They turned the corner just in time to see the man disappear into a two-story brick building directly across from the depot on Sixteenth Street. Gabe waited on the street while Harley went in. Harley found the office where the man had gone and listened from outside. He couldn't tell what was being said, but from the tone of the voices knew when the man was about to leave. He hurried down the stairs and he and Gabe found a door-way to back into just in time to hide from the man. Then, they followed. Sure enough, he went straight back to the telegraph office. After he left, they went in to see Hans.

"Ja, ja, here is message. But no telling how you get it. Big trouble for Hans if you do," he said, peering over the top of his wire-rimmed glasses. "Make promise?"

"Promise," Harley said.

"Promise," Gabe said. "Until you say different. See, someday, mebbe you're gonna be a hero for helpin' us like this."

"Haha. Hans no want hero. Just regular pay," he said.

Gabe and Harley looked the telegram over. It was a copy of the one sent to Cheyenne, but with an added request for more men, to stay back and out of sight. Their real interest was where it was sent. It was addressed to "Gen. Lee, Santa Fe Telegraph Office." Gabe immediately wired Daisy. He and Harley would head back home as soon as the message was sent. They both needed to be in on the plans for the prisoner exchange. Harley was heartsick. But he had no choice. He promised himself he would ride back to see Maddy Hayes as soon as Gabe's troubles were over.

36

THE COLONEL OUT OF JAIL

The day of the prisoner exchange came after much planning and specu-lation. At mid-morning on a fine, cloudless August day, a rider broke the usual placid feel of downtown Boulder, charging down Pearl Street on a big, brown Morgan. Thundering hooves scattered dogs and pedestrians, leaving behind curses muffled in a cloud of dust. The muscular horse was well-lathered, and blew and shook his head as its rider reined in in front of the Sheriff's office. Sheriff Taylor heard the commotion and stepped outside in time to see the young rider pull up. He quickly sent the boy who cleaned the jailhouse to get Gabe.

"Mornin', soldier boy," Taylor said casually, leaning forward with two hands on the hitch post. "You appear to be in some kind of a hurry. Appreciate it if you'd keep it under control here in town." He couldn't help noticing that the rider was dressed in the old Confederate "butternut" style, highlighted by a short-waisted coat with gold-colored buttons, black cotton shirt and jean-cloth trousers. He had a war-era Springfield rifle in his saddle scabbard and wore an older Army Colt on his hip. He appeared too young to have fought in the war, but sometimes a man couldn't tell. Towards the end, especially, the Grays were sending young boys out into the field.

"Corporal! You can call me Corp'ral Pyle," the young man declared in a deep southern drawl. "I'm here to pick up two riders for the trade. Two only," the young man said in a deeper voice and with a practiced air of authority.

"All right, then Corporal, you just stand by, my other man is on the way with the horses, and I'll be gettin' your Colonel out of the lockup. You can call me Sheriff Taylor."

Taylor went back into the cells and unlocked Fletcher's cell. "Well, Colonel, it looks like this is your lucky day. It's bright, sunny and warm, and you've got an eager young corporal out front says he came to fetch you out of here. We got all the outfit you came with and your horse is on the way. I took $20.00 out of your bags to pay your livery bill. Oh, and eight dollars to plant your friend Beau. You can leave another $20.00 if you want a stone." He waited for a response. "No? Didn't think so. The rest of your money's still there. Come on, let's go."

"I'll be glad to be shut of this place, Taylor," Fletcher said. "Bad grub, bad coffee, boring company. I do wish I was back in Dixie where the folks have a passin' knowledge of the social graces," the Colonel said.

"So do I, Colonel, so do I," Taylor said as he grabbed a pair of handcuffs off the top of his desk.

Gabe appeared at the front door. "Them social graces include praisin' the Lord on Sunday an' beatin' folks half t' death on Monday, Fletcher?"

"Oh, no, this damn darky isn't goin' with us," Fletcher growled.

"You can get back in the cell if you want, Colonel. Breakfast is in half an hour. Or, you can stick your hands out so I can put these cuffs on and we'll be on our way. Which'll it be?" Taylor said, growing impatient.

"Cuffin' me wasn't part of the deal, Taylor."

"Like I said, breakfast in a half hour. Your favorite, Colonel – biscuits and cold gravy, beans and ham." Fletcher stuck his hands out and Taylor locked them up tight.

Fletcher walked out into the sunshine, eyes squinting, trying to focus on the young "corporal". Taylor watched but didn't see any sign of recognition. He walked behind Fletcher with his Winchester. U.S. Marshal Tompkins arrived just in time to watch over the process. Fletcher looked at him warily, then acknowledged him with a slight nod.

Gabe brought up Fletcher's horse. "This 'un's ever' bit as skittish as the one I rode down t' your hole in th' ground, Colonel. You remember – your cave? Mebbe senses danger, eh, Colonel? Or, mebbe more'n likely horses just don' like you. You know where th' term 'horse sense' come from, right?" He laughed out loud at his own joke.

The young corporal looked shocked. He'd never heard a black man speak to one of his superior officers that way. He opened his mouth, then thought better of it. He remembered his mission. He saluted Colonel Fletcher. "General says we got to show up by noon. Meet at the field ever'body agreed to. With your permission, Colonel?"

Colonel Fletcher returned the salute, but it was Gabe who spoke up. "Jus' so's y' know, Corporal, your Colonel ain't in charge on this ride. 'e's still Sheriff Taylor's prisoner until we make th' exchange. This here's his party 'til that 'appens, so you better listen good when 'e's talkin'. Somethin' don't look right, sound right, smell right, Colonel's gonna get shot afore anythin' else 'appens. I've done it twice, I'm willin' to do it again. You understand?" The boy turned red with anger, pulling at his Springfield without thinking. Gabe swung the barrel of his Henry over to hit him on his jaw. He went down off his horse, landing on his backside on the street, now thoroughly humiliated. None of the adults said a thing for a full minute as they watched him get up and brush off. Then, Taylor looked at Fletcher with raised eyebrows.

"I see you're a good soldier, young man," the Colonel said. "I won't forget. But, for right now, let's be patient. We can always set things right some other time."

Corporal Pyle looked up at him, dusted himself off some more and revealed a slight, unpleasant smile.

Gabe rode up beside Taylor, and said in a hushed tone, "Did y' catch 'at, Sheriff? Sound like some kind o' mischief in th' works, all right. Like we figgered. I 'speckt Daisy's on the job other side o' Valmont by now."

The four men rode silently at a moderate pace for most of an hour. They passed by Valmont Butte east of town and then slowed when they approached the field at old Fort Chambers. They were just on the northeastern edge of Valmont. Sheriff Taylor held up his right hand in a signal for the riders to stop behind him. The group stopped and sat quietly while the horses stepped nervously. He looked in every direction, for anything that didn't seem normal, or for any kind of movement.

Gabe sidled up to Taylor, and said softly, "Sheriff, there's a signal mirror flashin' up on the Butte. We been spotted and whatever their plan is, they must be gettin' it ready."

Taylor thanked him. "I wouldn't be surprised if we were just about surrounded by now, Gabe. Sure hope Daisy and her group are on the job this mornin'," he said.

Gabe scratched his chin as he looked over at the two Knights. They weren't talking, but the Corporal was nodding towards the trees. Gabe said, "They seem t' want this Fletcher pretty bad. I'd think they wouldn' start nothin' 'til we get 'im off his horse an' walkin' an' mebbe out o' range." Then he saw some movement towards the agreed-upon site. "There, Sheriff!" He pointed. There were at least four men standing just inside a copse of large cottonwoods, partially shaded. Two of them quickly stepped back into the dark.

The air was still and silent. The usual chirping and warbling of songbirds here where Boulder and South Boulder Creeks met was absent. The usual quacking and honking of waterfowl was also noticeably missing. The unnatural silence triggered something in Gabe. He knew what the feeling meant. He braced himself. Please, not now. Please. He felt it. He immediately thought of Lin-Chi. He saw a quick image of the old man's gap-toothed smile, and heard his simple words of wisdom: "always do what is right in front of you. If your mind is clear you will know what it is." Gabe's mind cleared. The cannon that had already started to roar in his mind just as quickly started to recede. He was where he needed to be.

He glanced over at Sheriff Taylor, who was looking at him. "Gabe, you all right?"

"Yessir. I am now." Gabe pointed to the spot he knew they were supposed to start Fletcher walking.

"Yep, that looks right, Gabe," he said. Then, turning to Corporal Pyle, he said, "All right, Corporal, it's your time now. Go ahead and ride on over to your side. And tell them nothing's happening until they get General Burke out into the sun where we can see him." Pyle didn't acknowledge the order, but started out across the meadow.

The meeting place was well-selected by both sides. They each stood at the edge of the meadow, cottonwoods behind them. They were about 50 yards apart. The group slowed-walked their horses close to the spot when Sheriff Taylor ordered a dismount. They could see the two men on the other side of the meadow, but hadn't seen Avery Burke yet. Gabe got his field glass out for a closer look. Pyle was riding slowly.

"All right, Sheriff," Gabe said. They're givin' the signal." They waited until Pyle made it back behind the two men showing themselves. He disappeared into the shadows. Gabe looked back at the butte again.

"Damn, Sheriff. Look!" he pointed. The gleaming barrel of a Confederate field piece was now visible just over the lip of the cliff. "A 12-pounder. Th' way things look, we're about t' fight the next battle o' the war between th' states."

"What can they hit with that thing, Gabe?" Taylor asked. Fletcher stood by, listening.

"Sheriff, th' way they got that barrel elevated, it looks like they'd be shootin' at somewhere around downtown Longmont. I don' know what they think they're doin'. It'd be damn hard t' drop a ball down on us here." Fletcher frowned. Gabe saw that. "Fletcher, what you think, your boys know what they're doin'? Hahaha!" Just then, while they were looking, the cannon disappeared behind the edge of the precipice.

"Well, mebbe, they figgered it out, Fletcher," Gabe said.

The Knights on the other side of the meadow were now yelling, "Send him! Send him!"

Sheriff Taylor yelled back. "When we see our man!" Then he turned to Fletcher. "Colonel, you'd want to listen real careful now, your life might depend on it. Once we send you, if I say 'stop', you stop right now. When I say 'walk' you walk slow. If it doesn't look like you and the General are going to meet at about the halfway point because you're too fast, I'm going to yell stop. If you don't stop I'll stop you with this," he said, shaking his Winchester up and down. "I'm leavin' the cuffs on you and puttin' the key down your boot, you can take 'em off when you're done walkin'." He turned to Gabe. "Gabe, you got anything?"

"Thanks, Sheriff. Just this. Colonel, I'm a crack shot with this Henry. It'll surely be aimed at your back until you get to the other side. You remember. Okay, Sheriff."

Sheriff Taylor cupped his hands around his mouth and yelled, "All right, let's see the General!"

The two visible Knights looked behind them. One of them grabbed a man's arm, and pushed him forward, into the light.

Gabe looked through his glass. "Sheriff, I can't tell. I can't tell if that's Burke. Looks like the right size, and I'd say that's 'is hat, but that hat is pulled down so low I can't see 'is face. It's mighty concernin', I'd say."

"Ye-eah," Taylor drew the word out, scratching his chin. Then he yelled out, "Take the man's hat off, for Christ's sake! Get it off." Gabe watched through the glass. The two men were talking. One of them took the hat off and held it in front of him.

"Sheriff. That ain't Burke," Gabe said under his breath.

"Damn!" He turned towards the Colonel. "Well, Fletcher, looks like you'd be on your way back for a late breakfast. And trial. And then a rope after that."

Fletcher looked down at the ground, thinking. Then he raised his head. "Sheriff, let me walk halfway out, let me talk to 'em. What have you got to lose? I'll still be under your guns."

"What the hell good would that do?" Taylor shouted. He was getting impatient. "If they had Burke and they wanted to trade, he'd be standin' right there in front of us right now."

"I can find out what's happening," Fletcher said, unconvincingly.

"We know what's happening. They don't have Burke, they probably killed him a long time ago. You probably knew that before you proposed the trade. Now, they're stallin' for time to get around behind us. Get on your horse."

"You're not going to say anything to them?" Fletcher asked.

"What for," Taylor said, more as a statement than a question.

Fletcher yelled out to his comrades, "They're taking me back! There's just two of them!"

"Hold up over there! Hold it! We got Burke. Look. Here he is!" shouted a voice from the shadows.

The Sheriff squinted. "Gabe?"

"Sheriff, he don't look so good. Lost weight. But, yeah, I'd say this one is Burke. I guess they wanted both ends o' that trade. Also means they aren't too worried 'bout us bein' disappointed."

"You sons-o'-bitches try one more trick and your Colonel don't make it," Gabe cried out. He sighed and said, "Sheriff, it's your call. You willin' to try again?"

Taylor looked at Fletcher and then said to Gabe, "Yeah, I am so damned tired of listenin' to this dandified, pampered jackass complainin' down at the jail, I'm willin' to try just about anything."

"Don't make another mistake," Taylor yelled out to the other side. "Start your man!" He nodded at Gabe, who poked the barrel of his Henry into the Colonel's kidney hard to make him wince and get him started. "Remember the rules, Fletcher," he said with a slight, unfriendly smile. "Stop means stop."

General Burke started from his side with a few tentative steps. Gabe advised Fletcher, "Go. Move slow." Each side was ensuring its man was moving at the same pace as the other's. They walked self-consciously, each knowing he had guns trained on his back. Ten yards, twenty yards, then at the halfway point. As they approached each other, they stopped.

"Mornin' Fletcher," the General said.

"Hello Burke. Let's see now. Been some 22-23 years now, hasn't it? West Point, '52?"

"Sounds right. What the hell happened to you? You following a man like Shemp Lee? There was a time, long, long ago, you were respectable. Now, you're following a man who is a coward, a weasel, a charlatan and a drunk. You do see that, don't you, Fletcher?"

"Of course, I see it. He had the plan. He has the name. He's not going to last forever."

Gabe and Sheriff Taylor looked at each other. "Sheriff, what the hell is goin' on? Looks like some kind o' reunion."

"I don't know, Gabe. Must have known each other in another life."

Burke said, "Like I said, what the hell happened to you? I've been hog-tied, chained and half-starved by your so-called Knights, Fletcher. And while that was happening, I heard a lot. I know what they did to my man Gabe. You will die for that."

"That's not likely, Burke. Neither you nor your men scare me a bit," he lied. He couldn't help think of Gabe's Henry aimed at his back. Then he added, "By the way, your man Gabe came out all right. He's standin' right behind me with his Henry pointed at my back."

"In that case, sir, you'd be a fool not to be scared," Burke said. He tipped his hat and started walking again, now smiling at the news and straining to see Gabe. Fletcher started as well. They each made it to the end of their walk. Then a shot rang out.

37

SHOOTING AT THE BUTTE

No one on either side of the meadow knew who had fired. It sounded like it came from behind and to the east of the Knight position at the end of the meadow. Gabe and Henry knew there were more men on the Confederate side than had shown themselves. And there was enough on the butte to shoot that cannon. They also knew that Daisy Wood was supposed to be in the vicinity, and they further hoped she had with her a sizeable contingent from Fort Wallace. Besides Daisy, they would be backed up by Billy, Harley and Old Henry.

The Confederates knew there must be more men on the other side, too. None of the principals in the prisoner exchange itself could be certain of details, but they all could figure there were armed men all around. It was a dangerous situation.

It had been 11 years since soldiers had fired shots in or around Fort Chambers, Colorado. Then, it was a training exercise and shots rang out and echoed off the butte all day long. Company D of the Third Colorado Cavalry had mobilized and started preparing for what was to become the horrific attack on the peaceful Cheyenne and Arapaho village at Sand Creek. This time, just a single shot was heard. But it was an ominous sound because it was heard by an unknown number of battle-hardened men who were armed and ready to kill or be killed. Once the shooting started, it would be hard to stop unless and until one side either had a clear victory or abandoned the field.

Sheriff Taylor decided he would take one last chance at preventing bloodshed. He yelled out even as he heard the sound of riders coming up hard behind him. "Rebs! That shot came from your side. We don't need to restart the war here today. Mount up and ride while you have the chance!" There was no response.

Taylor had no idea if his bravado was justified, but he would deem it so when the approaching riders turned out to be Billy, Harley and Henry. When they pulled in their reins they dismounted quickly in the cloud of dust they had just rode in on.

"Good morning, gentlemen," Taylor said, turning and smiling at them. "Your timing's good, there may be some fireworks any minute now. Damn good to see you."

"Wouldn' miss it for th' world, Sheriff," Harley said, nodding to Gabe.

Henry strode over to Gabe and grabbed his arm while shaking his hand. "Whatever 'appens here today, friend, I jus' wanna thank ya for bringin' me along." He winked at Taylor, and turning to spit, let go a nice, long stream of black juice. "I'm ready," he pronounced.

Billy said, "Sheriff, we just came out on the Valmont road, there was quite a bit of activity off to our left, I'd say 50 yards or so – excited voices and horses snorting and stamping. Saw some gray. They certainly weren't ours. We need to either move or set up some kind of rear guard."

"Thanks, Billy. That means we're about to be surrounded. We're kind of hopin' Miss Wood is not too far off. You see any blue?"

"No sir. What's our move?" Billy asked.

"We have a general here now," Taylor said. Burke and Gabe were off to the side, talking. "General, I'm Sheriff Taylor of Boulder. How are you, sir?" Taylor called out.

"Fair to midlin', considering what I've been through. Thanks for bailing me out. But now we've got a new problem to deal with. I'd say there were some 20 soldier boys with us riding here, and there were more behind that they didn't want me knowing about. But damn! This is our chance to get Shemp Lee and maybe even that gold! Where's Daisy? Is she here?"

"General, we don't know. She was to be here in the area this morning, we hoped with some men from Fort Wallace," Taylor said.

"If she said she'd be here, she's here," Burke answered. "And to answer your real question, Sheriff, yes I'm in good enough shape to take command here. First thing we need to do is have someone get some high ground and do the reconnaissance necessary for us to know where all those damned rebels are. Then, at least we'll know where to dig in, if we have to."

"I'm on it, Gen'ral, I got a glass. I'm goin' up the butte, be right back."

"Gabe. Gabe!" Taylor yelled out. That cannon crew is still - " He was too late. Gabe was gone.

There was no sense in moving around now with the possibility that hostile guns were setting up all around them. They picketed the horses, organized their ammunition and set up behind what little cover they had, watching in all directions. And they kept their eyes on the butte. Taylor, who was familiar with the trail up the back side, told Burke, "If he doesn't run into trouble and takes five minutes to look around, best case is he'll be back in 15."

Henry said, "If we hear some shootin' off that way, I'm goin'." Burke looked at him with a slight frown. Billy and Harley watched the rear and they all listened as intently as they could.

There was a moment of silence. Then, the ominous "rebel yell". The wild, piercing howl Confederates had used during the war to intimidate their enemy on the field as they began their charge. A barrage of shots came from the left side just as horse soldiers attacked from the front. Burke, Taylor and Henry Haymond squared off to defend against the charge. Henry was the only one smiling. Billy and Harley hurried over to the left to hold the flank.

Two riders were down before the charge was about to overrun Taylor's position. Then – a thunder of hooves and five riders coming in hard and fast from the right. Wearing blue! Their pistol shots scattered the rebel cavalry, although it wasn't clear whether they had hit any of them. Some of the Confederates ended up behind Taylor, where they ran right into Harley and Billy's field of fire. The blue riders pulled up in front of Taylor. The rider in front wore a wide-brimmed slouch hat with gold cords and a coat that was two sizes too large, but had the bars of a captain on its shoulders.

"Mornin', Captain, it sure is good to see you," Taylor said as the riders started to nudge back into the trees. The Captain's hat came off with a flourish. And her hair fell to her shoulders. "Daisy Wood!" Taylor shouted. "It's *really* good to see you. Or, should I say Captain Wood."

"Mornin' gentlemen, and General, it's really good to see you, too. And Henry! Henry, don't worry, Gabe is the one who sent us over here. He's making his way back through the trees now. General, there are six total from Fort Wallace. The four I have here and two more covering the road these Knights came in on. Sharpshootin' Swedes. Do you have orders for us?"

"Take three of your men and go after that cavalry. Leave one here to help us defend this position," Burke said. "If the opportunity arises, help out on our left flank, be careful not to shoot our two boys out there."

"Billy and Harley," Henry shouted up to her.

Daisy put her hat on, saluted and motioned for her three riders to follow. At the same time, the grays were pouring fire into the flank. Billy and Harley weren't getting many shots off. They were busy trying when Gabe came running up behind with his rifle at the ready.

"You boys look like you could sure use some expert help over here," he said above the noise of the constant fire. "I'll be right back after I see th' Gen'ral."

"Gen'ral, sir," Gabe said when he made his way over to Burke. "I count some 25 troops to our northeast and another 10 to the northwest, including those horse soldiers – mebbe four left after that charge. No one to the south or west far as I could tell, but there is some brush cover back in that area."

"Thanks, Baker, what about that gun?"

"It 'accident'lly' got pushed over the cliff on the back side."

Burke smiled. "Good work, Gabe. Make your way back to that Harley and the other fellow. It sounds like it's getting hot over there. That's where the pressure is right now."

"Yessir."

"Gen'ral, looks like we run outta anythin' t' shoot at, want us to go help Gabe and them?" Henry asked.

"Exactly. Let's go."

Lead was still flying and the boys on the flank were having a hard time of it. Billy saw Burke, Taylor and Henry run up behind them and shouted, "General, if you can hold this position for a few minutes, I see a way around in a ditch over here." He pointed off to their left. "Harley, Gabe and I can flank the flankers and push them out into the open."

"Do it," the General said as he got settled in. "We'll give you cover for as long as we can, and that won't be long. Be careful of Daisy and her men, they're coming in from the other side."

Billy gave Gabe and Harley "the look" and they took off, crouch-running to the ditch. "Just like old times, eh, Harley," Gabe huffed.

"Looks like, an' I ain't complainin'," Harley said. "Billy, what now?"

"Let's keep crawling as long as this ditch doesn't get too shallow, and look for something gray to shoot at. Yep. Feels like old times."

"I see three of 'em firing at Burke, Billy. Look. Look over there," Gabe said, pointing.

"I see 'em," Harley said. "Let's take 'em outta commission." The three of them kneeled above the lip of the ditch and shot. Three soldiers went down.

But now they had lost the element of surprise. They were drawing fire from farther to their left. They all got back down low in time but were pinned down and below where the shots were coming from.

"We can't stay here," Harley said, stating the obvious.

"You two, quick, get up t' the edge an' roll over to those trees. I'll keep 'em busy," Gabe said. Billy and Harley complied and made it to cover again. Billy yelled out, "All right, Gabe, your turn." Gabe made it with the covering fire protecting him.

"Well, Billy, that was – uh – fun?" Harley said, with a faint smile. "Want to try somethin' different?"

"Yeah. *I* do," Gabe said. "These sons-o'-bitches, Knights, whatever you call 'em, I'm jus' gettin' so damn sick an' tired of 'em. They killed my friend Heck, they been trying t' kill me for months, they tried t' kill Nat an' Dundee, they'd be tryin' t' kill *Miss Daisy Wood* right now. I'm ready – to – you know – just -" and his speech got slow and low in tone, as he took in a deep breath, "to – take care o' bus'ness. Right now."

Billy and Harley had not seen this exact mood in Gabe before. There was a definite fatalism in his expression. But they both knew what he was feeling and what he meant. Billy and Harley looked at each other with understanding, and Billy spoke for both of them. "We're in, Gabe. You call it."

"All right. We quit messin' aroun' back here in the trees. We tell the gen'ral we're mountin' up and we go root 'em out, we find 'em, we shoot 'em where they are, an' we keep shootin' 'em until we're done shootin' 'em." He looked back and forth between his friends, who appeared confused. "Well, that's *it*," he said.

"All right, Gabe," Billy said, with a blank look on his face.

"All right. Let's get 'er done," Harley said. Everyone's mood had changed. They were all business. They made their way over to the General Burke. Gabe didn't ask permission. He said what they were doing, pointed the direction they were going and turned to go before the General had a chance to respond.

They heard him yell out as they galloped off, "Get 'em, boys!"

Gabe led as they crashed through the thickets at the edge of the trees the grays had been shooting from. They had all fought Confederates before although none of them had been in the cavalry. But they had fought Cheyenne on horses while guarding the wagon train they came west with nine years earlier. They knew how to do it. This time they rode into a hornet's nest. As soon as they emerged from the trees on the Confederates' right flank, all guns started pointing in their direction. They had surprised their enemy enough so that the initial shots coming their way were going wide or high. They rushed through the group, shooting down from their mounts, scoring hits right and left, and then disappearing out the far side. They quickly reloaded. They didn't say a word. They were all three breathing heavily.

Then, Gabe said, "Ready?" Billy and Harley just nodded. Back they went, straight through the group they had just cut a swath through. Again, shooting right and left with practiced aim, slowing as return fire diminished. Then, there seemed to be a lone shooter remaining. Gabe dismounted, walked around the man's position until he could see him. Gabe yelled out. The man turned to fire but wasn't fast enough. He shuddered when hit, silent, except for the crunching of twigs beneath him as he lay down slowly, one last time. It was young Corporal Pyle. Gabe walked back to his friends, who were now holding their place uneasily in the midst of gray-clad young men. Dead young men.

"What a waste! What a damned waste!" Harley let loose. "And what for?" But each of them knew, this day wasn't over yet. They mounted up, and again Billy and Harley followed their friend's lead. Out of the copse of trees and once again in the open. They heard hooves again and saw flashes of color in the meadow on the other side of some large cottonwoods from the clearing they sat in. It was Captain Wood bringing her men to a halt.

"Daisy!" Gabe yelled and spurred his horse. The three of them burst through a narrow space between two large spruce trees close to the creek and joined Daisy and three men she still had with her. She motioned to a slight incline on the other side of Boulder Creek.

"They're regrouping. Looks like bringing everything they have this time. The General's group is on their way to help out." She put her hand on her horse's flank, and patting him, looked back at her men. "Everybody loaded and ready?"

"Yes, sir!" one of them said. "I mean, ma'am, sir. Or, *ma'am* rather. And – but Captain? How we gonna play this?"

"The way my Pappy would do it. Straight up."

Gabe smiled and looked at Billy and Harley. He lowered his head a bit, raised his eyebrows and smiled. "Huh? See what I mean?"

"Yep," Billy said.

"I do reckon," Harley added, smiling.

38

THE COMING STORM

The Confederates were not trying to hide. They were on open ground and could tell they were being watched. The time for surprise or subterfuge was over. Both sides knew what was coming. The two "armies" would throw themselves at each other. Men would die. There would be a winner and a loser. But now, there was no other way. And Gabe would be on the lookout for Colonel Fletcher and General Shemp Lee. Before the men – and woman – slowly started riding towards each other, Gabe had a quick thought of Heck. This is for you, Heck.

The Knights of the Golden Triangle had the high ground, but would soon give up that slight advantage as they walked, then trotted their horses towards Daisy's position. General Burke, Sheriff Taylor and Henry now trotted their horses to join up and Burke took his place at the front of the group with Daisy and Gabe. They were all together now. Daisy looked to her right to see Gabe looking at her with a broad smile, which she returned.

"Soldiers!" Burke cried out as the Confederates' trot got faster. "March!" He turned to Daisy to say, "They are formed to charge. They will throw heavy fire at our center." He slowed and his troops slowed with him. "Gabe?"

"Agreed, General. They have us outnumbered two to one," Gabe said, staring ahead at the oncoming menace. He added with a smile, "They don't 'ave a chance."

The General smiled as he looked over the field. Then he nodded as if he had made a decision. "Everyone, close in on me," he yelled. As they gathered in, he said, "Keep walking. They are going to charge. Look ahead. We have cover. These rocks here," he shouted, indicating left and right, "the ditch here and the trees to the right. When I give the word, dismount with *all* your guns. Get your cover and commence firing. Make it count!" Burke leaned over to Daisy and said, "We will have them at our mercy for maybe 20 seconds before they can disperse. Let's shoot straight." She nodded in understanding.

The oncoming cavalry did, indeed, break into a hard gallop as it charged towards the slow-moving federals. Burke had it timed out so they would be close to cover as soon as the Knights reached pistol range. When they reached the spot, Burke gave the order, "Dismount! Get cover and fire at will! Don't miss!" The men obeyed well as the thundering onslaught of Confederate cavalry headed straight towards their center. But their dismount tactic seemed to confuse Shemp Lee's men. Most were holding a sabre or pistol, and the swords would now not be as effective as they would have been against mounted men.

The two groups clashed hard. They created a storm of blood and violence. But Burke's side, armed with repeating rifles and shooting from stationary positions with cover, soon gained the advantage. Most of the riders fell, a few rode away the way they had come.

One sat his horse on the edge of the woods. He wore a feather in his hat and held a sabre out in front of him. He called the next charge and galloped forward, apparently not realizing no one was left to follow him.

He was focused on Gabe Baker, who had just stood up from behind his rock. Gabe's heart raced when he realized he was now face to face with Colonel Fletcher.

The Colonel charged directly towards Gabe, his horse's hooves pounding hard. He raised his sword to swipe at him as a .45 slug from Gabe's Colt burned the top of his head and knocked him off his horse. Gabe's shot caused Colonel Fletcher to drop his sabre. It landed at Gabe's feet. Gabe picked it up instinctively and lunged towards his foe as Fletcher, now on his knees, struggled to free his Colt from its holster. Fletcher palmed the gun, and pointing it towards Gabe, cocked it while Gabe fell to his knees in front of him. Before Fletcher could get his shot off, he felt the blade of his beloved weapon enter into his own chest. Gabe thrust it all the way through, the sun gleaming on the bloody tip as it emerged from the other side before Fletcher went down on his back.

Fletcher stared up into Gabe's eyes with fear and hatred, grasping at the sharp edge of the sword and cutting his fingers to the bone as Gabe held tight and pushed harder, even up to the hilt, pushing into the ground. Fletcher's chest heaved once, then again, and then stopped. Gabe pulled the bloody blade out and threw the sword on top of his enemy before he scrambled back to his position. He was trembling, his heart pounding.

But Gabe wasn't done yet. There was still Shemp. He would never have expected Shemp Lee to take part out front where the shooting was happening, but he had to be close by and he would find him.

Just then, they heard more shots. They were coming from the trail the Confederates had ridden in on. Gabe heard Daisy shouting from that direction, "The Swedes! Gustafson and Berg. They are engaging on the trail." She spurred her horse without waiting for orders. The others went ahead while Gabe found his horse and followed, Henry close behind.

Suddenly, three new riders burst onto the trail from a hiding place behind a jumble of boulders. They were 40 yards ahead of Gabe. "Shemp Lee!" Gabe yelled out. "It's Shemp!"

General Lee shot out onto the trail first, leaving two guards behind to fend off Gabe and whoever was behind him. He was a small man on a good, rested horse and he took off fast. His men turned and fired, but shooting behind them with their Colts on rough trail at high speed made for a lot of wasted lead. Gabe gave a quick look behind and saw Henry closing on him. Together, they started to gain on Shemp's rear guard, trading shots as they went. As they closed the gap, Gabe hit one in the shoulder with his long Colt. The slug hit the man hard enough to spin him off his horse. He hit the ground hard as his horse slowed and sauntered off the trail. Gabe spurred his horse, rounding a corner that showed he was within 15 yards of the second man. He fired twice. He hit his mark and the man slumped, trying to hold on to his horse's neck before he fell off.

The trail now featured several tight turns and Gabe could not see far ahead, but he knew what was ahead. Or who. His horse, old Samuel, had never been fast. But he was sure-footed and always reliable. Gabe would spur him to his limit, but no further. No matter what, Gabe would not put his horse at risk. He knew Samuel would try to do whatever was asked of him, so Gabe had to be careful. After two more turns, Gabe saw Shemp ahead. He was gaining on him as Shemp's horse appeared to stumble. Now, Shemp turned to fire. His shots went wide.

Shemp crouched down low on his horse and leaned forward like a jockey. He would be hard to hit in that position. Gabe had two shots left in his Colt. Shemp sat up for a moment to take another shot at back at him. It was then that Gabe instinctively pulled his trigger, cocked, and pulled again, in rapid succession. Shemp kept riding, and Gabe started to slow as he sensed Samuel was laboring. But Shemp wasn't just riding low anymore. He was sliding off his saddle! Gabe slowed but kept pace with Shemp's horse. Then, Shemp fell. But his boot and spur on his right side were caught in the stirrup. The horse dragged him for a good 30 yards as Shemp bounced over rough and rocky terrain before he came to a stop.

Shemp was still stuck when Gabe rode up beside him, just off the right side of the trail. Gabe looked down at him and dismounted. Henry stopped with him. They could see that Shemp had been hit once in his upper right back. He was wheezing and coughing up a bloody froth from the side of his mouth, now drooling down his cheek. Gabe's shot had made it to a lung.

Shemp was on his side but rolled his head back and forth on the ground. He growled, gasping, "Well, get me out of this goddamned stirrup, man!" Shemp's shirt and coat were in tatters, having been dragged up around his chest, showing just how skinny and white and hairless he was.

Gabe kicked Shemp's revolver away from him and walked over to release his foot from the stirrup. The leg was obviously broken. He turned around to look at Shemp. He was flopped over on his back, one leg bent 90 degrees so the knee was in the air. The other was flat on the ground.

Gabe looked down on this man who had been his worst enemy now for some 18 months. He didn't speak. He just marveled at how weak and helpless he looked.

Then he saw. He got down on his knees to look closer. He touched the three round, dark spots under Shemp's ribs. He rubbed them with his fingers. Shemp started to object, but Gabe paid him no mind. Three round scars from long-healed puncture wounds just under Shemp's ribs. Evenly spaced. Like from a pitchfork. He immediately knew. His Mama had put them there. Gabe noticed the ribs on that side were caved in a bit.

Gabe looked up at Henry, his eyes now wet with tears. He tried, but couldn't speak.

"Gabe!" Henry rushed over to his friend, kneeling beside his friend and ignoring the man on the ground. "Gabe! What is it? Ya look like ya jus' seen a ghost," he said, grabbing his friend's arm and gently shaking him.

"A – a – ghost? No – no. Not a ghost. No - flesh and blood. Flesh and blood."

"What you talkin' 'bout, Gabe? Make sense!"

"This – right here – this mis'ble excuse for a man – this son-of–a-bitch – he raped my Mama."

"What? How you know that, Gabe?"

Shemp glared at Gabe in pain and confusion but was too weak to protest. He tried to lift a hand and point a bony finger. Henry was just confused. But Gabe was sure.

"Henry! See them three holes up under 'is ribs?"

"Yeah, Gabe. So?"

"My Mama put 'em there."

"What? Your Mama? Gabe. Those are old wounds. How you sayin'?"

"Yeah, they're old. 'bout 35 years old. Jus' 'bout nine months older than me. She tol' me. She didn't tell me who th' man was, but now I know. She tol' me, sure enough."

"Damn. Damn, Gabe," Henry said, shaking his head.

Shemp sputtered and coughed. He spit up more blood. He tried to lift his head. Gabe pulled his long Colt out, clicked the hammer back and put the end of the cold barrel against Shemp's left temple. His hand started to shake. Shemp just stared up at him.

"You got a right, Gabe. If anybody got a right, you got a right," Henry said.

Gabe stood up, pointed the Colt at the sky and shot into the clouds. "Not sure anybody got a right, Henry. Anyway, I reckon I can't kill my own - father." He convulsed when he uttered the word. He took a deep breath. "It don't seem right, somehow. Jus' don't seem right." He looked down on Shemp's face and saw him in a new light. Shemp Lee was struggling for air. His breathing was raspy. Gabe felt pity. "Besides, I don' think 'e's gonna make it much longer in this world anyways. An' if there's any justice, 'e ain't gonna be happy in th' next."

"Gabe," Shemp rasped. "I didn't know – before. I didn't. I mean, I was damned drunk."

"If you're tryin' t' make an excuse, that ain't - "

"And I've been drunk ever since."

"That don't make none of it right, Shemp Lee."

"Gabe - I got a – a bottle in the saddlebags. Bring it."

"I ain't of a mind t' do much o' anythin' for ya, Shemp Lee."

"Gabe. You think you're my *son*? Bring me the bottle."

Gabe pulled his Derringer out and shot twice, kicking up the dirt all around Shemp's head. "Damn. Don't you ever use that word with me, Shemp." But he got the bottle anyway. He poured some into the cup he had also retrieved and lifted Shemp's head. Shemp slurped greedily. Gabe lowered the cup.

"More," he said. Gabe carefully tipped the cup up to Shemp's mouth again. Then, he poured another cupful into Shemp as he coughed and gagged.

"Thanks," the dying man said.

"You can return the favor. Do somethin' right for once, Shemp. Where's the gold an' how many men you leave with it?"

Gabe didn't expect much, so he was surprised when Shemp said, "In a cave - down by Santa Fe. You get Fletcher yet? He's got - a map. Shemp twisted with pain and coughed and spit out a glob of thick, foamy blood. "Five men." Gabe gave him a puzzled look. "It's the truth, Gabe. All you need - is Fletcher."

"I killed Fletcher."

"Good. He was just waiting for me to die anyway. You got him - good. So, go look," he said, once again wheezing. Shemp's back arched up in pain, his eyes fluttered and the full weight of his slight frame thudded back down in the dust. He was done. Shemp Lee was dead.

39

A DYING MAN'S LAST WORDS

G abe and Henry stood silently over the body of Shemp Lee. Watching. Watching for what, neither man knew. Gabe took a deep breath. He handed Shemp's bottle to his friend. They passed it back and forth without speaking until Henry handed the last gulp over to Gabe.

Gabe slugged it down, held up the bottle, and said, "A father's legacy, eh, Henry?" It was supposed to be funny, but neither of them laughed, or even smiled. Gabe dropped the bottle on the ground next to Shemp.

"Gabe, you think we should go help the others now? Mebbe we could catch up."

"No, my friend. Not me, anyway. I just don't 'ave it in me. I jus' wanna be done with the killin'."

"What you do now, Gabr'l?"

"I wanna go home. Play some fetch with 'at ol' redbone hound. Read a good book, ol' John Henry and Tex down at my feet. But - " Gabe and Henry listened to the wind in the trees.

"What, Gabe?"

"I still got a job t' do. I got t' go back an' bury Heck proper. I got t' tell 'im what all happen. 'course, you know," he said looking over at his friend, "them soldier boys'll go down an' get that gold. I figger they're up t' it, don't need me for sure. What you do, Henry?"

"Mebbe jus' go back to m' boneyard. That ol' mis'ble buzzard prob'ly missin' me by now. An' I gots t' get my Sheba back afore she thinks I just plumb forgot 'er. Mebbe I can ride back with ya, Gabe?"

"I surely would like that, Henry. Surely would. Mebbe we find ol' Granny an' see 'ow she's doin' 'long with them two hill boys workin' for 'er back there."

They stood, looking at Shemp, lying in the dirt on his back. Shemp had closed his eyes with that last spasm of pain. "Let's take the mis'ble cur back t' Boulder t' bury 'im," Gabe said. Just then, they heard horses. General Burke, Daisy, Billy, Harley, Sheriff Taylor and two of Daisy's men.

The group reined in when they saw Gabe and Henry standing over the body of Shemp Lee. General Burke let out a big exhale. "Well, Gabe, looks like half of your mission with the Service is complete. I'm afraid we couldn't help but dispatch the rest of this rabble, so we don't have any further lead on the gold."

"General, I killed Colonel Fletcher. Shemp Lee's last words were Fletcher 'as the map t' the gold. It's in a cave close t' Santa Fe. Fletcher's just back down the trail here a might 'less the devil already come and got 'im. Shemp said five men were still down there with th' gold."

"Yes, good work. I guess we'll see. We have a man down there, we'll send a telegram, see what shows up. But why would he tell you, Gabe? You believe him?"

"I do, General. Dyin' man's last words . . . and, well, and – as hard as it might be to b'lieve, turns out Shemp Lee is – well – I'm his – damn, I can't say it."

"Shemp Lee is – *was* – Gabe's father," Henry said, trying to help his friend.

"What?" General Burke asked, looking confused.

"Gabe - what?!" Daisy asked, as she dismounted.

"Yeah, an' he was like a different man, those last two minutes of 'is life, seem like. I reckon it was th' pain, or mebbe jus' knew 'e was on 'is way t' judgment day."

Gabe explained everything to them the way he had been told by his mother. Henry agreed, he thought Shemp was telling the truth. And when they rode back to Fletcher's body they found the map in his pocket, just as Shemp had said.

General Burke said, "Well, looks like Deputy Chief Hiram J. Flynn, also known as Colonel William Fletcher, has finally contributed to the mission of the Secret Service."

The group rode back to Boulder together. General Burke and Sheriff Taylor went to the telegraph office to send the message to Santa Fe while the rest of the group went down to O'Neill's Saloon to wait for an answer. Burke authorized his man in Santa Fe to hire men to overtake the remainder of the Golden Triangle. They then walked to the Sheriff's office to talk.

Taylor sent his helper to get Dankworth the undertaker to come to the office. He would send him out with three wagons for the bodies.

"Let's see, General, how many were there?" Taylor asked, with a slight smile.

General Burke was in a good mood now. He played along. "Oh, Sheriff, you know, I don't know. It seems like I lost count somewhere around 18 or 20."

Dankworth rolled his eyes. "Gentlemen, I suppose I can give you an exact count when I bring those poor unfortunates in."

"Sir, I will need to see all of their belongings, as part of my responsibilities, before you, uh, complete yours," Burke said. "We must do our best to identify all of them. You understand?"

Dankworth nodded. "I'm gonna need help, though, this ain't gonna be cheap, Sheriff," he said.

"Well, just maybe we can get the federal government to pay this one, eh, General?" Taylor answered.

"Maybe so, Sheriff. This was not a local matter, and we do appreciate your local help. Depending on the answer to that telegram, there may be a lot of happy people in Washington soon anyway. Happy people are generous people. At least, with government money, I should say."

The group at O'Neill's was in a celebratory frame of mind. After a couple of hours of Harley buying rye, they were also getting more boisterous. They were still standing, though. In a tight group around the end of the bar. There was only one other patron in the bar as the sun started to dip behind the foothills. Harley started wondering about him.

"Hey, Gabe, d' you know who that feller is over there in th' corner? Seems like we saw him before," he said.

Gabe took a good, hard look. He walked half-way across the room to get closer. "Yessir! I do recognize th' gen'leman," he called out as he turned back towards his friends. "You boys don' even know, now do ya? Well, out east I'm one o' them famous fellers. You know, like Wild Bill Hickok. 'Cuz they write books about 'em."

"What, Gabe? You got a book about ya?" Harley asked.

"Yep. Just like my ol' friend, Wild Bill. It's called "Gabe Baker: Black Man of the West".

"Gabe, you are jus' funnin' us now, ain't ya?" Harley said. He looked at Billy, who shrugged. "Anyways, what's 'at got t' do with 'at scarecrow sittin' in the dark over there?"

"Hah! Well, I reckon he's th' reporter from Denver. Remember from the trial, Billy?" he asked, looking around Harley to Billy. "Anyways, he wrote that first book. I got a copy, you come out all right in it. Mebbe he's goin' for number two. Harley, if'n y' wanna look good in this one, ya should be extra nice t' me – or, jus' go over there an' give 'im your side o' things," Gabe said, with a big smile spreading across his face. He nudged Daisy with his elbow. His friends laughed.

Then, Billy got serious. "Too bad, Gabe, he can't just call it 'Gabe Baker: Man of the West'."

"Yep, thought o' that, Billy," Gabe said, with Harley nodding. "Someday mebbe, someday."

40

THE TREASURE

After an hour or so, Gabe and Daisy found a table where they could talk more privately. They were quiet for a while, the others looking over at them for a clue as to what was going on. When they saw the others looking, Gabe laughed nervously and Daisy chuckled – at him and his friends.

As the sun was going down, Sheriff Taylor and General Burke came into the saloon. Burke made the announcement, in a voice tired and raspy, but loud for all to hear. "Gentlemen. And Gentlelady," he said, bowing over to where Daisy sat with Gabe. We just heard from Santa Fe. The treasure trove of the lost Confederate gold has been restored to its rightful owner, the United States of America. One guard killed, four taken into custody. I'll be starting on my way down there tomorrow."

The saloon erupted in a joyous celebration. Burke motioned with his arms for all to quiet down. "This result is due to the Herculean efforts of the hero Heck McCabe who gave his life for his country, the hero Gabe Baker, who tried several times to give his, and our new honorary agent, Henry Haymond of Rockville, Maryland. And perhaps the hero of the day today, in 'the Battle of Fort Chambers', one Daisy Wood. I thank you all." The reporter scribbled furiously.

The General bought a bottle and carried it over to Gabe and Daisy's table. He set it down, and said, "I won't bother anyone tonight, but I'd like to talk with both of you tomorrow morning before I leave. Gabe, I want to make you a job offer. Daisy, there's an opening now that Colonel Fletcher is gone I'd like to talk to you about."

Daisy stood and started to say something, and the General asked her to just wait until the next day. She sat down and stared at Gabe.

"Daisy Wood, that sound like a mighty fine job for you, Deputy Chief. I'm confessin', I don' want you t' leave an' I want t' carry on like we 'ave been. And – well - and more."

"Gabe Baker," she said, with a slight smirk. "Are you proposing to me?" He looked down at his feet and back up at her. It appeared he couldn't make himself speak. But she wouldn't let him off the hook. "Well, Gabe? Are you?"

He struggled, and finally said, "Well, I – uh – I don' really . . . I mean, I never done it before an' so I don' know. I don' know *how* t' do it. Did I, just now? Did I just – you know – do it?" He looked so confused and helpless, Daisy couldn't help but laugh.

"Gabriel Baker! Only you can answer that question. So?"

"Well, I mean – I must 'ave. If you thought I did, yeah, I must o'."

"So now what, Gabe? Are you waiting for an answer?"

"Yeah, I'd think that must be how it goes, then. Yeah, then you'd – you know – say 'yes'." Then he hesitated. "Or – you know, 'no'. Whatever it was you was feelin' at th' time, o' course."

Daisy crinkled her nose at him. "This has got to be the strangest marriage proposal in the history of – well, marriage. I guess - "

"But. But Daisy. You know what it'd be like. For you. It wouldn't be easy, no matter where we were."

Daisy got serious again. "I know that, Gabe. I know. Of course, I think we got a lot of people around here accepting us so far. I know. I've thought about it."

"You thought about it?! You thought about it, Daisy?!"

"Well, of course, silly. The way I feel about you."

Gabe beamed and sat up as straight as he could. He quickly looked around like he was supposed to get up and do something. "Um, but you thought about it. Daisy?"

"Gabe, what did I just say?"

"Yeah, yeah, what was that? I mean, what *do* you say?"

She smiled and took a step to stand by him. She leaned over and as he looked up at her with shining eyes, she kissed him on the lips. "I say yes, Gabe."

ABOUT THE AUTHOR

Hugh Pixler is a retired civil rights and employment law attorney. He has always loved western stories, whether in books, on television or at the movies. He lives with his wife Deborah, and two cats, Jimmy and Gracie, in the foothills above Boulder, Colorado.